———————————— ★ ————————————

I knew better than to touch anything. I started to back out, started to yell, to call for help, then I saw a movement. A sign of life. Her eyes were staring straight ahead, but her lips, darkened with her own blood, were forming words.

"What is it? Rachel? What happened?" In a flash, I was on the floor with her. This wasn't a crime scene; this was my friend. "Are you hurt?"

The absurdity of my own words hit me. She was lying there, her body unnaturally still. My hand had landed on the red spot on her coat and the spot was spreading. Hypnotized, I stared at it. Watched it grow.

"Pah." Rachel's voice, barely a whisper, broke the spell and I kneeled closer.

"What is it, Rachel? What are you saying?"

I pressed my face closer, trying to understand, and held my own breath, the better to hear. Her lips moved like those of a beached goldfish. "Pah. Pah." And then they stopped.

———————————— ★ ————————————

Previously published Worldwide Mystery titles by
CLEA SIMON

MEW IS FOR MURDER
CATTERY ROW
CRIES AND WHISKERS

Clea Simon

PROBABLE CLAWS

W🌐RLDWIDE®

TORONTO • NEW YORK • LONDON
AMSTERDAM • PARIS • SYDNEY • HAMBURG
STOCKHOLM • ATHENS • TOKYO • MILAN
MADRID • WARSAW • BUDAPEST • AUCKLAND

Recycling programs
for this product may
not exist in your area.

PROBABLE CLAWS

A Worldwide Mystery/December 2009

First published by Poisoned Pen Press.

ISBN-13: 978-0-373-26695-1

Printed in U.S.A.

To Jon

PROLOGUE

I AM NOT A CAT. Beyond the obvious—no fur, no whiskers—
I'm not and have never been as fastidious as your average
feline, and I'm certainly not the clean freak that my own
Musetta is. I do not drop everything to bathe.

But as I looked down at the red-brown stain seeping into
the knees of my jeans and tried to rub the sticky liquid from
my hands, I began to understand the urge. Even as I wiped
my palms on the loose papers spread all around, I saw that
blood had gotten under my nails, had begun to dry in my
knuckles and under the band of my wristwatch. I wanted to
back out, to forget that today had ever happened. Looking
down at the mangled body that had once been my friend, I
knew it was already too late.

ONE

Two days earlier

"TUNA BREATH!" I recoiled in disgust.

"Excuse me?" The voice on the phone was too refined to sound insulted. Still, I owed Patti an explanation.

"Sorry, Patti." I sat up and pulled my plump cat into my lap—and away from my face. "Musetta was giving me a morning kiss."

"Oh, isn't that sweet!" It was, but my cat's bad breath woke me up more effectively than my neighbor's early morning call. "But anyway, Theda, I wanted to ask you about the whole cat food thing. I mean, Violet left me a message, and I've got some lovely chicken livers left over from my dinner date last night. I should tell you about him; he's a most interesting man. But anyway, we did a sauté with some sherry, and I just don't know. I mean, they say the alcohol burns off, but—"

"Hang on a minute." Who had been sautéed? I shook my head to clear it, sending Musetta, my black and white tuxedo cat, bounding to the floor. It was Tuesday, almost nine, but the regular work week meant little in my line of business. I'm a writer, a music critic who specializes in the club scene of this gritty little city, and I'd been out late the night before. A new British band, on its first US tour, had played the first of two gigs in the area. I'd interviewed them for the weekly column I write for Boston's *Morning Mail,* and although it wasn't necessarily part of the job,

I had stayed up with them long after their midnight set, sharing beers and industry gossip. What's a job without perks?

"Patti, I don't mean to be rude." At this hour, with this head, that was the best I could do. "But what are you talking about?"

"Didn't you hear? I thought Violet would call you first." I looked over to my answering machine and saw that it was, in fact, blinking. "There's something wrong with some of the commercial cat food again. Violet's cats have been poisoned."

"What?" That news sent me bolt upright, and Musetta's fluffy hindquarters cantering out of the room, but I focused my rapidly clearing mind on Patti. "Tell me what happened."

"I don't know the details, darling. I just got the call. But I was wondering if you think that livers, cooked with just a little—"

I couldn't listen any more. "Look, Patti, I'll call you back. I've got to talk to Vi."

"I understand, Theda. But if you can, ask her about—" I hung up and began dialing the shelter where Violet and her partner Caro cohabited with two dozen formerly healthy, happy felines. As the phone rang, I pressed the "play" button on the answering machine.

"Theda, it's Vi. Can you give me a call?" I half listened to the machine while waiting for my friend to pick up. "Something's up. I think I've got some bad cat food." The phone in my hand kept ringing. "Or just come by? And don't feed Musetta before—" I dropped the phone and ran into the kitchen. Musetta was already bending over her dish, lapping at last night's can. She looked up as I grabbed it away. The wet food had gone dry and crusty overnight, the half a can that was left.

"Musetta?" She sat and began washing her paws. "Are you okay?" She didn't respond and I hoisted her into my arms. God, she was getting heavy. "Kitty?" I turned her to look in her face. The round green eyes staring back into mine were clear and bright. Her nose, half pink, half black, was damp and cool. In response to my touch, her tongue darted out and I got another whiff of her breath. "Oh, kitty." She blinked. But halitosis aside, my cat seemed the picture of health. I put her down and refilled her water dish before running back to the phone. The line was dead; nobody had picked up.

Musetta pounced, grabbing my ankle, but there was no time for play. Violet was family, more than any remaining blood relatives. Pulling on sweats and galoshes, I grabbed my keys and headed for the door. It was April in New England. I wouldn't look any odder than most of my neighbors here in Cambridge, and I was making tracks to help a friend in need.

"YO! VIOLET? CARO?" I'd driven over to Vi's, but by the time I tromped around the back of the sprawling green and gold Victorian known as Helmhold House, officially the Helmhold Home for Wayward Cats, the mud had managed to seep up to the ankles of my new yellow boots. Which were leaking already. "Hello?" At least it wasn't snow. But the lack of response was worrying me more than the creeping damp. "Vi?"

I hopped in the mud, trying to balance on my warmer foot while peeking through the back door. Nothing, despite my repeated knocking. If I reached up, I could just grab the top of the door frame and—yes—see into the enclosed porch. But before I could examine the living room beyond, I fell back, barely righting myself before I landed in the muddy yard.

Catching my breath, I looked around one more time. Patti lived beyond the hedge, her neat-as-a-pin split level a strange contrast to the colorful shelter. Would Violet have given her realtor neighbor a key? My punk rocker friend was as different from her prim neighbor as their properties, but I needed a way in. Unless…yes, there was one large rock back here. If I could roll it over, I bet I could at least get a clear view into the house. I caught myself trying to dry my wet hands on my jacket before reaching for the muddy rock and shook my head. What was I thinking? Life before coffee wasn't sensible. But as I grabbed the stone and rolled it, I remembered. This was Violet's not-too-subtle hiding place. Sure enough, taped underneath the miniature boulder was her back door key.

"Hello?" I called softly as I let myself in. No sense giving anyone a fright. A marmalade short hair came running. Head butting me, he began to purr as I scooped him up and closed the door behind me. "Vi? Caro?"

I kicked off my boots and wiped my wet bare feet on the well-scratched sisal mat before proceeding into the living room. "Anybody home?"

Sprawled out on a sofa was my buddy. Her mouth was open, her purple hair matted, and her face pale, dead to the world.

"VIOLET!" I DROPPED the cat, who skedaddled with an annoyed mew.

"Wuh?" With a snort, my friend awoke and blinked. "Oh, man."

Seeing her put her head in her hands, I had to ask. "Hangover?" After years as a straight-edge no-booze, no-drugs, no-meat purist, Violet enjoyed the occasional beer and burger. Maybe, if there'd been a tragedy…

"What? No, just no sleep. What time is it?" She squinted toward the sunny porch.

"Just after nine." Crack of dawn to folks like us, and Violet suddenly focused, taking in my odd attire in the morning light.

"And you? Oh, sorry. When I got your machine, I figured you were at Bill's, you'd get it when you got home."

"Not to worry. You didn't wake me. Patti did." I didn't want to get into why I had been at home. My long-term guy and I had been on the outs for weeks now, and I suspected that Violet secretly sided with him. "But she said something about your cats being poisoned? So then, when I heard your message and I couldn't reach you—"

"Oh, sorry." My diminutive friend stood and stretched, all five-foot-one of her. "I wanted to warn you. Didn't mean to cause a panic. Though, I'll tell you, last night things got hairy."

"Tell." The marmalade cat returned and flopped on the floor in front of me, his thick short fur warm against my bare feet. He was obviously healthy, and whatever crisis had occurred seemed to be under control. Breathing easier, I settled into the sofa and pulled the purring cat onto my lap.

"Well, I got in late. We had that gig out in Worcester." Violet's band, the Violet Haze Experience, was building a reputation all over New England. "We headlined and what with loading out, and getting everything back to the practice space, it must have been around three-thirty, close to four by the time I got in. Caro was out like a light." Violet's partner worked as a contractor, a mostly diurnal job. "I was creeping around with the lights off, when I first heard the hacking. You know, like a hairball?"

I did, indeed. Musetta's fine medium-length fur came up regularly, no matter how careful I was about brushing her.

"So, I didn't think much of it, not until I heard another cat—and then a third. Then, I figured at the very least I should clean up a bit. Why let Caro wake up in the morning to little wet piles of felt and puke?" Violet kept talking as she wandered into the kitchen. I let the cat jump down and followed her. Coffee was definitely in order.

"So I turned on the hall light, hoping it wouldn't wake her and, man, what a mess." Violet shook her head as the grinder got busy with an excellent aged Sumatra, dark roast. Bit by bit, bean by bean, she and Caro had been upgrading the shelter. "Cat vomit and diarrhea everywhere—and I mean everywhere. Half the cats hidden away under the furniture like something was attacking them, the other half lying around so listless I started to really worry. That's when it hit me that they must have eaten poison. There must have been something making them sick like that. But I didn't know what. I called Rachel's beeper and left a message with her service and started the most out-of-it cats on subcutaneous hydration drips. I figured it couldn't hurt 'em. It's just saline, right?"

I shrugged. Violet would be finishing up her undergrad degree this spring, with a heavy emphasis on "pre vet" courses.

"Anyway, they started to perk up right away. Murray— your golden boy over there?—he was totally out of it, and look at him now.

"At some point Rachel got back to me, must have been close to dawn. She said it did sound like they'd eaten something bad, so I should just wrap everything up, keep them on plain water. The good news is, she said that if they'd gotten at rat poison, or, more likely a poisoned rat, they'd have been a lot sicker. I didn't lose any of them, Theda. They're all as healthy as Murray today. But I was still up cleaning and checking sub-Q bags when Caro's alarm went off this morning. She helped with the rest of it, and I was just going to truck the food dishes over to Rachel's office when I thought I'd sit down for a minute—and here you are."

"Wow, that sounds horrible." I took two oversize mugs from the cabinet and helped myself to milk from the fridge while Vi poured. She kept the real stuff for me; soy is fine, but not in coffee. "But why do you say 'poison'? I mean, couldn't it just have been something that went bad? A kitty stomach flu or something?"

"I wish." She threw back the mug as if it were toxic. The soy milk, I was sure. "There are a lot of cranks out there, Theda." She reached for the real stuff this time, as she refilled. "You should see the letters. I'll show you later."

She knew me well enough to know that I'd ask. I'm a journalist, not a private investigator, but sometimes the two fields overlap. "Well," I savored my own coffee. "I'm glad everyone pulled through. Sounds like a horrible night." I looked back to see Murray groom, extending one leg to work on his toes, revealing the pink pads beneath the dark orange fur. "I must say, the place looks good. Smells fine, too." Only a few of us hardy cat lovers, I realized, would be able to enjoy a fine brew while sniffing for cat poo. "Simple Solution?"

"That and leaving the windows open since dawn." We took our coffee back into the living room. This time I checked the sofa before I sat down. It was clean. "But I need to get all their food and toys checked out before I have a riot on my hands. Who knows what was in the food, or where else it is. Wanna help?"

I thought of Musetta, who had been working it hard—rubbing aggressively against my shins—before I left. She hadn't understood why I'd removed her food dish and not replaced it. I thought of her sick, her green eyes dull. Her white belly heaving, her stout little form writhing on the floor. I began pulling on my boots.

TWO

"FINALLY! I WAS WONDERING when you'd make it in." Rachel met us in the city shelter's waiting area and, once we'd squirted some hand sanitizer into our palms, led us down the main hallway to her tiny, cluttered office. "I should have known 'first thing' meant closer to noon for you two." She softened her words with a smile, and as I followed my two friends past the big quarantine rooms I was struck by their similarities. Rachel was all business, her curly black hair tied back in a ponytail that bobbed over her white lab coat. Violet was, well, violet, from her spiked hair down to her hightop sneakers. But stylistic choices aside, they could have been sisters—both short, both intense. Kind of like cats.

"So, what have we here?" Stepping over a miniature air purifier, Rachel put the bag Violet handed her on her desk and pulled out several cans. "These all look intact." Violet and I looked at each other.

"I hope we don't have another China situation." I said it. It was on all our minds. The fact that the cans hadn't been tampered with only meant that any toxins could have been there from the beginning. After examining a few more, Rachel put the cans aside and took out an opened bag of dry food. "The sick cats all had access to this?" Violet nodded. She was being strangely silent, considering her suspicions, but maybe she didn't want to bias Rachel. The vet pulled on thin plastic gloves and looked over the bag. "Free feeding?" Violet nodded again.

"Well, then." With a frown of concentration, Rachel plucked a pair of goggles off a shelf. "Let's start here." She shook out one of the kibble nuggets and began to scrape at it, chopping at the fragments and pausing occasionally to add drops of some clear liquid. Preparing slides is tedious work, and I knew the time she was giving us was stolen from other pressing projects, but I was bored. Violet had collapsed into Rachel's desk chair so I poked about, trying to stay out of the way as we waited. Rachel's office was little more than a converted alcove, a tiny workspace between the main hall and a sterile treatment room. She'd compensated by covering all the available wall space with shelves and work notices, so there was plenty to explore.

"Cute." Even my busy buddy couldn't be all business. Tucked beneath one bookshelf hung a tiny reproduction of a vintage poster. "Hang in there, baby, Friday's coming." The kitten suspended from a tree branch looked more startled to find itself there than seriously concerned. Right underneath, I spied a stack of pads, unlined but irresistible, thanks to the shelter logo, the profiles of a cat and a dog, back to back, in an ever so slightly darker cream in the corner. "Very cute." Aren't all writers paper fiends?

"Help yourself." Rachel didn't even look up, so I took two. As a freelancer, I could no longer raid the *Mail* supply cabinet.

"Dr. W?" A tech stuck her head in the back door and, after a brief exchange, Rachel followed her into the treatment room. I fought back my growing impatience. Violet and I both considered Rachel "our" vet, but in truth, she had a full-time gig with the city, overseeing a staff of five and at any given time about a dozen volunteers at the shelter and its clinic. Testing kibble, as she was doing this morning, might be considered part of her job—public pet health, and all that—but the fact that our concerns had trumped at least a dozen others was due to friendship. The least I could do was wait quietly. I looked over Rachel's desk and started browsing a plan to foster kittens. The first bit addressed kittens who were too young to be adopted. The really little ones, I read, would go to people who were prepared to bottle feed them. Slightly older kittens would stay in private homes until they were mature enough for their vaccinations. I nodded. Distemper, panleukopenia, could wipe out an entire shelter's worth of kittens if they hadn't yet gotten their shots, and by all accounts the disease was a miserable way to die. I moved the page to read more.

"Cat PAT?" I hadn't realized I'd spoken aloud until Violet started in her seat. She'd been dozing.

"Pet-assisted therapy," said Rachel, closing the treatment room behind her. I heard a loud thump as something was dragged into the back hall. "Sorry about that." She went back to her microscope. "We're getting some new equipment tomorrow, and Bari and Sue need to clear space." Rachel ignored the noise and adjusted the focus on her microscope. "Usually, it's former show cats. They're used to being handled. I'm quite optimistic about our program. We've got so many friendly old timers here. If I can get the volunteers, it'll give them another lease on life."

"Sounds good." When Violet woke up for real, I'd have to talk to her about this. At this point, in Rachel's chair, she was breathing deeply, almost snoring. Rachel went back to jotting notes. I picked up another folder and began to skim. The words I read—"kill," "pests," "bomb"—jerked my head back.

"Yow, what are these?" I held the folder gingerly, as if it were contagious.

"The usual." Rachel barely glanced up. "Nut jobs and people with more time than sense." I flipped past the one I'd started reading. Sure enough, the next one was written in crayon, though the vocabulary was startlingly adult. "I'd toss them, but the board says I should hang onto them."

I nodded. "Makes sense to me. I didn't know you could spell 'murderer' with an 'a.'" Rachel gave a ladylike snort. "Don't you think you should give them to the cops, too?"

"The board does. That bomb one, especially, and so we did. But, you know, it wasn't specific. It was printed out on the kind of printer that every library in the city has. And there was no return address, so it wasn't like there was much the police could do." She looked up, her dark eyes blinking from the change in light. "Dr. Massio, over at WellPet, has all his mail screened, but they're private. They've got money. That was the only one that spooked me, but it's been weeks since that came in. Now we're just getting the normal kooks. People telling us we should get rid of all the 'pests' in the city, or the ones that call me a murderer because I do euthanasia."

"Euthanasia?" Violet jumped up with a start. "I thought you were going to stop—"

"Hey," Rachel turned to face her. "We do what we can. Sometimes animals come to us in such sad shape that it really is a mercy."

"But, what, like ninety percent of all animals euthanized in shelters are perfectly healthy and—"

"I *know*." Rachel was glaring. "Believe me, I'm hearing it. I have the letters to prove it. The calls, too. Kitten season is just starting and we're already near capacity. So, yes, I know it's a crisis. We're trying, okay?"

"Euthanasia." Violet spit out the word, and I jumped in before she could go further.

"I always thought that would be a good band name," I said, trying to lighten the mood. It was a small office. "You know," I made air quotes with my fingers to separate the words, "'Youth in Asia'?"

"Been done." Vi didn't look amused, but at least she sat

back down. Rachel accepted the truce, as well, turning back to her microscope, and for a few minutes quiet reigned.

"So, you talking to the folks at WellPet?" Violet's query had an edge I couldn't identify. "You thinking of going for-profit?"

"We're colleagues, Violet, that's all. Wait, I think I have your problem here." Rachel motioned us over to her microscope, but even when I was able to focus on what looked like crystals, I didn't understand.

"What is it?" Violet adjusted the sights. "Did something go bad?"

"Not naturally." Rachel raised her glasses and began sealing her slides in plastic bags. "Someone put some kind of alkaloid on the kibble. I don't know what yet, but my best guess would be theobromine, probably from cocoa or chocolate, or some derivative. I'm surprised they ate it. Maybe there's something else in there, too, but it fits with the vomiting. You're lucky you didn't have any cats with weak hearts." She reached for a label and started scribbling. "These will have to go to the city health lab, but I've seen enough to guess that's what made your cats sick last night. How did theobromine get into their food anyway? I assume you got this closed?" She held up the bag. KittyLuv: a popular brand.

"Yeah." Violet reached for the bag. It was heavy paper and appeared intact. "This is the good stuff, too. Pricey." She paused to think. "Not what we would have bought. This must have been a donation."

"Some gift." Rachel pulled off the gloves. "I don't think there was enough there to kill a cat, but it doesn't look good. And who knows what would've happened if any one particular animal had pigged out—or was already in poor health. It sounds like you've passed the crisis, but we should schedule a housecall anyway. Talk to Amy." That was the receptionist.

"Tell her two hours for all the cats. And watch for any more vomiting or even excessive purring."

I looked up at that, and Rachel noticed.

"It can be a sign of discomfort or pain. Nobody knows for sure, but it may be a way for an animal to comfort itself, or comfort others. I've heard it myself when we get injured animals in."

"Purr therapy?" I had an image of a Musetta lying next to me on a couch. "I like it."

"It is being researched." Rachel was less fanciful. "But for now, we'll stick with Western medicine here. Now, ladies?" I didn't realize I was still holding the letter file until she reached for it. "Some of us have work to do."

As she walked us out, I managed to ask Rachel about Musetta. Was my kitty at risk from food poisoning, too?

"You're halfway through a bag and she's not showing any symptoms?" I nodded. "Same thing with the cans—same brand, no problems?" I waited. "I think you're fine. This looks like an isolated contamination issue. One bag, perhaps one batch. Watch her, though. Vomiting—I mean more than usual. Excessive thirst. If she stops grooming, straining at the litterbox. Anything like that, you give me a call."

"I'll be doing that anyway, Rach." She looked back at me. "She's due to have her teeth cleaned."

Rachel nodded once. "See Amy." She turned to go, but called back to me. "And no worrying about excessive purring!" I resisted the urge to salute. If Rachel held to a near military mode, it was because only her efficiency kept the shelter running. That she could see me or Violet, or private patients like Musetta, was all a bonus, the payback for giving up small talk now.

WE LEFT THE CANS with Rachel; she'd send them out for further testing, but the dry food seemed the likeliest candidate.

"So, how do you think that stuff got into that bag?" As I climbed into Violet's van, I breathed easier. What had happened was horrible, sure, but, as Rachel had said, it seemed to be isolated. A mug of cocoa overturned at the wrong moment, maybe.

"Who did I get that bag from, you mean?" Violet shoved the old vehicle into gear with a vengeance, and I realized how angry she was. "Who would want to poison my cats?"

"So you still think it was intentional?"

She shot me a look.

I sighed, and pieced it together. The bag wasn't watertight, but it had been sealed. "Kill off the cats with a so-called gift? That's pretty harsh." I glanced over at my friend for a reaction.

"Yeah, well, you saw what type of nuts are out there. And that was only Rachel's mail bag."

"I thought you were asleep back there?"

Violet shrugged and reached for the CD player. Her transmission might need attention, but the old van's sound system was up to date. "It's no big deal. Nothing I can't handle."

"Those letters." I'd almost forgotten "Anything in them about poison?"

She shook her head. "*That* I would've told you about. Just the usual creeps and haters." I waited. As a lesbian couple, she and Caro took some grief, even in super-liberal Cambridge. Instead of explaining, she turned up the volume. I was expecting a guitar attack, something raw and loud. What I heard was a distorted funk bass line, rubbery with wah-wah. *"Reach out…"* A feather-light falsetto, vintage '70s, soon topped the beat.

"What's this?" I wanted to push Violet about the threats, but she'd talk when she was ready and not before. Besides, I was intrigued and started poking around for a CD case. Vi dug one out from between our seats.

"Buzz Grammers, real old school." Her eyes were back on

the road, but I had a feeling she was watching me in the mirror. "Bill had him at his place last night. Didn't you go?"

I looked out the window. Not only hadn't I been there, I hadn't even known about the show. "Nope. I had a gig last night, the Infallible Mystics." Not that far back, Bill would've told me if he was having an act he thought I'd like. Not that long ago, I'd dropped by regularly enough to know what shows were on the bill. "I gather you did."

"Caught some of the sound check, before we left for Worcester. But I thought—" She fell silent. I didn't feel like answering. "Theda? I know it's none of my business."

"I had to work last night. I've got my job, too. Let's leave it at that, okay?" She shrugged. We'd been friends long enough for her to know I'd talk when I was ready to. Instead, I turned the volume even higher and let the singer tell me about love and happiness.

"MAY I BORROW THIS?" As Vi pulled up to the shelter, I popped the CD out. It wasn't just the music. At some level, I wanted a reminder of what Bill hadn't told me.

"Even better," she reached for it. "I'll burn you a copy." We walked in through the back, and Vi handed me a trash bag.

"More puke?"

She shook her head. "Cleaning house." I followed her into the pantry, as did five eager cats, tails up. Five large bags of dry food were lined up on the lower shelf. She pulled one off and a cream-colored darling, at least part Siamese, stood up to beg. With a deep sigh, Violet ignored him and placed the food into one of the garbage bags. The Siamese questioned her: "Ow wow?" But Violet reached for a second bag. "These were all donations. I can't take any chances."

"Wet food, too?" I held up a plastic-wrapped tray of cans, retail price at least twelve dollars. The cats, no fools, turned to me. A softer touch than Violet, I pushed the tray back on the shelf and bent to stroke the Siamese and an all-black adolescent with green eyes. "Maybe we could wait until Rachel's tests come back?"

"Yeah, for now." Violet looked relieved. The shelter had an endowment from its founder, and Caro and Violet took care of the building themselves. Still, it relied on donations to make ends meet. If she had to start spending cash, Violet would be forced to turn away some of the strays and abandoned animals that the neighborhood kids brought by. "But the dry food? These bags are just not that secure. Until I figure out where that one bag came from—and how the theobromine, chocolate, or whatever it was got in there—I want these out of my house."

"Fair enough." I grabbed a small sack of dry food. It was a store brand and I remembered the bright red and blue KittyLuv logo. "But don't you have any way of tracing that one bag? Could we find out who it came from?"

"There'll be something in my office." Violet pulled two more bags out. One was open, half gone, and I could see her wrestling with the idea of throwing it away. "But you know my filing system." The food went into the garbage bag.

I did. "Hey, I could help you, you know." I thought through my day's duties. "Sort through the paperwork, see if I could trace that one bag. And besides, I really would like to see what hate mail you've got." I wanted to believe this had all been an accident, but those letters of Rachel's had scared me.

"I'll see what I can pull together." Violet looked distracted—and exhausted. "I need a few hours at least."

"Maybe you could get a nap in, too."

She didn't answer that, and together we humped the garbage bags out to the curb. It was almost midday by then, the sun was warm, and my feet were sticky inside my rubber boots. Besides, Violet's charges had made me think of my own little furball.

"You set for the rest of the cleaning and everything?"

"Uh-huh, Tess is coming by, and she'll probably bring Francesca." That was good news; our friend Tess was still fragile, following a stay in rehab for a drug problem that had snuck up on her without any of us noticing. Working with animals would do her as much good as it did the cats. Francesca was another up-and-coming musician who'd begun to do a little volunteering, and probably a little networking, at Vi's.

"Okay, but don't forget those letters. If you don't have time to get your paperwork together, you can just let me loose in your office."

She laughed and we parted. But any plans of getting to work were interrupted as soon as I slipped off my muddy boots and opened my own door.

"Meh!" Musetta came running up to greet me. "Mrrup." She pounced on my foot, and I could feel the touch of teeth.

"No, kitty!" I clapped to reinforce the message and she let go. But as I lifted her into my arms, I knew I was to blame. Sure enough, a small array of cat toys had been deposited by the door. She wanted to play.

"Miss me, little girl?" On her back, her fluffy white tum exposed, she was the picture of innocence. But a squirm and a kick revealed the power in that small body. And her claws. I put her down.

"Manicure time." I reached for the clippers that I keep in my key bowl, but she was having none of it. Instead, she cantered off to the kitchenette, stopping just out of reach to look back at me. "Meh?"

"Have I been ignoring you?" I came after her and she reached up, catching her claws on the top of the lower cabinet door. "Breakfast, right. Sorry." I was hungry, too, come to think of it. But the lady of the manor came first and I so enjoyed watching her lap at the fresh can that I almost forgot my own dearth of groceries. A quick survey reminded me: Cold pizza. Peanut butter. A hunk of parmesan from the last time Bill and I had cooked together, already petrifying.

Had it been two weeks? Three? I used my one good knife to whittle some of the cheese onto the pizza, popped it into the microwave, and tried to figure. Eighteen days, I counted back. We'd gone to a matinee at the Harvard Square and come back to my place for a quick pasta dinner before Bill went off to his club. He'd brought that incriminating hunk of cheese, a good Parmesan-Romano, to jazz up our supermarket sauce. We'd been laughing, I remember that. Holding out a paring for Musetta to sniff and joking about her approval of our meal. The movie had been a good one, too, though I couldn't for the life of me remember anything about it now.

So what had happened? The microwave pinged and I retrieved my slice, heading into the living room to eat. Musetta, already finished with her breakfast, was carefully washing one side of her face. The club, it must have been the club.

When Bill had taken over the Last Stand, back in January, I had tried to be supportive. Not long before we'd met, I'd given up a secure job as a copy editor at the *Mail* to write full time, freelance, without any kind of a safety net. It had worked out, with a few rough spots along the way, and now I wrote a weekly column for my former employer. After twenty-something years on the force, my sweetheart was retiring on partial disability. He had a nice nest egg, and had earned the right to make the same leap of faith. In his case, that meant indulging a passion for live jazz by taking over a small club.

I hadn't thought he'd make a go of it, frankly, but seeing as how I'd jumped off the same cliff only a year before, I'd kept most of my reservations to myself during the planning phases.

Besides, the tiny bar he'd bought into had existed long enough as a cop hangout so that I wasn't too worried that he'd lose all his savings, nor were his pension and disability payments—he'd wrecked his knee—subject to the vagaries of the music scene. And the first month had been fun, all the passion and adrenaline of a start-up, with the added incentive that Bill was, to some extent, entering my world. Clubland.

Maybe that was it. Because after the first flush of excitement died down, clubland had become his world, too. Maybe more his than mine: I've written about music for a while now, been a critic, an important but ultimately peripheral part of the scene. But he owned and ran a live music venue. Hired the musicians I commented on. And even though his specialty was a far cry from the loud 'n' fast music I favored, there was enough crossover so that I felt, well, not threatened exactly. But intruded upon. As a single woman who has made her own way, I like to keep my life neat. Was that so big a problem?

Maybe it was. I thought back to the pasta night. It had been a Monday, blues night at the Last Stand. Blues being a catch-all for anything rougher, rowdier, or more rock and roll than the club's weekend fare. Bill had started it in part as a sop to my taste. Mondays were when my friends could come by and jam, and when some of the older musicians we both loved—blues, but also soul and zydeco—would find an eager audience. But, as last night's show apparently proved, the series had grown to take on a life of its own. Mondays at the Last Stand had a certain prestige; as an off night, they drew a wide range of musicians who came for drinks and conversation as well as to play. And people I'd known for years were starting to ask me to talk to Bill on their behalf. Even Ralph, the *Mail*'s pony-tailed staff critic made it a regular stop, quite a stretch for the dyed-in-the-denim rocker. The result was…uncomfortable, at least for me. And when I'd said something to Bill, that night as we slurped up our fettuccine, he'd nailed me on it.

"You're jealous." He hadn't looked at me as he'd said it, which somehow made his accusation worse. "You were hoping I'd fail and that would make you feel better about your success. You can't believe I'm making it work."

"That's ridiculous." I'd spat that out by reflex. But even as I said it, I knew I wasn't being entirely honest. "I mean, okay, maybe a little." Bill knew I'd had a few months of scrambling, of unpaid bills, before I'd gotten my feet under me. "But it's not just that. It's your attitude."

"My *attitude?*" He'd looked up at me then, and I'd had to fight the urge to wipe a bit of red sauce from his chin. I was trying to think.

"Yeah, I mean, I love the scene." My feelings weren't coming together in sentences, or not quickly enough.

"And I don't?" He challenged me, and I struggled to find the words. Clubland—the loose community of musicians, fans, and assorted other folks—was home to me. Family. For Bill to just buy a liquor license and barge right in was....

"It's too easy for you." As soon as the words were out of my mouth, I knew they were the wrong ones. "You don't love it like I do."

"You're saying I haven't paid my dues? Like that band?" He was referring to Swann's Way, a group of pretenders I'd caught trying to buy their way to headliner status only a few months before. Bill had been proud of me, then, even as he'd lectured me about taking risks. I could see the beginning of a smile at the corner of his mouth. I could have salvaged the evening then, only that smile meant something more to me.

"You think I'm just being sentimental. That I romanticize the scene." He did, I knew, and maybe he was a little bit right. But that was also his convenient way of dismissing me. "But you don't know the history. You don't know where everybody's coming from." I was gathering steam. "You have instant access because you've got money to spend and a stage where people can play, so you think you are a part of everything. Which is great. Good for you!" I'd dropped my silverware by this point, and threw my hands up in the air. "But that doesn't give you the right to be so damned patronizing!"

That had been it. He'd gone off to the club and I, for once, had stayed home. We'd spoken a few times since, but each time it had been tense. And each time, we'd both made a point of how busy we were—and where we were going, alone. But I guess we hadn't spoken yesterday, or—I did some quick calculations—since last Friday. Had we really missed an entire weekend together?

As if she knew, Musetta chose that moment to grab my ankle. "You got me!" I reached for her and she scooted away, stopping halfway down the hall to see if I'd come in pursuit. I found one of her favorite cat toys, a crumpled ball of aluminum foil, and tossed it. She intercepted it easily and sent it skittering back to me. "Goal!" I threw it again and watched her chase it several more times, before her attention flagged and my stomach began growling in earnest. She was purring; a good healthy purr, I was sure. My pizza had gone cold again by then, but it helped my appetite to know that at least some living creature cared about my well-being.

THREE

Writing up my column carried me into the early afternoon. The band had been fun, and chatting with them after their set had given me insight into their music and motivation. The small club show had been their first Boston appearance, but the five musicians weren't kids, far from it. Instead, they shared histories with some of the biggest near-misses of the last ten years. NME picks that never crossed the Atlantic, pub bands without a hit, and one one-hit wonder had all contributed members to the Infallible Mystics. Unapologetic throwbacks all.

"We've chased every trend," Sean, the drummer, had told me. "We've never caught one yet."

"So this time, we'll let them double back to us." Guitarist Liam had finished the thought. Looking at my transcription, I wondered how to use it in my preview for next week's big radio concert. The show would be free and a madhouse, the Infallible Mystics just one band of seven. And every band claims to be playing for the fun of it, just as each of them deny following the fads and fashions of the pop world. The quotes, by themselves, were useless. I closed my eyes.

Music, that's what I needed. Not only to wake me up, but to make my case. If I have any talent, it is for describing the sounds I love, translating the aural experience to the page. I'd enjoyed last night's set considerably, and not just because Liam had been sweetly flirtatious, with the kind of lean, dark

Celtic look I adore. Whether or not Bill remained in my life, I liked to think that I was experienced enough not to swoon over touring musicians. No, there was something in the songs themselves that had gotten me going: a bit of '80s New Wave edge, a little '70s swagger. A solid blues foundation. If I could give that to my readers, they'd believe the band members when they made their declarations of faith. I'd believed them, hadn't I? My job then, was to explain what I'd heard, and that would suffice.

I put on the CD and started dancing around the room. Musetta took refuge under the sofa and watched me with caution. But I'd gotten my blood flowing and soon I was singing along. *"Man got the blues, the blu-u-ues."* Okay, it wasn't great poetry, but I didn't have much of a voice either. I cranked the volume to drown myself out, and Musetta fled to the bedroom. At least I didn't have to worry about my neighbors. Midday Tuesday, they were all at work.

Or so I thought, until in the lull between tracks, I heard the pounding. I hit mute and danced over to the door to see Reed, my upstairs neighbor. As was usual, he was holding the sax from which he derived his nickname.

"Oh, sorry." The Mystics were a far cry from Reed's jazz roots. "Were you trying to practice?"

He smiled and my concern melted. "You'd hear it if I were, darling. No, I'm on my way into town. Thought I'd stop by, though, and see how you're doing, if you need anything."

"Thanks, Reed." This was nice, but unexpected. Except that Reed worked with Bill, handling the business end of the bookings. "Is this because I missed that show last night?"

"I admit I was wondering where you'd gotten yourself off to. Thought maybe you were out of town until I heard your stereo." So it did carry. "Then I thought, maybe you've got that cold that's going around."

"No, not exactly." I hung on the door, my newfound energy suddenly gone. He must have seen something in my face.

"Everything all right between you two?"

"I don't know, Reed." At one point, I'd considered the gallant New Orleans transplant as a romantic possibility. Tall and lean, with a Duke Ellinton fashion sense and the kind of creamy chocolate skin and cheekbones most male models would kill for. Now, he was a neighbor—and a link to Bill. "I'm not sure what's going on."

He looked at me, his dark eyes homing in until I felt a flush creep up my own pale cheeks. "You might consider coming down to the club tonight, Theda." That look was trying to tell me something. "Some things are worth fighting for."

"Really?" What did he mean? "I'll think about it."

"Don't think too long." He looked past me, and I turned, too, to see my answering machine blinking red. "And start picking up your phone calls."

"Thanks, boss." I smiled to take the edge off and he rewarded me with one of his elegant half bows before heading back down the stairs. Now usually, I confess, I'd watch him. Reed's easy on the eyes. But the blinking machine was beckoning me. It was Bill, it had to be, and as I crossed the room I kicked myself for not calling him sooner. Our squabble had been so silly.

"Hi, Theda. It's Patti." Ah well. I'd give her thirty seconds. "I wanted to tell you that my pussums lapped up those leftovers and everything seems fine. But call me anyway. I really have to tell you about this new man—" I hit the button for the next message and was rewarded by a male voice clearing his throat.

"Krakow? Call me." Not Bill. I sank onto the sofa with a sigh. And not only was the caller not Bill, it was Tim, my editor at the *Morning Mail*. What did he want? Deadline wasn't for hours yet, and for a variety of reasons I was very tempted to ignore his terse demand. How dare he not be Bill?

But he was my boss, or at least as much of a boss as I had these days. As a freelancer, I get paid by the piece, and I can write for anyone I chose. Still, my old paper and I had come to an agreement; each Tuesday I turned in 800 words on the local club scene. Every Thursday, "Clubland" ran in the arts pages. And one week later, on Saturday, I got a check in the mail. It was an arrangement I could live with, even if it was informal.

These days, with buyouts and threatened layoffs, my gig was as secure as just about any in the newsroom. As long as I held up my end. So while I could put off Patti, I should call Tim. On the off chance that my column was being killed this week—or discontinued for some reason—it would be good to know before I worked on it any longer.

"Mrup?" Musetta came up and bumped my shin. She always could figure out my moods.

"You're right, kitty. I'm being overdramatic. It's probably nothing." I reached down to rub behind her ears and was rewarded with a purr. "Maybe there's a new way to submit photos or something." She started to knead and I reached for the phone. I'd call Tim, and then I'd call Bill. I needed to break this absurd silence.

"Tim? Theda here." Much to my amazement, the phone hadn't gone direct to voice mail. But the silence that followed made me wonder if some circuit had gone astray. "You called me?"

A thud and a rustle told me the line was still live. "Tim? You okay?" For anyone else, this might be more overreacting, but I'd had a couple of run-ins with violent crime in the past year. If my editor was being held hostage, but had somehow managed to get to a phone…"Tim?"

"Budget meeting." I looked up at the clock. It was coming on two o'clock. "Call you back."

"Wait!" If there was bad news, I wanted to know it now,

or at least before I put more time into this week's column.
Maybe the buyouts hadn't been enough. Maybe the freelance
budget was getting slashed, too. "Give me the thumbnail,
Tim? Please?"

"We may have a position open. You'd have to talk to
people, and it might not be music. More after budget, Krakow.
But, Krakow?" I nodded, but he didn't wait for a response.
"Wow me this week. A lot of people will be reading."

MY HEART WAS POUNDING in my ears, and not just because Tim
had hung up with his customary vigor. A position? On the
staff? I'd tried to get off the copy desk and into a writing job
for years, when I'd worked at the *Mail*. At that point, it seemed
impossible; nobody wanted to hear that a copy editor could
write. It was, I realized as my stout pet leaped into my lap and
began to knead, as if Musetta had tried to bark. When I'd quit
last spring, I'd hoped that I could prove myself independent
of the paper, redefine myself as a writer. I didn't think I'd end
up back at the *Mail*. It seemed particularly unlikely now,
when so many senior writers were being forced out, told in
essence to take the buyout or be sent back to the bureaus, the
suburban wastelands where school board and zoning meetings
were the daily fare. But then again, maybe that was part of
the deal. If Tim brought me in now, I'd be both a proven com-
modity and a newbie. Cheap and yet reliable.

I winced, and not just because of Musetta's claws. Did I
really want to be replacing old timers? Did I have a choice?
And what did Tim mean when he said I should "wow" him?
Didn't I always?

Much as I wanted to talk to Bill, right now I needed more
information. My friend Bunny still worked in the newspaper's
library, although her advancing pregnancy had made her noc-
turnal outings with me a thing of the past. At least I knew she

was less likely to be wandering the grimy hallways of the downtown plant. But luck was running against me today.

"You've reached the desk of Barbara Milligan…" I left a message at the beep, and sat there, holding the phone. Musetta jumped down, leaving me to think. Tim had said to wow him. My column was lacking a lead. I needed something more substantial to eat than cold pizza. And, if I really thought about it, the one-bedroom apartment I shared with Musetta needed a thorough cleaning. So many things to do.

I looked over at my cat. Using her particular feline talent, she'd managed to find and completely fill the one place on the sofa that caught the sun, and the long guardhairs in her coat glistened. She was the picture of contentment, while I was its polar opposite. It was time. I dialed.

"You've reached Bill Sherman's private line. If you are calling about Bill's Last Stand, please call the club during business hours. If you are calling about booking—" I hung up. I knew he wouldn't show at the bar until five or so. Could he have not come home last night?

That way madness lay. I'd been up and out early, and Bill was more of a daytime type than I was. He was probably at the gym. Following the knee injury that ended his police career, he'd embarked on a rigorous discipline of weight lifting and swimming, with the goal of being able to run again, at least slowly, by summer.

A small murmur caught my attention. Musetta was yawning, one white paw extended in a leisurely stretch, her head and body turned to expose that white fluffy belly. I reached for it and her eyes opened, round, green, and accusing.

"Sorry, kitty." The eyes blinked. "And yes, you're right." I hit redial.

"Bill, it's Theda." What could I say? I wasn't sorry. "I'd love to talk with you. Call me?" My own eyes were smarting as I hung up, and I blinked away the tears. This was ridiculous. We were adults; we cared about each other. We'd either work it out or we wouldn't. And now I had a piece to finish.

Fifty minutes later, I had something cobbled together with the requisite quotes and me weighing in as a critic. It wasn't what I'd hoped for, and I doubted it would "wow" anyone, even Tim. I was distracted, and even some more high-volume therapy hadn't gotten me back into the mood. I hit print and grabbed the pages. Sometimes reading things through in hard copy lets me see a piece in a different way, and I didn't feel quite comfortable sending in a column I felt so ambivalent about. But as I collapsed back on the sofa, waking Musetta, I couldn't seem to focus on the papers in my hand. What was going on with my life? And had somebody really tried to poison Violet's cats?

WITH A BEAT RECYCLED *from the ragged funk-punk '80s and a strong blues spirit, the Infallible Mystics conjured up a vintage dance groove*…Was the contamination specific to that one bag of cat food or would we be hearing of other poisonings soon? Would Bill call me back? *"The Jam, Gang of Four, the usual," said guitarist Liam, admitting to those 30-year-old influences.* Acknowledging, not admitting; I made the change before the copy desk, my former colleagues, would. There was no shame or blame here. *But before you can say "new wave," keep in mind*…No shame or blame except that which I felt reading my own hackneyed prose. Could this get any worse? I had a story here, but not the one I'd written. I needed air, a dose of adrenaline. A glance at the window showed me Musetta had found a new perch, stretched out on the sill and soaking up the sun that streamed in. I needed a run.

"In the heat of the night…" I found myself singing as I laced up my sneakers. It had been too long. *"She's gonna push, push…"* I finished the other shoe with a flourish of air

guitar. Poison. Well, we were talking '80s bands here. But the song—too late, I recognized "Love on the Rocks"—was a sour reminder. On any other day, with the sun baking the morning's mud, I'd have sprinted to Bill's place first, just to see if he'd power walk a block or two with me. I pulled a sweatshirt over my head and silenced my iPod. Just in time to hear the phone.

"Bill?" How could I be breathless already?

"Sorry, Theda." It was Bunny. "Just me."

My heart sank, and for a moment I mistook my own mood drop for concern. "Everything all right? When you didn't answer—"

"I'm fine, Theda. The baby's fine." A few months earlier, we'd had a scare. These days, I felt more concerned about her pregnancy than she was, even though it was her first. "It's just that this last month I have to pee like every twenty minutes. And going up and down those stairs, oy."

I remembered the circular stairs that led into the *Mail*'s morgue, or library. At some point, an elevator had been added for ADA compliance, but it was so slow that even folks on crutches tended to hobble by it. Still, last time I'd seen Bunny, she hadn't been able to see her feet. In all fairness, some of that was the baby, but my zaftig buddy had also taken full advantage of her state to indulge.

"Well, you take care of yourself."

"Thanks, Mom." I heard her crunching on something. Maybe it was a carrot stick. "But what's up? You had a question?"

"Yeah." I flopped back on the sofa. Musetta came over to sniff my sneakers, and I realized I had a more pressing concern than *Mail* gossip. "Do you remember the cat food problems a year or two ago? Some kind of contamination?"

"Do I!" She made a noise that made me picture her ample flesh all aquiver. "That was awful."

"Mmm." I agreed, but my mind was on the present. "Well, I don't want to scare anyone, but have you heard anything about a new problem? About dry cat food making people's pets sick?"

"Theda? Tell?" I could hear her leaning in.

"Remember your blood pressure, Bunny! Don't worry! It's probably nothing, but some of Violet's cats got sick last night. Nothing serious, they're all fine." Even as I filled her in, I decided against sharing Violet's theory; it still seemed far-fetched and a little paranoid. "It might have been a complete accident." I wanted to keep an open mind. "A case of something going bad."

"But it might not." Either Bunny heard my unspoken thought or she and Violet worked along the same lines. "You know, sometimes I feel like if I were a good mother, I'd make the cats' food myself. There are all those recipes out there now."

"Bunny, I really don't think that's necessary." At least she couldn't see me roll my eyes. "Half those recipes are nutty, anyway. I mean, they're not healthy, not any healthier than store-bought food."

She sniffed. "They can't be worse."

"Actually, they can be." I cut her off. "When you're dealing with raw meat, you've got bacteria to worry about, not to mention getting the nutritional balance right. Please, Bunny, don't get all extreme on me." Silence. "I mean, you're going to have your hands even fuller soon. But, if you could check for me?"

"I'll get right on it. Globally." With Bunny's computer expertise and the *Mail*'s access, she meant that. If kitties in Kathmandu were getting sick, my friend would find out. Which left me with my own good intentions. Giving Musetta a quick squeeze—"meh!"—I headed for the door and down to the street.

Vintage soul made a good choice for a running soundtrack, the wah-wah guitar and intricate bass lines providing a compromise between the rock I'd been writing about and the mood of my muscles. Thirty-three, almost thirty-four, and feeling it, as I started off at a slow lope, I pondered age. The sun was out, its bright light mirrored off every puddle on the street. But this last winter had seemed longer to me than those past. Was the freelance life wearing me down? Did I want to "come in from the cold," so to speak? Or was I just fretting over the situation with Bill?

A puddle loomed and I leaped it with only a slight splash. Nothing was set in stone. Maybe we were meant to move on— a new season, a new life. *"I know we can, I know we can..."* The next puddle was smaller, and I cleared it with ease. *"'Cause better days are very near."* Maybe my life was changing like the season, but as I turned the corner and headed down Putnam, I began to see the other side of that metaphor. *"Spread your love for a brighter day..."* Maybe things were getting brighter. Maybe it was time for me to commit. Maybe Bill and I would work it out. Maybe Violet was wrong and the cats had been sickened by a mistake. Rachel wasn't sure what the contaminant was. It could have been something accidentally spilled on a batch of food—or on the porous bag itself.

By the time I finished a circuit of the neighborhood, the combination of sweat and fresh air had pulled me out of my own personal brand of funk. "Mighty people of the sun," indeed! Even if I had to stand bent over, hands on my knees, to catch my breath, I felt better than I had a half an hour ago, maybe better than I had in days. Older didn't mean old, not yet. Buoyed by my freshly pumping blood, I was only a little disappointed to hear Bunny, rather than Bill, on my answering machine.

"Didn't get much, which is good I guess. What I did find, I've sent." Bunny could be cryptic at work. "And I've been meaning to ask you, do you know anything about pet psychics?"

I looked over at Musetta, who looked back. I'd often suspected her of being able to read my thoughts, but if she had an answer she wasn't transmitting it, and I went off to shower, unenlightened.

Twenty minutes later, I was no closer to solving any of my mysteries. The few clips Bunny had e-mailed didn't seem related to Violet's cats: a dog in Spain had gotten drunk on fermented fruit, a Brooklyn cat had to have its system flushed out after eating a poisoned rodent, and one case on the South Shore of multiple pets that had gotten food poisoning from an overzealous home chef with refrigeration issues. I thought about calling Bunny—she should take note of that last item. But I didn't need Musetta's paranormal powers to tell me that what really needed my attention was my column. Luckily, the break had indeed cleared my head. Reading my rough draft through again, I saw the problem: too many quotes and not enough description. Like so many of my colleagues, I loved the interviews—nearly always found myself drawn to the interviewee—but words on a page don't have the zing of a real human voice. Better to paraphrase, to describe, to suggest. Save the quotes for spice. And that realization let me trim the piece down to size, too. One spell check and a final read-through and with the push of a key it was gone. Time to tackle bigger problems.

FOUR

IF I'D THOUGHT THAT I'd be rescuing Violet, the scene that greeted me at Helmhold House proved me wrong. While my friend still didn't look as if she'd gotten any sleep, she was on top of her game, managing a cleaning crew of four, most of whom I recognized from the clubs. Back in the pantry, another volunteer—Tess's friend Francesca—was wiping down shelves with what smelled like ammonia. Even more of the stored food was gone.

"Hey, Theda." One of the cleaners looked up at me. Mona? Mina? I smiled and gave back a generic "hey."

"Guess you don't really need any more help." Maybe I should have gone for a longer run, hit the river.

"Not so quick, cowboy." Violet waved me over to the old house's curving staircase and I followed her up to a small office. "You offered to track that food down, right?" A stack of paper was piled on a desk by the window. A solidly built chocolate-point Siamese was luxuriating on top, a regal feline paperweight.

"Come on, Simon." Violet clapped her hands. Two blue eyes blinked in disbelief at the effrontery. I walked over and lifted the muscular body to the floor. "This is it. Our official correspondence. I guess we're lucky. Simon's litter mate Sushi would've eaten three or four pages by now."

I began to leaf through the pile. Most of it looked like letters, some handwritten, obviously by children. On a pad nearby Violet had started making some notes, but I couldn't discern any order in the stack. "All of these are about food donations?" I hadn't realized how large a task I'd taken on.

Violet shook her head as she collapsed into the desk chair and the air seemed to go out of her. "Nope, this is the paperwork on everything donated. We're just too vulnerable. I've been thinking about it all day. We take everything. You know."

I did. All my old towels went to Violet's shelter, and after Bunny's neighbor lost her cat, we'd help her pack up the twenty-year-old tabby's remaining low-ash and special diet cans as a donation.

"Well, I'll get started here." I waited for Violet to give me the desk chair. "Maybe you could let yourself take the rest of the day off? Take a nap?" I snuck a look at her notes and saw a list of numbers. Numbers and dollar signs.

"There's no time." She stayed slumped in the chair, looking beat. Even her spiky locks were listless. "It's too dangerous. We're too open. From now on, we've got to buy everything, and let people know that any donations have got to be in cash."

"Not even towels?" With kittens, sick cats, and injured animals in need of emergency swaddling, the shelter went through terrycloth as fast as litter. She shot me a glance. I'd hoped for a smile, but her pale face was too sad and tired.

"I don't know, Theda. It's just all too much." She dropped her pencil on the pad in front of her. "Or too little."

"Well, what if that one bag was an isolated incident?" I was winging it, but my bout of exercise had boosted my optimism. "What if it was just an accidental contamination, a sack of food that got stored in someone's pantry. I don't know, and someone spilled some hot chocolate, or something, just by mistake, and you can trace it to its source? Won't that be the end of it?" She looked up, those green eyes small and sunken inside heavy, blue-purple rings.

"I can't take any chances. Theda."

I pulled my own yellow legal pad out of my bag and motioned for her to get up. "You may not have to. I'll go through these and see if I can spot anything. I'll figure out where that bag came from and why it was contaminated. Keep in mind, it may still have been an accident."

"Better to know than not know, I guess. Speaking of which," she pulled a blue file folder from a drawer and tossed it on top of the pile, "here's our lovely 'hate mail' file. At least, the ones Caro made me keep. But you'll see, they're too flakey to take seriously. What worries me are the ones who act instead of writing." And with that, Violet finally surrendered her chair, leaving me alone with the towering stack.

AN HOUR LATER, I'd made some headway. Of course, I'd dived into the blue file first, but I'd come to the conclusion that Violet was right. Of the seven handwritten letters, three were typical homophobic rants, complaining about Violet and Caro cohabiting in what had been a "perfectly decent" neighborhood. One of these accused my friends of engineering the state's gay marriage law, though, as far as I knew, they hadn't tied the knot. Three were anti-cat. Two called cats "pests," saying they spread disease and shouldn't be allowed to run around. From the theme and the handwriting, these looked like repeats. Someone had too much time on his hands. The other complained about the noise, as if any of Violet's cats would have been left unneutered to caterwaul in the night. The final letter confounded me. In big, loopy letters, it seemed to accuse Violet of witchcraft, but also seemed to confuse her with the shelter's previous owner, a nice older woman named Lillian. Maybe the writer had thought that Lillian had used her powers to transform herself into a young purple-haired punk? These were nasty, no doubt. But compared to the specifically violent ones that had been addressed to Rachel, they seemed silly. Jerks and kooks, maybe, but not capable of actually doing anything.

In a way, that was a relief. I was still pushing for the accident theory. But I agreed that tracking down the source of the contaminated food was key. With the blue file tucked away, I made myself start on the more mundane pile, with the idea of making order out of chaos. I'm not the neatest person by far, but over the next hour I managed to clip together the related correspondence—the letters asking for receipts and the little shelter's copies of the receipts—and sort it out by year. After that, I pulled all notices of food donations, working backward in time. Violet of necessity stockpiled food; donations came in waves. But it seemed reasonable to assume that the contaminated sack had been dropped off sometime within the last few months.

Working through the food-specific letters wasn't easy. Some were illegible, many were undated. A few were smeared beyond recognition by some liquid, long dried, and I put some of them aside to look at again later. Had someone been using this pile as a litter box? Perhaps Simon wasn't the gentleman he appeared? I lifted one yellowed page up for a quick sniff. It smelled clean. But the page below it caught my eye. It had stuck to the water-stained letter and it, too, was faded. Maybe Caro hadn't gotten around to fixing all the leaky windows? I held the paper close, but the writing—brown now, and fuzzy at the edges—was no more legible than the page on top. Still, there was something. Up in the corner, was that a water mark? The stain of a drip that had dried? Or was it the profile of a cat, the logo of the city shelter? The letter referred to sixty dollars value and I thought I could make out the word "kibble."

"Hi, this is Theda Krakow, calling for Dr. Rachel?" I didn't know if the tainted food had come from Rachel's shelter, or if

the contaminant—whatever it was—had been added before or
after it came to Violet's. But I'd promised Violet I'd try to trace
the source of the food, and as I dialed, I realized I had other
questions for the vet. Between my fatigue, her hectic schedule,
not to mention the storm brewing between my two friends, I
hadn't followed through that morning. Rachel had been
looking at the food, but we'd left the bag that it came in with
her, too. At the time, I hadn't thought about it. The brand wasn't
anything special. KittyLuv was just a fancy supermarket brand.
But maybe the packaging had an expiration date on it, crimped
on the end to indicate freshness. Maybe it had some code or
stamp that would help us identify when it had been sold.

"She's busy?" When the volunteer came back to the phone,
I realized I wasn't going to get my answers today. It was past
five already, and although the shelter stayed open into the
evening, most of the office staff would be packing up. "Would
you tell her that I called? No message." The letterhead, some
old notice that may have been tied in with a donation…it was
too complicated to explain. "No, wait! Tell her not to throw
out the cat food bag. Tell her I can trace it!" I'd explain later.
As long as that bag didn't get tossed, maybe I had a lead. In
the meantime, I could show Violet the questionable letters.

"Hey, Violet?" Three young women were still at work
with rags and a mop, but the first floor of the shelter was as
clean as I'd ever seen it. Even Sibley, Violet's nearly constant
companion, looked freshly brushed, his gray tail wrapped
around his white paws to make a neat package. The Siamese,
who had followed me down, stopped to sniff the floor.
Murphy's Oil soap: the faint memory of my own last house-
cleaning came to me.

"She's taking a nap," a voice answered from the corner.
Francesca, with her delicate build and long dark curls, could
have been Tess's younger sister. She even had a guitar out

now, and was absently fingerpicking a chord for a soft, sad sound. "We told her we'd finish everything up here and she needed the sleep."

"I'm glad. The place looks great." It did, and I automatically reached for Simon to walk us both around one damp spot on the floor, settling us both on the worn sofa. "Working on a song?"

"Yeah, 'Shiva's Lament.' But it's for me. Not for a critic to hear." Her smile softened her words. "Not yet. You're Theda Krakow of 'Clubland.' Violet talks about you all the time. Bill, too."

My face must have registered shock, because she laughed gently. "In a good way, I mean." She gestured at the guitar. "I've been talking to him about starting an acoustic night, I mean, now that the blues night is such a success."

I smiled back at her, but I could feel my cheeks ache with the strain. Such a success that Bill couldn't tell me who was playing?

It wasn't this woman's fault. "Good idea. Let me know if it happens, I'll try to do something." Not that I could write about Bill's club. But I could drop a hint, and as long as Bill ran a bar tab for Ralph, our official pop music critic, he'd guarantee coverage. I ran over the possibilities as she continued to pick out notes, forming them into a familiar pattern and then taking it apart. I wanted to follow the tune. There was something interesting going on, something unresolved. But the cat on my lap began to purr and knead. The room was warm. I didn't know how long had passed before my own nodding jerked me awake.

"Oh!" The papers in my hand had fallen to the floor. Francesca reached to retrieve them.

"Anything I can help you with?" She looked at the pages. "Taxes?"

"No, I'm trying to figure out where the bad batch of food came from. I meant to ask Violet about a couple of the donations. Specifically, about this." I showed her the waterlogged letterhead. "I could be wrong, but it looks like it came from the city shelter." The cat jumped down as I grabbed my bag from the floor and tucked the papers inside. "I need to look at these again when I'm not half asleep, though, and I can ask her later. Are you done here?"

"Pretty much. They're just finishing up." She motioned with her chin to the three remaining cleaners. "I'm supervising."

The three cleaners are all wearing earbuds, but I wasn't going to question her. She must have seen something on my face.

"Really I'm just trying to work out a plan," she went on. "Violet has said she doesn't want to take any more donations of food or anything else, if she can help it, which is great. I want to get her into the healthier stuff anyway. And we were talking about the shelter endowment. I know it's good, but she's going to need a quick influx of cash to replace her stores. So, I was thinking of a benefit. I mean, hey, we all love Violet and most of us on the scene love cats, too."

I nodded in agreement. A fund-raiser for the Helmhold House made perfect sense. What didn't was that this newcomer was now Violet's confidante in running the shelter. Was the pretty musician a romantic possibility? I couldn't see Violet and Caro breaking up, but then again, I hadn't been around much recently. What else, I wondered as I grabbed my bag and looked around for my coat, and who else, had I been missing?

FIVE

"Wow!"

"Hang on!" Even before I could unlock the door, Musetta was making her demands known. With reason: I was late, I knew it. But all those papers had made me hungry, and the pizza had worn off hours ago. The Central Square diner didn't make tuna rollups as well as the lifers in the *Mail* cafeteria—something about the pickles—but the counter man had only raised his eyebrows a bit when I asked him to chop the dill slices and layer them in. I'd thought briefly about getting the sandwich to go, but it was a two-hander, not the kind of meal you could eat while driving, and I was too hungry to wait.

"Wow! Woo-wow!" Someone else had a thing about waiting. As I stepped in, the purring little linebacker threw herself against my shins. Clearly she'd been wanting to play. I was looking down at the pile of toys, considering my options, when she decided for me, pushing her head into my hand, her nose wet against my palm. I hoisted her in my arms, her dense middle stretching out as I lifted her like a Slinky.

"Oof, kitty, you're getting chubby." Rachel had warned me of this, of course. She'd even marked Musetta as "overweight" at her latest checkup, three months before.

"What do you mean, overweight?" Rachel had been writing up her bill when I had noticed the word on my pet's chart. "You didn't say anything!" Yes, I was a little oversensitive. As I progressed into my own thirties, I was finding it increasingly difficult to fit into my own jeans. But this was my pet she was talking about.

"For a pampered Cambridge housecat, she's well within the normal range." Rachel didn't even look up. Obviously, she'd had this conversation before. "But you've got to start watching her intake. No more free feeding, no more cans on demand. Do you know how many cases of feline diabetes we're seeing these days?"

"A lot?" My voice had gone soft. I'd thought of Musetta's weight as a vanity issue. A soft cat is a thing of joy, an obese one a joke. "She's not—" I couldn't even say it.

"No, her blood tests have been fine." Rachel looked up, handing me the bill, but also reassuring me. "But she's an adult cat, now. The only growing she'll be doing is sideways."

I THOUGHT OF THAT now as I hefted my pet up. "Musetta, do I have to start measuring your food?" Bunny, I knew, scooped out a careful cup each morning for her two cats. But since one was a glutton, the other as finicky as that famous commercial feline, her care didn't pay off. Pangur Ban looked like an orange ottoman with ears these days, while Astarte remained an Audrey Hepburn gamine. "Kitty?"

In response, she turned her sweet round face to me, reaching her nose to touch mine and giving me another dose of that foul breath.

"Okay, kitty, that's it. We're making that appointment." In response, Musetta blinked her green eyes. The more I talked to cats, the more I became convinced that they do understand. The placid cat still in my arms, I made my way to the phone, edging around a coffee table covered with papers, CD cases, and, yes, yesterday's coffee mug. I should clean. I should also call Bill again. But first things first: My pet probably just needed a cleaning, but I knew that bad breath could be a sign of other health problems, too.

"Hi, Amy." The regular receptionist must have been closing up. "Theda again. I need to make a dental appointment." I remembered my earlier query about the cat-food bag. "And is Rachel still around? I left a message for her earlier, too, with one of the volunteers. Do you know if she got it?" During the moment of silence, while Amy looked, Musetta began to knead. I was glad I'd trimmed her front claws as she worked first one and then the other paw deep into my thighs. "She did? Damn! Sorry." I must have missed the dew claw. "And she's not taking calls now?" I must have flinched, because Musetta prepared for a leap right toward my coffee mug. "Oh, hell. Well, don't let me keep you. But when you come in tomorrow, would you let me know when the next available appointment is, please? And tell her I called, okay?" I hung up in time to catch the mug, but the papers it had balanced on went flying onto the floor.

Having had her fill of loving, my cat now wanted to play. "Go, kitty!" I tossed a ball of aluminum foil and saw her leap for it, her white mittens grabbing at the air. "Go long!" Her feet slipped and scampered as she dodged and jumped, making me work to keep up. "One more, okay?" How out of shape could she be? I was out of breath before she stopped, mid-chase, to wash one white boot.

That's when I noticed the answering machine.

"Theda?" It was Bill, finally. "I got your message. I've been meaning to call. Yeah." There was a pause so long that I checked to make sure the machine was still running. "I'd like to talk. Try me at the club?"

I CHECKED THE CLOCK—nearly six. Beginning of the busy time over at Bill's. He'd have no time for a call, but if I dropped by, maybe we'd be able to chat. And so, despite her protesting "meh," I dislodged Musetta from my lap and headed for the door.

"Going over to the Stand?" As I locked my front door, I heard Reed descending the stairs above me.

"Yes." It was a relief to say, and he smiled back. "And you?"

"I've got a gig in Watertown. There's a bistro thinks I'll lend the dinner hour some class." He raised his eyebrows. "But I'll come to the club later." He paused at the base of the stairs. "Welcome back."

"Thanks." Had the entire world known of our fight? It didn't matter, my step was light as I headed down the street. Pizza or no, that was my only question. That tuna roll-up had been awfully small, and a shared slice behind the bar would be cozy, an edible peace offering. I didn't mind being the one to offer the metaphorical olive branch. With pepperoni.

But if I didn't bring food, and Bill could sneak away for an hour after the rush and before the music, well, we might be able to have a more intimate meal. Or whatever. That thought, as well as the nip in the air, made up my mind, and I dug my hands in my coat pockets as I trotted directly to Bill's Last Stand.

"Hey, Theda!" The heavy door was pulled open for me by a familiar face.

"Hey." I ought to know the name. Good looking, shaggy blond hair, and a jaw like chiseled granite. Played guitar—bass? no guitar—in a new garage band. "Peter."

"Piers." He smiled and held out a hand big enough for a bassist. "I guess I didn't make that much of an impression." I'd written up some news about his band in a scene round-up a few weeks back. We'd talked about doing a column.

"No, it's me. Crazy day and not enough sleep." I slipped past him, but he remained by the door. Was Bill employing a bouncer now?

"No sweat." He nodded toward the rear. "Bill's in back."

The long, narrow front room was full enough to make my heavy coat uncomfortable, and I slipped it off as I threaded my way through the crowd. "The back" either meant the music room, which had probably once been the private part of this ancient bar; the tiny backstage dressing room beyond; or the cluttered storage area-slash-office off that. If Bill was setting up already, maybe he would have time for a break.

"Hey, stranger." I purposely cast my voice low, not angry, not whiney, as I stepped through to the music room. "How've you been?" But if I expected to find my sweetheart alone, assembling mike stands, I was mistaken. The music room was empty.

"Hey, Theda!" A voice called from the backstage area. Francesca, looking a little flushed, was just getting to her feet. Behind her, I saw Bill, kneeling on the floor.

"Uh, hi." I walked over to the smaller room.

Francesca seemed to be blocking me. "Bill?"

"He's not coming out." Bill seemed to be talking to the floor. "Sorry."

"Bill!" Francesca's rising tone finally caused him to turn around.

"Theda." He stood, slowly, still a little creaky as he unfolded his long legs. "You know Francesca, right?"

"Yeah." I'm not the jealous type, but none of this was making sense. Why wasn't Francesca letting me pass? "Is something going on?"

Bill shot Francesca a look, and she moved aside. "I'll get the treats."

We were silent until she'd left the room. "It's a cat, Theda," Bill said, finally. "Francesca brought over one of Violet's recent acquisitions. I think she wanted to adopt him, but he wasn't really friendly. She thought he'd do well here, keep some of the rodents at bay. But something, maybe the noise, has spooked him. He's gotten himself wedged behind these boxes here and I'm not sure what to do."

A club cat? Maybe a feral? Well, I knew weird bookstore cats aplenty. "May I be introduced?" Bill smiled, and I felt a rush of warmth as he reached out to me. "Please. Theda? Meet Ellis. Ellis, Theda Krakow."

I knelt where Bill had been a moment before, but all I saw were two yellow eyes. Someone was not happy.

"Ellis like the writer? Or, no, Marsalis, right?"

"I'm not sure." With an audible crack from his knee, Bill lowered himself to my side. "He came with that name, it's a good masculine name for a big former tom, and I figured it had a sibilant, so he'd hear it, right?"

"Yeah. 'The naming of cats is a serious matter…'" I drew out the "s" and, sure enough, a round black face turned up toward me, sleek and curious. "How long has he been here?"

"Since yesterday. Francesca called me this morning, asking me to check on him. I gather there was some trouble at Violet's?"

"Yeah, there was." I turned back to the cat and began drumming my fingers on the wooden floor. The rhythmic sound caught the cat's attention, but I really did it for an excuse to turn away. "Funny, I tried to reach you this morning, too."

"Yeah, well, things have been weird." I looked over at him. He collapsed back on his butt and I, too, turned to sit. But not before taking a quick look over my shoulder. Francesca had made herself scarce. "I needed to think about things before we talked. It's been hard."

I nodded, my throat tight.

"I was really hurt, Theda. I mean, it seems like every time we are on the verge of getting closer, you pull away. With the club, with all this," he gestured at the room around us, "I thought out of everybody, you'd be supportive. You'd be there for me." Like he had been for me. He didn't have to say it.

"Bill, I'm sorry. I—"

"No." He held up one of his big broad hands, and I noticed that he'd stopped biting his nails. "It's a big change. Everything—our timetables, who we are, when we can be together—it all got mixed up."

"I want to unmix it." I didn't realize until just then how much that was true. I loved this man, and I wanted to work it out.

"Do you?" That crooked smile broke my heart.

"Yeah." I swallowed. "I didn't realize how territorial I was, or how much my ego was tied up with being the rocker. You know," I tried a smile. "The 'hip' one. But I miss you, and I'm willing to share." I meant it as a joke.

"Are you?" He leaned forward. I waited for the kiss, but he kept talking. "Are you sure you can deal with this? 'Cause sometimes, Theda, I wonder if you're always going to back away when I get closer. I wonder if you really want me in your life."

I took his hand in both of mine. "I do, Bill. I'm a work in progress, I know that. But I've missed you. I want to keep trying, Bill. I do." Just then I felt the softness of fur. Ellis, an enormous black cat, had emerged while we were talking and was now brushing up against me.

"Well, I guess you still have the touch." Bill freed his hand and reached over to pet the big cat. In response, Ellis craned his large head up, pushing it into Bill's palm and I saw a slight dab of white on his chest. "You got this guy out of hiding, and you found me in my den, too." I reached over to stroke the sleek black back, and Bill put his hand over mine. "I'd say this has another life in it, don't you think?"

I smiled my answer, tears smarting in my eyes, and this time he did kiss me. Between us, the big black cat started to purr.

WE DID GET PIZZA, eventually, when someone in the first band offered to make a food run after sound check. I didn't mind waiting. Maybe I had been away too long, but it seemed to me that everyone in the club was energized by our reunion. Reed certainly was, when he came by during the second set.

"So nice to see you here, Ms. Krakow." Reed passed his sax case over the bar to Piers; the muscular doorman had taken over drinks duty after the dinner rush.

"And you as well, kind sir." I was giddy with happiness. It wasn't just Bill, I'd felt isolated. While he'd helped the headliner set up, I'd even poured my heart out to Piers. For a big guy, he was sensitive, and a good listener, and he kept my mug of Blue Moon full.

"I do my best." Reed gave Piers his order, and the cute bartender set off down the bar to fetch Reed's call brand rye.

"Making friends?" Reed raised an eyebrow. Ralph had shown up, too, and begun to sidle over, but when he saw Reed settle in he turned instead to a red-faced blonde.

"Feeling happy." I raised my mug to Ralph, just as a gesture of friendship, but he was engrossed in the blonde. When she turned to greet a familiar face—Mona, that was it—with a big hug and a kiss, I couldn't help but smile. Piers had returned by then, bringing himself a soda and the two of us clinked glasses. Bill waved from the music room. The headliner would be going on soon, and Reed and I made our way toward the back.

"See you soon." I slid a five across the bar. Nobody charged me here, but Piers was working. Besides, I'd enjoyed talking with him.

"Hey, stranger." Bill wrapped an arm around me as I passed through the doorway, drawing me back to him. "Thought I might lose you out there."

"Yeah, right." I was feeling the booze, but I was sure he was joking. "Speaking of—we've been MIA for too long. Bunny and Cal want us to come over."

"Not dinner—"

I cut Bill off. "No, they know that you're still here every night. Maybe by the summer." I didn't think it likely my sweetheart would ever take a night off, but I wasn't in the mood to argue. "Bunny was talking brunch. Sunday, maybe?" I tilted my head back to look up at Bill, but he was busy watching the stage.

"Sounds good." He wasn't listening. The band hadn't started yet. Was he concerned about something I couldn't see?

"Cal will make those killer banana pancakes." I didn't care if he was paying attention. I was feeling good, envisioning our renewed domestic bliss. "Maybe we can go back to your place after, curl up with the papers."

"Uh-huh." He was definitely watching something. "Wait, did you say Sunday?" I nodded. "Sorry, Theda. Can't do it. I promised Francesca I'd do some strategy session with her. Start planning for the big benefit."

"What?" Suddenly those large drafts seemed like a bad idea. Had I missed something? But Bill was gone, up toward the stage where the singer was struggling with a recalcitrant mike.

"Francesca." I'd noticed her hovering, but hadn't thought anything of it. "You've already planned the benefit for Vi?" I asked, leaving out my bigger question: why are you getting together over brunch to discuss it?

"The fund-raiser? Oh, yeah." She was staring at the stage. With Bill's help, the band got going, swinging into a Brazilian groove. The singer's warm voice joined the mix, easing over the Portuguese lyrics like she was enjoying something delicious. She was eye-catching, but my gaze turned back to Francesca. Did she know the singer, or was she looking at Bill? "Vi's really worried." She turned toward me, her dark eyes huge and, I had to admit, very pretty. The swirl of the music seemed to fit her. Exotic, lyrical. Even her voice had fallen into the rhythm, matching the singer's cadences. "You know she needs to replace everything that was donated. With a shelter, you're not just taking care of individual animals, you're watching over an entire animal population. It's just too great a risk to keep everything. So I asked Bill if we could have it here."

"But here? This is a jazz club." That second beer had definitely been a mistake. "And, besides, the room is too small."

She was shaking her head. "It's a *music* club, and Violet's cool with the idea of some of us doing acoustic sets. Maybe between the bands. Besides, the bigger places in town are all booked, like, months ahead of time. And the fact that we know Bill just makes everything easier."

Just then, the band amped up the volume, saving me from having to reply. "We know Bill?" I was mulling that one over, as our Bill returned from stage side. "That cable's shot and the spares seem to have gone missing. I've got to ask Reed to pick up some new ones." With a smile, he went in search of his dapper partner, leaving me feeling vaguely sick and wondering just what had happened while I'd been gone.

SIX

My headache the next morning came from more than the beer. I'd wanted our first night back together to be perfect, but I was enough of a realist that I knew to defend my turf, too. So despite my rapidly sinking mood, I'd hung around till closing, chatting with Reed and Piers, and trying not to shoot daggers at Francesca's slim back. I don't like feeling jealous. Love is about connection, not competition. But I also knew I'd been away for a while. Maybe too long, and I had some lost ground to make up, none of which makes the best setting for a romantic interlude. Bill and I, our chemistry was good. And I like to think that we had more between us, too. So by the time we fell asleep, we were both warm and happy, and Musetta completed the picture—jumping onto the foot of the bed with a thud. But the next morning, as I let the shower beat down on my head, all the night's worries came back in force.

"Bill? Honey?" I'd needed the time to think, but as I reached for a towel, I couldn't help a pang of disappointment. There had been a time when he'd have joined me. "You want to grab some breakfast?" No way was I going to sound desperate.

"I'm making coffee." The whir of the grinder cut off any more, and by the time I emerged, toweling my hair, the aroma spoke for itself. "I can stay for a cup." He gave me a quick peck. "But then I've got to run." The shower curtain scraped back, the water started, and with a sigh I walked into the bedroom to get dressed.

"What are you up to today?" At least he had the grace to ask, fifteen minutes later, as he reached for his own mug. I'd buried my face in the paper to hide my mood.

"I told Violet I'd help her track down the source of that bad cat food." Bill made a noise, either curiosity or the coffee was too hot. "Didn't you hear?"

"Just that there had been trouble. What happened? Are the cats okay?"

"They're fine." As if to stress the point, Musetta chose that moment to leap from the floor to the table via my lap. Coffee slopped over the Living section. "Oh, great." I mopped up the spill with the proffered paper towel, and Bill reached to top off my mug. "Thanks." I tried to sound gracious as I caught him up on the possible poisoning and Violet's impending financial crisis.

"That explains a lot." He looked thoughtful. "Francesca seemed really intent on scheduling the benefit as soon as possible, but I must have missed the back story."

That was my opening, but I had to be careful. "So, is Francesca helping out a lot? She and Piers are close, right?" It was a shot in the dark, intended to distract. Bill wasn't buying it.

"If they are, she's got reason to hate you after last night." His grin took the sting out of his words. "You and my hunky bartender were getting pretty tight." I started to protest, but he raised his free hand. "No, don't say it. I was busy. You were happy. But to answer your *other* question. No, there's nothing going on with Francesca. She's just trying to establish herself on the scene. She lost her own cat not too long ago, too, and she's still really broken up about it. I think she's trying to keep busy." He must have seen the relief that flooded my face. Pet loss was something I could sympathize with. "She probably doesn't want to go home to an empty apartment. You understand."

"Definitely." I put down my mug and walked around the

table to wrap my arms around my sweet man. "And I think you're a good guy for keeping her distracted. Not to mention offering the club to help Violet out. I'm proud to know you."

"The pleasure is mine," he said, before kissing me back, as I tried to put the pretty dark-haired Francesca out of my mind.

ONCE BILL HAD taken off, the day looked strangely empty. I had made that promise to Violet, sure, and I had phone calls to return. But my apartment seemed lonely and dull suddenly, rather than cozy. Wednesday, hump day. Even Musetta had made herself scarce and when I found her, napping on top of the file cabinet by my computer, she dismissed me with a sleepy glance. "Neh." And that was that.

Nothing for it but to hit the phones—or leave the house. But the bright clear day outside still looked too cold to be officially spring, and I hadn't made a go of freelancing by shirking work. Grabbing the receipts I'd taken from the shelter yesterday, I plopped onto the sofa and reached for the phone.

"Hi Amy, Theda again. Is Rachel in?" The combination of that questionable receipt and my need to make an appointment for Musetta gave this call priority. "No? Well, do you know if she got my message?"

"Sorry, Theda. I put it in her box." Amy sounded harried. I knew better than to push her.

"Of course, thanks. But while I have you here, have you found me an appointment time yet?"

"That's right. Sorry." I heard pages turning. The shelter kept its calendar the old-fashioned way: on paper. "It's been crazy. One of our regular volunteers quit with no notice. We've got a new aide starting. Plus, kitten season has kicked in in earnest, and we're trying to do as many of the combo distemper shots, the FVRCPs, as we can before all the new animals come in. More and more, people are saying they don't want 'em."

"The kittens?"

"The shots." Behind her, another phone was ringing. "They hear about vaccine-site sarcomas and they think the shots are going to be worse than the disease. They should come in here when we get an outbreak. Wait, looks like, let's see. Fifth of May? That's a Saturday, first free appointment, 9:00 a.m.?"

Saturdays at nine I would prefer to be asleep. But this was my cat we were talking about, and, besides, once the annual spring flood of new litters started coming in, Rachel's days would be more than full. "Sure, I'll take it." I flipped my own calendar forward a page. "May, wow." Hard to believe that real spring—the kind with flowers and warm weather—was just around the corner.

The busy receptionist misunderstood my surprise. "If I get an opening earlier, I'll let you know." I knew she meant "sooner," but who needs to be the grammar police? I winced.

"That would be great. Good luck with the vaccinations, Amy, and thanks."

I'd barely hung up before my own phone rang again. But if I was hoping for fast news of an opening in Rachel's schedule, I was disappointed. It was Tim, my editor, sounding breathless as usual.

"Krakow? Good. When you come in, I need you to bring a résumé and some of your non-music clips. At least the dates, we can pull them up here."

When I come in? Tim knew that I filed via e-mail, and that he already had my column for this week. "Tim? Did we have an appointment?"

"Yes! The staff job! Your interview. Didn't I tell you?" Well, no, but I wasn't surprised.

"You had to run off to the budget meeting, Tim. You said you'd call me with details." My editor might have been as overworked as Amy, but he was certainly less organized. And less sympathetic.

"Well, I'm calling you now. The head office wants to act on it right away, and they're meeting with candidates this afternoon."

Candidates? Plural? "Tim, you didn't even tell me what the job is. I mean, I don't even know if I want it."

"Arts reporter. You remember reporting, don't you?" He was trying for humor. "You were keen enough on it last January when you did that big drugs story."

"That was club related." It had been, and I also had never meant to get that involved. "And, Tim, I'd have to think about taking a staff job. I mean, I'd have to give up a lot of freedom."

His guffaw made me start. "What a joker you are, Krakow! That's why you're my top stringer. Three o'clock today. And wear something that makes you look like a grown-up."

Great, I was competing with people I didn't know for a job I wasn't sure I wanted. But maybe I could find out more about the position itself.

"Bunny?" This time my friend picked up on the first ring.

"Theda! I'm so glad you called. You got those clips, right? So, do you have any thoughts on the pet psychic?"

I'd forgotten entirely about her odd request. "Sorry, Bunny, you're going to have to tell me more. A pet psychic—not a psychic pet, right? Like one of those 'dog whisperers'?"

"Sort of. I was reading about one who helps find lost pets and resolve squabbles, like when you get a new kitten?" I murmured what must have sounded like assent, because she kept on talking. "So I was thinking. Pangur Ban and Astarte have been like my babies for so long, but soon they're going to be replaced. I mean, not replaced, but unseated."

I had to break in. "You're not thinking of getting rid of your cats, are you? I mean, I know you've been having Cal deal with the litter, but all those old wives' tales about cats hurting babies—"

"Theda!" This time, she cut me off. "Who do you think I am? My kitties are more than my pets. They're my *familiars!*" Usually, I take Bunny's Wiccan beliefs with a grain of salt, but this time I felt relief. "They help me commune with my feline side."

"I'm glad. I know you love them. But you've never had any problems communicating with them yourself. So why are you asking about cat whisperers?"

"Well, it's just that there's going to be a lot of change going on. And I want them to understand it—and *know* that even if I'm too busy for pets and all, that I still love them. And there's this one pet psychic, she does all her work by phone and she only charges eighty dollars for a session."

"Bunny!" For a smart woman, one who worked at a newspaper no less, my friend could be gullible. "Are you hearing yourself? Save your money. Better you should spend it on a nice dinner for you and Cal. First you talk about cooking for your cats and now this. You can make your cats understand. And I promise, if they start to feel neglected, I'll come over and play with them." Musetta wouldn't be crazy about that, but it beat babysitting.

I heard a sigh commensurate with my dear friend's weight. "You will? I guess I've just been worried."

"Bunny, is everything going okay? I mean, otherwise?" I knew she didn't like to talk about problems—thinking bad thoughts gave them power—but I was a believer in getting things out in the open. "Is there anything up with the baby? Is Cal good?"

"Yeah." I heard something in her voice, and waited. "Oh, I don't know." She wasn't going to spill.

"Bunny, tell you what. I've got to come down to the *Mail*

this afternoon anyway. Can I grab you for a coffee—I mean, a juice—break? Maybe around two?"

"That would be great, Theda." Her voice dropped half an octave with relief. "What are you coming in for—that arts job?"

"Yeah, I think so." I'd find out more soon enough. "In fact, I was hoping you could give me the scuttlebutt."

"I'll see what I can dig up." If anyone could, Bunny would, and the idea of a project had put some life back into her voice. "See you soon!"

THAT LEFT ME WITH a couple of hours to kill and too unsettled to do much with them. Another run would clear my head. But so, I realized, would food. Even if Bill had to dash off, there was no reason why I couldn't head down to the Mug Shot. If I needed to, I could switch to decaf, but the fresh air and a lemon-poppyseed muffin might help me sort out my options.

A walk might also help me stretch out those muscles. As soon as I started down the stairs of my second-floor apartment, my calves started crying out in pain. It had been a brutal winter, and I'd been lazy too long. Maybe it was just as well Bill had taken off; he'd gotten positively religious about his fitness regimen, once his various casts and crutches were gone. I was limping as badly as he'd been back in February when I hit the street.

The kinks were nearly gone ten minutes later, when the Mug Shot came into view. City living had its drawbacks—my rising rent was only the latest reminder—but as long as I could walk to a coffeehouse, a club, and a bookstore within fifteen minutes, a city girl I'd remain.

"Decaf latte, and one of those." I pointed to the top-heavy golden muffins behind the counter. The tattooed barista, the latest successor to Violet's old job, wiped down the counter in front of me and went to fill my order.

"Hey, Theda!" I looked up and saw Piers a few stools down. He grabbed his mug and slid down with a big smile. "Off to work?"

"Sort of." His grin turned quizzical, so I gave him the thumbnail. He knew I wrote, but the whole freelance-staff writer disconnect was new to him. "And now they say there's some kind of job I might be right for," I concluded. "But I don't know what I'd have to give up—or what exactly I'd get."

"I get you." He shook his shaggy head. "One of the reasons I'm a contractor is because of the freedom." That explained the muscles. I wondered if he and Caro knew each other. "I mean, I've got the Last Stand gig now, for some steadiness. But that's just part-time. My drummer, he's working for his dad's business. Does the same work, really, and earns a lot more. But he's got someone looking over his shoulder."

"Whereas you can while away the morning at a coffee-house." I smiled to soften what could sound like criticism. After all, I was here, too.

"Actually, I'm heading out now." Maybe I had misspoken. "Doing some volunteer work at the shelter."

"Violet's?" How much had I missed?

"No," he shook his head as he stood up. "The city shelter. I'm fitting the back room with shelves. Used to be a stock-room for supplies and stuff. We've already insulated it and it's almost ready for cages."

I couldn't imagine him in the uniform scrubs, not that he wouldn't look dandy. Maybe carpenters were exempt. "Just in time for kitten season, huh?"

"Yeah." He grabbed his coat and looked up at me. "The more animals they can take care of, the better."

The alternative, we both knew, was not pretty. "Well, good for you. I should give them some of my time, while I have it."

I thought of Rachel. Maybe I could drop by after my meeting at the *Mail*. "Do you know Dr. Weingarten?"

"Rachel, yeah. She's the reason I'm giving it away." His grin turned on the wattage then, his blue eyes crinkling up in pleasure, and I realized that whether the strait-laced vet knew it or not, she'd made a conquest of another long-haired creature.

WHATEVER HIS MOTIVATION, if Piers could build shelves for the city shelter, I could do a little more paperwork for Violet. Getting my refill to go, I picked up the last tangy sweet crumbs with my fingertip and trotted, a little more easily, back home.

"Oof!" I'd only been gone about forty minutes, total, but that was too long for Musetta, who jumped into my lap with a thud. "Hang on, kitty." Heaving my hefty cat temporarily up in the air, I was able to reach the pile of papers. She took the disruption in stride, kneading me as I settled back to read and sip the swiftly cooling latté.

With a little effort, I was able to make out more of the shelter receipt. The signature was long gone, but the typed name on the bottom looked like Weingarten. And I was more confident than the day before that the body of the letter referred to sixty dollars' worth of kibble. But why would Rachel have made a donation to Violet's shelter? She did enough by making house calls. And dry food lasted, well, not indefinitely, but long enough so that the city shelter might have wanted to keep these bags on hand. Besides, since when did Rachel's staff have money to spend on a heavily advertised national brand? I tried to picture the back room of the shelter, where food and litter were stacked. Had I seen the bright red and blue KittyLuv logo there? Somehow, I couldn't conjure up an image of the bag, with its heart-shaped cat's face, on any of the shelves.

It was all too confusing, and in desperation I found myself

looking back through the few older receipts I'd taken. Here was one for a twenty-pound sack of prescription cat food. Someone else had donated an almost-full case of Science Diet; a local bookstore had raised money for a flat of generic low-ash food. But these contributions made sense: someone had lost a pet and didn't want food to go to waste. Or a group had raised money to buy something Violet's shelter needed. Which was, to be honest, just about everything. But why would Rachel be giving away ordinary cat food? Didn't the city shelter need it?

I didn't feel any closer to understanding what was going on. If Rachel hadn't called me back by the time I got done with the *Mail,* I needed to head over there and get some answers.

SEVEN

MUSETTA HADN'T WANTED me to go. As soon as I got up from the sofa, she knew, and spent the next half hour twining around my ankles. Doing her best to convince me that she'd pine away without me, she was more persuasive than she had a right to be. How many other cats had a person who spent most of the day at home? Still, I enjoyed the attention while I browsed through my closet, looking for something interview-worthy.

Black, black, denim, and leather: my wardrobe had only become more rock and roll over the past few years. By the time I hit forty, would I have any colors left in my closet at all? I pushed a hanger aside; my vintage CBGB T-shirt was more of a keepsake than a garment, worn thin and faded. What about the cowboy shirt with the mother-of-pearl buttons, a souvenir from that road trip to Austin? Three days in a van with the Road Workers, and I was ready to jump ship. But the music festival had been astounding: scrawny LA punks jamming with Tejano vaqueros, music everywhere. I remembered wandering into a boot store, thinking I'd try on a pair, when I'd heard the band in the back room, something between rock and soul, with a garage rocker from Boston sitting in on keyboards. I'd gotten a wonderful piece out of it, as much about the surprise camaraderie as the music. I'd bought this shirt that day, and boots, too.

I pulled the shirt from the closet. Not too wrinkled, and the embroidery on the front gave it a more feminine look than my usual. With black jeans and a jacket, yes, it would work.

I left the apartment with a renewed sense of optimism. Maybe this would be a good thing. Commitment. A job, a steady paycheck. The memories of that Austin trip prompted thoughts of paid vacations. Even, maybe, travel assignments. There was a festival in New Orleans every April I had my eye on.

AS SOON AS I SAW Bunny, that dream burst. I'd called her extension as I walked up to the main entrance and in hushed tones she'd told me to meet her in the cafeteria, over by the private dining room in the alcove we used to call "lover's lane."

"What's wrong? Are you worried about people seeing us?" I was half joking as I settled in, sipping at my fruit smoothie, but she was looking around surreptitiously, her cat's-eye glasses glinting.

"Not seeing. Hearing." Bunny had gotten in good with the women who ran the message center, and I knew that meant she caught more gossip than anyone back in the newsroom. "There is a posting. It's pretty vague, as usual. Reporter, level 1, full time, for the Living/Arts department. Not an arts writer. Living/Arts."

We both mulled that one over. As a music writer, I fell solidly into the "arts" category, and a reviewing job, like the one Ralph had, would have been classified as a "specialist," at least one pay grade higher than a reporter. Tim was in charge of both departments, and the boundary could be pretty flexible. Still, he'd warned me that the job wouldn't be straight music writing. "Living," after all, was what we used to call features: lifestyle stories and fashion. On the copy desk, we'd used to joke that when we reached a certain age, they'd rename the department "Dying." But Bunny didn't look like she was in the mood for a chuckle. She leaned closer in. "And that guy Cash is here today, and he's holding meetings with all the departments. It's gotta be connected."

"Cash?" I'd have remembered that name if I'd heard it before.

"He is, believe it or not, the money guy." Bunny wasn't smiling. "But he's from New York. There's something going on with the new owners." I knew what she meant. We all called the News Corporation of North America, NewsCo for short, the "new owners," even though they'd bought the paper close to four years earlier. So far, they'd been noticeable only in their absence, which had suited most of us just fine. "Mandating massive budget cuts, is what I hear. And not that far down the line."

"So he's behind the latest round of buyouts?"

She nodded. "I hear that's only the beginning. Overtime and some of the health benefits are next. The pension. You got out of here just in time."

"But Tim called me in about a job. So now they want me back?" It didn't make sense. "Am I replacing someone?" I thought of Ralph, who pulled in a good salary, and all the extras, doing not much more than I did for "Clubland." "Someone more expensive?"

"Maybe." She shrugged. "I've seen a couple of new faces around, and they all look pretty young." I pushed the remainder of my smoothie away. Discipline, that was key. "It's got to be a money thing. I mean, no offense." She raised her hand. I smiled.

"None taken." Bunny's support for me and my writing was never in doubt. And, besides, the way the bean counters thought, she was right. If I was being considered for a job, there had to be a budgetary reason. "I mean, I'm cheaper as a freelancer. So what's up?"

"I wish I knew. All I can figure is they want someone who can cover a variety of beats. Maybe they want copy they can use at a couple of their papers?"

I thought that one over. I wouldn't mind being read in more cities, though it would be nice to be paid more for it.

But I didn't think I'd feel comfortable taking someone else's job. Maybe I was one of the "younger" faces. Or the job meant writing fashion. I looked down at my getup, which now looked more Dale Evans than Austin hipster. Well, too late now to do anything about it. And the sight of my friend, large as a house, but still decked out in a purple sweater with spangles down the front—glitter that matched the sparkle on her glasses—made me smile. The *Mail* was hardly fashion central.

"So, what's up with you?" It would be good for me to get out of my own head for a while.

"I don't know, Theda." She reached into her bag and pulled out a Ziploc of carrot sticks. "Maybe it's just nerves. Waiting, wondering how our lives are going to change."

"Everything's copacetic with Cal, isn't it?" Her husband had always seemed comfortingly stable.

She nodded. "Yeah, it's more me than him. I mean, I don't know if I'm ready to give it all up yet."

I looked around. Right outside our alcove a janitor was mopping the floor, moving slowly to fill these off hours between the lunch and dinner rushes. Despite his efforts the floor was as dull as the rows of empty tables. "Too much excitement?"

"Not the *Mail,* Theda." Her voice brought me back. "My *real* life. The music, the *life.*"

My longtime friend was being unusually inarticulate, but I knew what she meant. For people like us, the club scene was more than nighttime fun. Bunny, Cal, Violet, and I had all been misfits, more or less, and we'd all found a kind of surrogate family out there. To top it off, six of the eight women in Bunny's Wiccan circle were in bands, last I checked, the nature-based religion fitting well with the creative music scene.

"We'll still be here." That was the wrong phrase; it was Bunny who didn't want to leave. "And Linda's a mom, and

you still see her." It was true, at least one of Bunny's sister
Wiccans now had two children.

"Yeah, but…" Bunny's voice trailed off. I could hear the
rest of the thought. Linda had a ton of energy, and, rumor had
it, enough money so that she didn't need to work full time.
And Linda was the exception. We'd lost more running buddies
to suburbia than I cared to count. Even I, single, childless, felt
too tired to go out some nights.

"Well, I'm still here. As is Violet." I thought of mention-
ing Tess, but she'd withdrawn from the scene because of her
own problems. "In the scene or out, your friends will stay
your friends."

"Thanks, Theda." A big sigh made the spangles sparkle.
"Anyway, it's not like I have a choice anymore, do I?" She
shoved the baggie back into her purse and pushed her chair
back. "But you, Theda, may have some decisions to make.
Call me after. And good luck!"

A BRIEF STOP in the second floor ladies' let me check my teeth
for foreign objects and try to calm down my hair. The hint of
spring humidity, a relief after a winter of overheated dryness,
had brought back its natural curl with a vengeance. I patted
one stray lock into place. I was who I was, wild hair and all.
Tim had called me, and he'd certainly seen me looking worse.
Nothing for it but to head downstairs and over to the management side of the building. I wouldn't have minded stopping
by Living/Arts. Maybe someone in the department would
know a little more. Maybe I should touch base with Ralph.
But Bunny and I had lingered. I'd have to leave the catching
up till later.

The glass-lined Conference Room B ran along the front of
the building. From the hall I could see across it and out its wall
of windows over the boulevard toward the harbor. Just beyond

the windows, a seagull floated on the breeze, and for a moment I considered bolting. But if I could see in, the folks inside could see me. I pushed the door open and stepped inside.

Tim sat on the far side of the long oval table. Not at the head, I noticed, or what would have passed for the head if not for the lack of corners. That position was held by another chubby, balding white man who, despite his shiny scalp, looked a few years younger than my boss. He glanced up as I came in, but it was Tim who greeted me.

"Hello, Krakow—Ms. Krakow. Thanks for coming in." I stepped forward and when he nodded took one of the seats on the other side of the table. To my right sat Glenna Rawls, the paper's managing editor. Next to Tim was Randolph "Randy" Williams. I didn't know what exact job Randy held, but had heard from Bunny that the women in News took the bearded editor's nickname seriously, making a point to avoid supply closets and dark corners when he was around.

"Krakow, I mean, Theda." Tim was nearly stammering and, against my better judgment, my heart went out to him. I nodded encouragement. "I don't know if you've had a chance to meet Rudy Cash, the new liaison between NewsCo and the *Mail.*" I hadn't, and nodded to the stranger. "He's here more in an advisory position, but he's very interested in the allocation of resources."

This is what Bunny had warned me about. I'd known of the sale of the *Mail,* we all did. But it seemed like the new owners were finally looking in the sack to see what kind of animal they'd purchased.

"So, Ms. Krakow, you write a freestanding feature on local pop music?" The balding newcomer looked up at me, for confirmation. I could see my latest pieces on the table in front of him, and his voice, strangely cool, didn't sound like there was anything he didn't know.

"Yes." I answered anyway, wondering what his game was. "'Clubland' is one of the most read features in Living/Arts." Last year's "youth initiative" had given Tim the resources to conduct the reader surveys that had saved my little patch of turf—and made my editor realize what a valuable resource I was.

"Interesting." That voice, and the way he flipped through the papers in front of him, indicated otherwise. But suddenly he stopped and held up one page for a closer look. Probably too vain for reading glasses. "But you've done some reporting, too. Drugs?"

I couldn't help it, I preened. "Yes, I uncovered the source of a new designer drug. My investigation helped convict several of the people involved." That story had started as part of "Clubland," since that was where the drugs first surfaced. But this didn't seem the time or place.

"So what have you been working on lately?" He didn't mean my music column. "Anything else…substantial?"

I didn't have anything, not really. But I'd been in the business long enough to have competitive instincts. "Pet food contamination." I looked over at Tim. I'd been careful to use the more inclusive "pet," rather than cat, but he'd still winced. He wanted me focused on young readers, not their pets. Cash nodded slightly, waiting for more.

"Isn't that old news?" Randy broke in. Either he had a favorite in mind, or I was simply too long in the tooth to spark his interest.

"Not if there are new cases. Local cases." I was spinning this out of nearly nothing, but I wanted to be taken seriously. "Possible poisonings."

That got their attention. "I'm following something up from a local shelter." Tim knew of my connection with Violet, but he kept his mouth shut. "The city shelter may be involved." I gave him a pointed look, and he nodded slightly. This wasn't just about my friends. "The chief vet is looking at contaminated cat kibble."

"That sounds more like a story for Metro." Randy was interested now. "Or even foreign, if it's the Chinese again."

"Now, wait a minute." Tim's territorial instincts were kicking in. "She's my writer, the anchor of my weekend section. If there's a pet angle, we want it. We can play it as a safety story. How to protect little Fluffy, or something."

"But—" The two of them went at it, Glenna chiming in occasionally about women readers and the most threatened demographics. I let myself relax. Mission accomplished, if all I wanted was to be taken seriously. But would I have to come up with a story? Violet had asked me for help as a friend, and going public with the bad food might have all kinds of repercussions for her tiny shelter. And what about Rachel? She wasn't implicated, not really. I just needed to find out if the bad food had come through her office, and why. If I had to cover this as a news story, it would create no end of hassles.

No point in worrying now. I made myself breathe in, slowly, and then let it out. Often enough, potential stories fell between the cracks. Leads evaporated, and the news cycle moved onto the next crisis. I waited for the discussion to burn itself out, but Cash wasn't that patient.

"Gentlemen, Ms. Rawls, I don't believe there is any reason to argue jurisdiction. This," he pointed to me as Exhibit One, "is a perfect example of what I've been telling you about. Interdepartmental cooperation, work assignments made by pay grade. If we can loosen our outdated sense of departmental boundaries and create more floating positions, we can turn the *Mail* into a leaner, more efficient news gathering organization."

I swallowed, hard, but nobody was looking at me now. I'd

come in here today hoping to be offered a job as a writer. But I had just made the case, it seemed, to insert myself as a cog in some new kind of machine.

EIGHT

OUT ON THE STREET, I told myself I could breathe easier again. Of course, as soon as I tried, a truck roared by, spewing gray smoke into the brisk salty air, and I found myself coughing up who knows what. So much for the city waterfront and the illusion of ocean freshness. Not that the air out here was any worse than the air inside. Should Bunny even be working at the *Mail* in her condition? The printing presses rumbled and shook the entire plant every night, and whatever they cast off probably made that truck exhaust look wholesome.

But the money was good, as I knew, too. Ah well, that was something she and I would tackle in a later conversation, maybe after I had let my own reactions to that interview settle. I'd been too scattered to seek her out again, and had ducked out the side exit so I wouldn't have to go through Living/Arts, wouldn't have to greet the writers and editors I'd known for so long. Some of those people were goners; nobody had to spell that out. At least one position was going to be scrapped to make room for the reporter position that had been dangled in front of me. I hadn't caused it, and I didn't know if I'd accept it, but that didn't make me feel any better about the whole deal. What I knew was that I had to think through everything I'd heard.

A writing job. On staff, back here at the *Mail.* On one side were several plusses. The idea of a steady paycheck was tempting. As was, if I were being completely honest, the validation of being hired, finally, as a writer by the biggest paper in town. But money only went so far, and flattery was a bad reason to commit to anything. If I thought about it objectively, the job had a lot of drawbacks. It wasn't only music, or even arts, and that whole floating thing sounded iffy, too, like I'd end up working for a bunch of masters, and having no beat to call my own.

Speaking of beats, what did the job mean for "Clubland"? In a way, it might not even matter. Although Tim hadn't said anything, I knew how these things worked. If I turned down a staff job as a writer and they hired someone else, why should they keep paying me as a freelancer? Why wouldn't they just give "Clubland" to whomever they hired?

Realistically, I didn't have much of a choice. Tim, the *Mail,* and that bureaucrat Cash were backing me into a corner. If I were Musetta, I would growl, the deep rumble starting somewhere back in my throat and my ears flattening against my sleek head. But even as I imagined her reaction, Bill's face came to mind and I knew in a flash what he'd say.

"Theda, isn't it possible you're overreacting? Fear of commitment, perhaps?" He'd be asking as gently as he could, and there would be some truth to what he was saying. But this was a big move. I knew this field better than he ever would, and I had also learned to trust my instincts over the years. They had gotten me some good stories—and even saved my life. No, I didn't need to go with the flow right now. What I needed was space and time to think things through.

Less than half a mile from the *Mail* was a city beach. The water, this close in the harbor, wasn't anything I'd ever want to swim in, but the waterfront itself was pretty. Coarse, tan sand belied its nickname, Gravel Beach, the wide crescent of beach proper bordered by dune grass that would grow waist high by summer. At this time of year, the little park was

probably abandoned, and cold as anything. But I turned into
the wind and made my way there, even waiting for the traffic
light before darting over to the water side. Sure enough, the
snack shack was still boarded up, but the sky was open and
clear, and the sand made a gratifying crunch beneath my
boots. Down at the far end, where a small pier stuck out over
the gray water, a young woman pushed a stroller. I wasn't the
only one seeking fresh air and the opportunity to be alone with
my thoughts.

A seagull swooped low over the snack shack. Seagulls soared
alone. Then again, seagulls ate trash. It squawked, angry that I
had no snacks to share. I sighed. My cell phone rang, its old-
fashioned ring startling me out of my thoughts. For a moment,
I was tempted not to answer, but I recognized Violet's number.

"Hey." My mind was still on the paper, and on the ocean.
I should come here more often.

"So, what did you find with the receipts? The poison? You
should have woken me, Theda, I'm having a crisis here. Can
you hear me?" I turned away from the harbor and began
walking over to the shack. It would be easier to hear her, and
to think, sheltered from the wind.

"Sorry, Vi. I'm down at Gravel Beach. Just came from a
meeting at the *Mail*." She didn't respond, so I kept going. "But
I think I found something in those receipts. I'm pretty sure
that bag of food came from the city shelter."

"Rachel, man, I'm not surprised—" The rest was garbled.

"What?" The wind had picked up and I huddled close to the
shack's weathered wood. "I'm having trouble hearing you."

"Rachel!" Violet was shouting. "I said I'm not surprised
that she's involved! You remember when we were there yesterday?" She didn't wait for my answer. "The letters about euthanasia? Well, they're doing it."

"Vi, I know that." Nobody wanted to put animals to sleep,

even the sick ones. But the spring kitten season was the worst. Too often, shelter overcrowding meant that even healthy animals were euthanized once their shot at adoption had run out. "But you know what they say, 'For every no-kill shelter….'" I didn't finish the thought. We'd been over this ground before. In order for a shelter like Violet's, a no-kill shelter, to exist, there had to be someplace else that would take the overflow—and deal with it as humanely as possible.

"Yeah, but this is new."

The wind must be making it difficult to hear. "What's new? I'm not getting you."

"They're giving up!"

"What?" I started walking to the road, trying for a stronger signal. "Violet, I don't understand, and I'm losing you." I stood on the sidewalk, the cars whipping by adding to the noise.

"Last year, Rachel made a big deal about how they were going for a hundred percent adoption, you know, like that shelter out in California? 'We will not kill healthy animals, blah blah blah.' She got a ton of press about it and I know their donations went way up." I nodded. I remembered the press conference, and the feeling of hope that had brought a new wave of volunteers to the city shelter. "But actually following through? Forget about it. Oh man, this makes too much sense."

"Wait a minute." I wasn't following Violet's logic. "Back up. How do you know anything about Rachel's plans? You were half asleep yesterday." I hadn't even read the file. Had I passed it over to Violet while Rachel did her thing?

"I've got my sources." It's true, Violet was connected and I didn't always want to know how. I thought of all the people who had come down to help the day before, and that led me to another thought: the Helmhold House had virtually no security.

"But, Vi, aren't you jumping to conclusions? Even if Rachel did donate that bag, maybe someone got to it while it was in your pantry." I thought of all the new faces I'd seen. "You've got people coming in and out of there all the time."

"Come on, Theda. They're my volunteers. Why would people who are giving their time want to hurt animals?"

"But why would Rachel? I mean, even if the food came from her place—"

Violet interrupted me. "This raises her profile! You heard her, she's talking to WellPet."

"Wait a minute, you think this is about a job?" I couldn't see it. Rachel was too dedicated to abandon the nonprofit, even for the glossy new animal hospital that had opened downtown. "She's not leaving the shelter."

"So she says." Violet was insistent. "But even if—think of the donations. You heard what she said about new equipment, right? It's all because of the new no-kill campaign. Word gets out that she's not sticking to it, she'll stop getting those nice checks. But if cats are getting sick, or even dying at my place, well, that makes her shelter look pretty good, doesn't it? I'm the bad news, then, and she's still the star."

"I don't believe it." The words came automatically, but I couldn't help thinking about how difficult it was to reach Rachel these days. How slow she was in getting back to me about Musetta and about the bag that held the poisoned food. About that letterhead. Just then a truck flew by and I staggered back from the force of the wind. "I've got to get out of here, Vi. I feel like I'm at the Indy 500. As soon as I'm home, I'll call Rachel again."

"You do that." Violet had a head of steam now. "And ask her about those tests she was going to have done. I haven't heard anything, and I've been home all day. Maybe I never will."

In a way it was pleasant to have a distraction. I'd rather think about cats, or shelter politics, than my own confused career.

But what Violet had told me was disturbing. A lot of cities were trying to reduce euthanasia rates, and everything pointed to Rachel being in the forefront of what had become a national movement. Yes, she was pulling money in, but that money was going out, too. Only a month before, she'd announced plans for a Spay/Neuter Wagon, a small operating room on wheels that would regularly visit neighborhoods, doing low-cost neuters. Between projects like that and the plans I'd read in her office, the fostering and pet therapy programs, it didn't sound like money was being wasted.

But I hadn't seen these plans come to fruition, either. Could Vi be right?

To think that Rachel was giving up was discouraging. Sure, the economy was tanking, but had donations fallen off? Was the goal of placing every healthy animal just too difficult? Another, darker thought hit me. Had Rachel's PR campaign been just that from the start? I'd heard stories of shelters that claimed not to kill healthy animals, but then stretched the definition of "healthy" to give themselves freedom to do as they pleased. All a dog had to do was have one accident, all a cat had to do was scratch, to be reclassified. In a new and stressful situation, like a crowded city shelter, it would be easy to label even the sweetest former pets as problematical and, thus, not salvageable. No, I couldn't believe that my vet, who worked so hard, would simply take the money and give up the animals—or use the publicity to leverage a job in the for-profit sector. But I needed to speak with her. Rachel would explain. She had to.

I was so caught up thinking about her that when my cell rang I almost automatically said her name. I was climbing up the stairs from the T, and didn't even look to see who it was.

"Krakow!" It was Tim. I was disoriented. He didn't sound like himself.

"Tim?" Hadn't we just spoken?

"No, Perry White. Krakow, enough fooling. That story you were talking about. Pet poisoning. I like it. What've you got on that?"

With everything else going on, I'd almost forgotten my speculative news story. "I don't know, Tim. I'm going to follow up, but I haven't been able to reach the vet in charge." Wrong words.

"*Haven't been able?* Aren't you a reporter? Isn't this your beat?"

Well, no, actually. I'm a music critic, and my beat is the local club scene. "If you want me to do more reporting for you…"

"Krakow!" I was toying with him, and he knew it.

"Actually, Tim, I was about to try the vet again. There's something else I need to ask her about anyway."

"Does it add to the story? Do I care?" This was his mantra—"make me care"—but for once I took his words literally.

"You might." I was thinking aloud. "I don't know if there's anything in it. I mean, I hope not. But there's a possible tie-in with kitten season."

"Kitten season?" From the sneer in his voice, I thought he was imagining fluffy baby animals, cavorting in the grass. "Should I get my rifle?"

I tried not to groan. "It's when intact animals breed, Tim. It's when the shelters are flooded with young animals, most of which end up being killed because there's no space for them and no chance of a home." He was quiet, waiting for the link to his story. "Anyway, the city shelter started a big campaign last year. There's a national movement to stop euthanasia of healthy animals, and Dr. Weingarten signed on. She got a lot of attention, and probably a decent amount of money for it, and if she's dropping it now, well, that's a bad thing."

"You mean, like the shelter has been taking donations

when they don't mean to follow through? And that could be related to the poisoning?"

He had it, but hearing my editor spell it out gave me the creeps. "Well, it's just a rumor and I wouldn't want to write anything until I knew. I don't even like to ask, really. I mean, it's kind of harsh."

"That's the job, Krakow." The job? *What* job exactly? I bit back my response. I did want to talk to Rachel, needed to talk to her, really, and not just for the *Mail*. There were too many questions floating around, and feelings were running high. I was pondering how to broach this latest powder keg, but Tim misinterpreted my silence.

"Krakow?" His voice sounded tentative, the usual bark gone. "I need you to do this. For me." Tim needed something from me? As much as we'd fought, he had been my ally, giving me my column and letting me write it how I wanted to, more or less. And besides, I realized, having an editor in debt to me couldn't be a bad thing. Especially if I did take that job.

I STOOD IN the Square, the first of the rush hour commuters beginning to swarm out of the T. Like them, I wanted to go home, play with my cat, have something to eat. Make a few calls. I pride myself on my phone skills. A good journalist can reach anybody within three calls. But if you're trying to winkle the truth out of someone, or just get someone to talk at all, broaching him—or her—in person works best. With a sigh, I walked back down to the T entrance. At least I had a monthly pass, and besides, going up and down the stairs would probably be all the exercise I'd get today.

The shelter and its attached clinic stayed open till seven on Wednesdays, and sure enough the beginning of the post-work rush was hitting there as well, as nine-to-fivers picked up their pets or browsed the adoption area, hoping to find some four-legged love. The din in the reception area was considerable. The phone ringing nonstop, while a printer behind the front desk rattled, unbalanced, as it spewed out invoices and whatnot on its rickety stand. Two young girls squealed with delight over a huge white rabbit. Over by the cages, layered three deep up the far wall, a young teen stuck his finger through the bars, letting a gray-spotted kitten bat at it. The kitten, wide blue eyes still too big for its face, had a look of intense concentration—that finger was going down—while the youth wore a smile that belied his grim gray hoodie and anonymous denim. Those two were going to be good for each other.

I was a little less certain about the little boy in the corner. From his tears, I could only assume he'd recently lost a pet, and when I heard his mother say something about a puppy, I was sure. Maybe the missing puppy would turn up, brought in by a concerned neighbor or picked up by city Animal Control? Amy, sitting at the front desk, was handling the calls. Moments later a volunteer in bright pink scrubs came out to greet the mother and son, walking them back through the far door to where new animals were kept in quarantine.

"Busy day?" I sidled up to the front desk to be heard.

Amy rolled her eyes. "Everything on two and four legs. You want Rachel?"

"If I can." The family with the rabbit had started filling out paperwork. That bunny was getting a home, but even as I stood there, another family came in. The shelter had the feel of an old jalopy cruising way too fast. One false move, and this place was going to fall apart.

"Hold on." Amy ignored the two blinking lines to page Rachel. I stepped aside to watch the frenzy, both human and animal. Would Musetta like a colleague? The spotted kitten was adorable, but he had a litter mate sleeping in the back of the same cage. All black, I thought, until he woke up and yawned a ferocious yawn, revealing a white bib down his front. A variation on Musetta's own coloring. What would the male version be, Musetto? Marcello? Or would my timid housecat react with horror, regarding even a tiny newcomer as some kind of foreign invader, a usurper in tuxedo fur?

Mulling over the possibilities, I didn't notice Rachel come up beside me.

"Theda." The utilitarian bun that pulled her hair back tight did nothing to hide the fatigue in her face. "I got your calls."

"I know you're busy, but I wanted to follow up about the food from Violet's shelter." I didn't want to jump in with accusations. Like Violet, I wanted to know why she hadn't called us back. But perhaps the bustling reception area was reason enough. "About your tests."

"I've sent some of the kibble over to the city labs, but there are a few other things I can do here." She smoothed her already flawless hair with a sigh. "It's been crazy. Kitten season. Plus, of course, we're expecting the usual flood of abandoned animals when all the colleges get out."

"I'd forgotten about those." We both looked around at the crowd. Usually Rachel would invite me back into her office. Was she trying to get rid of me? "But I hear you're prepared?"

"Why? What did you hear?" Her voice grew sharp and she looked up at me. I'd been thinking of Piers, of the extra room, but the edge in her voice made me wonder if Violet had been right.

"Hey, relax." I hate it when people say that to me, but Rachel looked so fierce the words just popped out. "People talk to me." She stared at me, not speaking. "And I'm a journalist, Rachel, so I have an obligation to ask. I mean, I heard about the work you're doing here. Piers was telling me."

"*Piers?* You're talking to Piers?" Her voice rose in volume.

Amy looked over at us and a woman pulled her little girl close. "What do you know?"

"Why? What's wrong with you seeing Piers? Rachel, what's going on?" There was no reason for her to be so sensitive. He was a nice guy, and if he was willing to help out, so much the better.

"It's nothing. He's—I don't want people talking. It's complicated." She browsed through the papers in the printer tray, selecting one before she turned back toward her office.

"Wait, Rachel!" I reached for her, bumping the teen aside. Why was she acting so touchy? *"Rachel!"* People were staring. I dropped my voice to a whisper and moved closer. "Look, I don't care if you and Piers are an item. I'm happy for you. Really. But what's going on here? Are you going to start—"

"Don't say it!" She spun on her heel to face me, positively hissing the words. "Don't you have any sense at all?" She looked around and I followed her gaze. The room was filled with families. Another volunteer, this one wearing mint green, was even holding up a toddler so she could see into a puppy cage. Not the place to talk about killing cats or dogs.

"Sorry." She was right. "But Rachel, talk to me." I moved in close so we could have something like privacy, and saw Amy start to rise from her seat. Were fights that common here? Between the humans? "What aren't you telling me?"

Her dark eyes spoke volumes, if only I could translate. "Not now, not here." She ran her hand over her head again, and I couldn't help thinking that the gesture was for comfort, as if she were stroking a cat. "Can we talk later? Why don't you bring Musetta in tonight after closing? Ring the after-hours bell at the back. I'll be here. We can keep her overnight and I'll do her teeth early tomorrow, before the clinic opens."

That was a peace offering if I'd ever heard one. "Thanks,

Rachel. That would be great." I smiled in relief. "You wouldn't believe how foul her breath is. She's a little dragon."

"Fire breather, huh? Well, we'll take care of that. Ring the bell on the back door. I'll be in my office till ten at least." Some of the fatigue lifted as Rachel smiled back. "But look, I've got to run. I'll see what I can do about the other stuff." A glance around warned me she didn't want to talk. "I should have some results by the end of the day, okay?"

"That would be great." A load slid off my shoulders. "Thanks so much."

She shot me a grin, her old self again, But I couldn't help noticing the puzzled look Amy gave me, as her boss—my friend—disappeared back through the security doors. Too late, I remembered the cat food bag. Whatever she did with the kibble, wherever it came from, I wanted that bag. I banged on the little window, tried rattling the door. It was locked, though, and when I turned back toward Amy, she turned away, unwilling or too busy to be bothered with a troublemaker like me.

"Someone's going to be hungry." I was talking to myself, imagining my plump kitty, but the woman next to me shot me a look. Even the hooded teen ducked his head and stepped aside as I walked to the front door and out.

NINE

I RETURNED HOME to a call from the copy desk and a sweet message from Bill.

"Hey, babe. I was sorry to run this morning. Any chance of catching up later?" It wasn't much, but just the fact that we were in touch again warmed me and I longed to call him back. Six o'clock. No, he'd be at the Last Stand already, any chance of a leisurely phone chat was long gone. Better I should deal with my column, bring my kitty in to Rachel, and then trot on over to see Bill in person. There was another band I needed to check out tonight, a retro garage unit—all guitar and tambourine. But if I started my evening at the Last Stand, there was a better chance that I'd be ending it there, too, or at least with my guy. I knew I'd miss Musetta tonight, and I could use the consolation. But if I was going to go anywhere, I had to take care of my column first.

"Theda Krakow here. You had some questions on 'Clubland'?" Not that long ago, I'd have known every copy editor on the desk, and they'd have known me from my years checking commas and clauses. But in the year I'd been gone the desk had changed as much as the rest of the paper.

"Hi, Theda. I'm Jesse, just come over from news." I was glad she couldn't see me roll my eyes. No matter how interchangeable upper management thought we were, there was a world of difference between editing news and editing arts. I mean, we didn't necessarily know where Whitten Avenue crosses from Dorchester to Roxbury, but we couldn't trust them not to condense a concertina down to a concert, or to differentiate power chords from power cords—or power pop, for that matter.

"I wanted to ask you about some of the terminology here. In the second sentence you've got what looks like 'emo.' Is that a typo?" This wasn't going to be easy, and sure enough we spent the next fifteen minutes compiling a glossary of contemporary rock. Musetta, with her feline sixth sense, must have known something was up, demanding access to my lap and kneading me throughout the edit.

"Comping, it's just, you know, *comping*." I should explain that it referred to the pianist's rhythmic chords, the bottom that allowed even the bass to solo. But I was tired. Musetta settled down, her purr fading as she fell asleep. "You know, like in jazz?"

"I believe you. I really do." She sounded exasperated. "I'm sorry, Theda. They're floating me around this week and they just threw this at me. These aren't even my questions."

"Wait a minute, Jesse." Something wasn't making sense. Tim knew me, knew my work. "Whose questions are in my piece?"

"Hold on." I heard keystrokes as Jesse tracked back, looking to see whose electronic footprint had stepped on my copy last. "The logon's RCASH. That anyone you know?"

I must have started, because Musetta jumped down. "Yeah, I do."

Twenty minutes later, we were finally through and I was wrung out. Time for a snack, but when I walked up to my tiny kitchenette, Musetta was there before me, waiting by her bowl. Poor kitty, I'd made her as food fixated as I was. But I wasn't having anesthesia in the morning.

"Neh?" In any language, it meant "dinner." In response, I stroked her smooth black head and chucked her under her chin until I could feel a purr start and then I walked away from the kitchenette. My stomach rumbled with hunger, too, but if I couldn't show a little solidarity, what kind of human was I?

MUSETTA DOES NOT go quietly. A half hour later, we were in the car and I was hearing about it, with a series of chirps and mews that increased in volume the longer we drove. "Are you trying to tell me something?" A loud howl greeted that question, but as I'd also gone over a pothole I was more inclined to echo her complaint than to question it.

What with the last of the rush hour traffic clogging up the South End and parking, it was nearly eight by the time I walked up to the back exit, trying very hard not to swing Musetta's case. A bright safety light made a puddle of illumination around the steel door, but the building otherwise looked dark. I rang the bell. It should have buzzed all through the back hall, which ran from the offices all the way past the wards and storage rooms to the loading dock. But there were no windows on this side of the building and everything seemed still. Even the loading dock, off to my left, looked dark. Rachel wouldn't have forgotten, would she? Quiet now, Musetta moved in her carrier, causing the box to tilt.

"Whoa, watch it kitty." I righted the box and tried the bell again. "Getting dropped will be less pleasant than getting your teeth cleaned." Through the metal grill, she stared up at me. "Kitty, this is for your own good. Really." She blinked. I leaned on the bell and heard a noise within.

"Sorry about that." Rachel pushed open the heavy door and stepped out. "We've got a new alarm system on this door. It's a bear. Everyone's just been using the dock. Nippy, isn't it?" The temperature hadn't gotten out of the forties all day, but she probably hadn't come up for air since lunch, if then.

"Doesn't seem like it's almost April, does it?" I moved

toward the open door. Rachel stepped in front of me and reached for the carrier.

"I can take her." Our hands met on the wire handle and Musetta hissed. For a moment, I fought the urge to yank my cat back. Vocal as she was, Musetta wasn't usually a hisser. Something was wrong. But Rachel was unfazed.

"It's the smell." She glanced down at Musetta and smiled. "No matter how often I wash, I smell a little like every animal I've seen today. I won't take it personally." We were both shivering by then, and I peered down at my cat. Even Musetta looked surprised at her own outburst, her fur fluffed and her green eyes, staring back at me, wide open. Despite her silent plea, I released the cage.

"Rachel, what about the tests?" She looked up, puzzled. "The cat food? From yesterday?"

"Of course. I'm sorry. I'm still working on it."

I shook my head. "Rachel, I know the food came from your shelter. That's not—"

"What?" She stepped back, jostling Musetta's cage against the door frame. I reached for it automatically. "No." Rachel held up a hand. "Please," her tone softened. "It's complicated. Give me a little time to sort things out."

I stood there, dumbfounded. Was this about Piers? I didn't care. Hell, I was happy for her. Still, she seemed awfully worked up. Was there something in Violet's theory? Was something wrong with the shelter? The desire to grab the carrier back and run was intense.

"She'll be fine, Theda." Rachel must have read my mind. "You can pick her up around eleven tomorrow."

I looked up at her and back down at my pet. This was Rachel, our vet. She'd done surgery on Musetta. Helped out both me and Violet a dozen times before. I needed to trust her—with my pet and with my questions—at least for the night. I stepped back, raising my hand in farewell. "Well, okay, then. She hasn't eaten since before I got home, around six at the latest." Musetta was licking her chops. I swear she was trying to send me a message. But I'm not psychic. "You'll take good care of her?"

"Of course, Theda. We'll just have our girls' night out tonight, and tomorrow you'll see her again."

"Bye!" I tried to smile, but they were gone.

MY STOMACH WAS still rumbling, but now I was too upset to eat. This was silly; Rachel knew Musetta, she knew me. My hunger did nothing to improve my mood as I walked up to the Last Stand.

"Hey, darling." Reed was seated by the bar, writing up a schedule. "Want some pizza?"

I looked over at the open box on the bar, pepperoni and something white. Mushrooms? "No." I did, but in addition to the guilt was my growing awareness that if I didn't run, then I shouldn't pig out on carbs. "No Piers?" I looked around. Maybe that was Rachel's secret. I wanted it to be so.

"You disappointed?" Bill had walked in right behind me, carrying a bag from Tags hardware. "And here I thought you'd come to see me."

I caught my breath. There'd been an edge to his tone. Reed heard it, too. "Nonsense, my man, the lady is here for my company. Here." Reed took the bag and walked quickly into the back room, leaving us, for the moment, almost alone.

"I just dropped Musetta off with Rachel." I wanted to explain. "And she was acting odd, and I thought it had to do with Piers."

"Maybe it did." Bill raised his thick eyebrows. "He's quite the favorite of the ladies here."

"You don't think—" I moved in to wrap my arms around

him. At forty-five, after eight weeks of physical therapy, he was as lean as a twenty-year-old. "You can't."

He made a funny face and I was reaching up to kiss him, when the door opened again, forcing him forward and out of my embrace.

"Hey, girls." Tess and Francesca both laughing and rosy-cheeked from the cold, made their way in. I noticed they had no problems reaching up to my tall boyfriend for a friendly kiss. So, Tess was up to clubbing again? I knew her drug problem had as much to do with work, with wanting to be "on" and awake, as with the music scene, but still, there was an awful lot of temptation here. Bill must have noticed the look on my face.

"Theda just had to bring her baby over to the vet." He turned back toward me. "Nothing serious, I hope?"

I shook my head and tried to smile. "Dental appointment. My Musetta has terrible fish breath."

"You should brush her teeth. I've got some vegan dental paste left. Herbal. I'll bring it in." Francesca reached over to pat my arm. Maybe she was just a touchy-feely person. I smiled to avoid answering. Anyone who knew Musetta wouldn't suggest brushing her teeth, particularly not with herbs. Luckily, Francesca didn't seem to expect a response. "Is Piers around?"

"I think he was going over to the shelter. Theda, you've got some competition." Bill wrapped his arm around me to soften his words. I leaned into him, not answering. But, yes, claiming my territory. Tess corrected him. "He might come by at some point, but I think he's got a gig tonight over at the River Bank."

I nodded, lost for a moment in thought. So Tess was back in the scene full swing. "That's right," I finally said, realizing that I'd been staring at her. "I thought I saw his band among the openers. I'm actually heading over there later myself." The

tiny club with its postage-stamp stage had four bands booked
and it was only Wednesday. If that wasn't a scene, I wasn't a
reporter. As I spoke, I could feel Bill's eyes on me, so I looked
up. "But I had to start my night here, right?"

"Of course." Now I got my kiss, though it was more of a
peck than a real greeting. "But some of us are working." With
that, he released me and walked off after Reed. I stood there,
feeling a little like a fool. Wasn't I working, too?

"Something going on?" Tess sidled up to me as Francesca
slipped behind the bar. Moments later, Francesca emerged,
holding a can of cat food and a bowl. That's right—the shelter
cat. At least that was her excuse to follow the two men into
the music room.

"I don't know, Tess. I really don't." I watched Francesca
glide through the growing crowd, slim and agile, and tried to
turn my attention back to my friend. "Are you doing okay?"

"I'm fine, Theda. Francesca's got me on a new cleansing
diet. She's really strict about things like that, and it's helping.
One day at a time, and all that." She smiled and I searched
her face for any sign that she was forcing it, for that worn, wan
look that should have been a warning the last time. "Maybe
you should turn that look on your own life." There was a
slight sting in her words, and I sighed.

"Yeah, sorry. But if you need anything…" She nodded at
my offer, that smile warming up her face. "Speaking of my
so-called life, Tess, anything I should know?"

"Depends what your intentions are regarding a certain
blond guitarist who's been changing his habits." There was a
playful lilt in her voice, but I still felt my head snap back.
"Piers?" She said the name as if it were obvious. I almost
laughed. But if Piers and Rachel were keeping things quiet,
I wasn't going to spill the news.

"Not my type." I tried to sound certain. She looked at me,

eyebrows raised. "Not anymore, anyway. I'm with Bill. At least, I hope I am."

She nodded, taking that in, and bit her thin lips. "Well, then, I don't want to tell you your business. But are you sure you want to take off just now?"

"Yes," I faked a conviction I didn't feel. "I've got my own life to take care of."

TEN

I'M TRUSTING, BUT I'M not a fool. I hung around for a while, spent some quality time with Ellis the cat before the music caused him to retreat, and made sure I got—and gave—a real kiss before I took off for the River Bank. Yes, I was reporting on the scene. Yes, I had a life. And since I didn't have Musetta to worry about, I could happily suggest adjourning to Bill's Inman Square condo at the night's end.

Once we made plans to meet, I should have been free to reclaim my evening. But as I rounded the corner to head down River Street, the wind off the Charles whipped up to greet me, and I found myself rethinking my priorities. Maybe it wouldn't have been so bad to stay at the Last Stand. How much did I really need to see these bands? My own question made me smile. I might as well have asked myself how much I wanted this gig. In response, I ducked my head and forced my way into the frigid blast.

"HEY, THEDA." Ten minutes later, Guy, the bouncer, was holding open the heavy door, letting out a few smokers and welcoming me into the club's warmth.

"Guy!" I smiled back and stepped to the side, looking up at the posted set list. Piers's band, Allston Onramps, was on second, at ten. Guy saw me looking.

"Didn't they used to be the Phantom Tollbooths?"

"Yeah, but they got sued." The first time I'd written about

Piers, I'd learned all about the cease-and-desist order. "Then they tried Allston-Brighton Tolls, but everyone just called them ABT and there's a hardcore band out of DC called that, and they were getting sued by some ballet company. Then they tried the Onramps…"

"Oh yeah, I read your piece. Some job search engine?"

I nodded. "Anyway, yeah, same band."

"Well, if the guitarist doesn't show soon, they're going on as a trio." Guy took my hand to stamp it. "You didn't see him out with the smokers, did you?"

"No, sorry. He hasn't been in?"

Guy shook his head. "His bandmates loaded in and did soundcheck without him. Should be fun." Just then two couples came in, and Guy started checking IDs. I walked up to the bar. Maybe Piers had been at the shelter. Or maybe he'd stopped in at the Last Stand after I left. I hadn't come to see him, no matter what Tess had hinted at, but I didn't want him to screw up a gig, either. The Allston Onramps were beginning to grow a fan base. I started to look around, but just then the first band started up.

I moved up toward the stage to see five beefy guys, all dressed up in vintage Ts from clubs long gone. Their first number started with a guitar attack. Fun, if a bit generic, with the kind of shouted gang vocals that I'd thought had gone out with the Fleshtones. Still, as they kept going, the sheer raw power of it got to me, all rhythm, beaten hard.

"Rawr, rawr, rawr!" That probably wasn't what they were singing, but with four of the musicians shouting into two mikes the sound wasn't going to get any better. "Rawr!" A drum roll broke in, the wiry guy in the back pounding the set so hard it swayed. He grabbed a cymbal, sweat flying off him, just as the two guitarists jumped back to begin a dueling solo, trading pyrotechnic licks like old school rock stars. The small crowd roared. I laughed out loud. God help me, this was my music, overwrought, outdated, or not.

"Good stuff, huh?" I turned and realized Guy was behind me. I guess nobody checked hand stamps during the sets.

"Great." I shouted not only to be heard, but because I meant it. "Did Piers show?"

"Just came in!" He nodded off to the left, and I turned my head as he patted my shoulder and retreated. Even this little club couldn't be that casual. The band began another song, the bassist thrumming out a deep tattoo, and I craned my neck, looking for Piers. Instead, I saw a familiar head of curls, bouncing up by the stage light. Tess, or so it seemed, and was that Francesca standing right by her? The stage light shifted and I lost sight of the two.

I stretched to see over the crowd, searching for the two wispy brunettes. I didn't want to be anxious about Tess. I loved her, and that meant wanting her to have a life and some fun, too. But why hadn't she mentioned that she was coming over here? I'd seen her not a half hour before. She could have offered me a lift.

She probably thought I'd taken my car. I tried to dismiss my concerns. It could be anything, I knew. A last minute decision. Maybe I'd even given her the idea. Maybe I was just jealous, seeing how close she was to her new friend. But she had nearly killed herself with amphetamines not that long ago, and I had heard scary things about recidivism rates. I didn't want to lose her. Plus, the Tess that I knew had been a singer-songwriter, a lover of melody and subtle harmony. Seeing her at Bill's club made sense, but here? Dancing to such loud boy rock? Could this be Francesca's influence? She did have that delicate look that made men go all protective, but she sure liked to be in charge. Maybe I was misreading her. I started to make my way over to the other side of the stage, but the middle of the floor had turned into an impromptu mosh pit, and I hesitated, unsure how to proceed.

"Theda!" I turned and saw Ralph. He was gesturing me over, pointing to a space by the bar. I waved him off. We'd catch up later. Until the whole job thing was cleared up, I felt odd about drinking with him. If it all worked out, he could buy me a beer to celebrate. If not, we'd commiserate. I turned back toward where Tess had been dancing, working my way around the center of the floor. But by the time I'd circled it, she was gone, as was her curly-haired colleague. Had I imagined them both, my own fears putting pictures in my mind? I could have checked outside, among the smokers. But the crowd had gotten thicker and I had a good spot now, right up by the stage. I didn't want to be an overanxious friend. Tess was a big girl. If I repeated it, I'd almost believe it. Besides, I was working.

Half hour later, Piers was on that stage, smiling down at me with a high wattage grin. I knew we were becoming friends, but I bet that smile would win him a lot of fans, too. I wished I could say the same for his band. Although they'd started off with the same kind of garage aesthetic, loud guitars and not much else, it seemed that some artistic pretensions had snuck in. They'd added a keyboardist since the first time I'd heard them, always a bad sign for a rock band. And the solos now seemed full of the kind of aimless noodling I hated in jazz. I looked back at the bar. Ralph was deep in conversation with a short guy I vaguely recognized. Lee something. Dark hair and nerdy glasses that were probably supposed to remind people of Buddy Holly, he wrote for one of the free weeklies. Probably just as well.

"So, what do you think?" I jumped. Francesca was standing right behind me, yelling in my ear. "Aren't they wonderful?"

"Well, it is interesting." She could read my real opinion in print, if I wrote about the Allston Onramps again.

"It's Bill's influence." Francesca sidled up next to me. "Piers has been listening to a lot of the bands that come through."

I nodded. Jazz wasn't a good idea for such a basic rock band. But pretending to concentrate kept me from having to respond, and we stood in silence through the rest of the set, Piers's broad grin taking us both in the next time he looked our way. I looked around for Tess and thought I saw her, up front. But then the band finished and the stage went black.

"You sticking around?" Francesca moved toward the door as the house lights came on.

"Yeah, I might be writing about the next band."

She already had a cigarette in her hand. I couldn't help but stare. "Tobacco's macrobiotic," she said, shaking her head. "Anyway, I'll be back."

She hadn't returned by the time the slapped bass and wahwah of Micro Brewster started up, but by then the club was so full it was difficult to move. Out of habit, I looked around for the fire exits. Only about a dozen people stood between me and the side door. Considering that it was a mere six feet away, that would be where I'd head if anything happened—or if the crush just got too great.

Not a pleasant thought, and my feeling of being trapped only got worse when I imagined my kitty, stuck in a strange place, hungry, and alone. I should have been listening to the band, hearing its wiry retro sound. But all I could hear were her plaintive cries. "Wow." That was the sound she made whenever she was waiting for me to come for her, to rescue her. "Wow!"

I was losing it. I shook my head and pushed back toward the main door. Micro Brewster would have to wait. "Wow."

"What did you say?" I hadn't realized I'd been speaking aloud until Guy questioned me. Had I been mewing like Musetta, or simply trying to comfort her?

"Nothing. I just need some air." He nodded and I stepped backward, almost falling as someone outside pulled open the door. "Come back soon!"

It was lack of sleep. Had to be. I wasn't psychic and my cat couldn't be in a safer place. My insecurities about Bill, my questions about the job and all the turmoil with Violet's cats were getting to me. I needed quiet. And food.

So much for solidarity. I walked back up to Central Square. Exchange Pizza was so greasy, people called it the Oil Change, but it was open late and by the time I was letting my second slice—onions, green peppers, mushrooms—drip on to the paper plate, I knew my mood was lifting. A dash of red pepper and grated parmesan and this was a meal fit for a queen. A queen of the rock age, anyway. Wiping my hands on the thin paper napkins, I considered my next move.

Odds were if I walked back to River Bank the Micro Brewsters would be off already. I could go into the Last Stand, wait for Bill to finish up. But, no. Now that I had some food in me, I felt more myself again. Hanging around seemed too possessive, like I was watching him or rushing him to close up early. I'd just go to his place and wait for him there.

But I had time, and although the idea of a third slice was tempting, I knew that resisting was the better part of valor. No, the only sensible response would be to head home, briefly. I could change clothes and be ready to go straight from Bill's in the morning. I piled my napkins on my grease-spotted plate and headed for the door. Maybe I'd pick up that Cuba book, too. I'd been meaning to learn more about those fun, funky rhythms and the island that spawned them....

With one thing and another, I didn't end up leaving my own place until close to three. First there was the silence. Even though I knew Musetta was in good hands, I found myself acting a bit frantic. First, I turned on the stereo. Loud. Then, before the phone could ring, I turned it off and switched on the TV, just for the noise. Of course, even though I didn't mean to look at it, I found myself entranced by yet another "Law and Order" re-run, one of the old ones with Adam Schiff as the D.A. Was this the one where the director dismembered the film producer? By the time I found out, I'd already spilled ice cream on my clean shirt, dessert being one of the few things that could comfort me for the lack of a cat. And so with a supreme effort of will, I put the rest of the pint back in the freezer and went to change again. By the time I'd figured out something I might want to wear the next day, and found both the Cuba book and the Donna Leon mystery I'd probably really read instead, an hour had passed.

I locked up and walked down to my car. The street was deserted, any late-night clubgoers had already gone to ground, but I loved this hour. So quiet, the city felt like a private preserve, and I felt a kinship with the cats I loved. As if on cue, a rat ran across the street. Okay, not that much of a kinship. But this was a city, and considering the proximity of the river such wildlife was understandable. I let myself into my car and felt the Toyota sputter a bit before sparking into life. It was funny. When I was young, I dreamed of living like this, single in the city. But I'd never thought that I'd still be doing it as I neared thirty-four. Three weeks till my birthday, and I was still living more or less like I had just after college. Would any of that change soon? As the car warmed up, I tried to imagine the possibilities. Making a home with Bill, that was feasible. Children? Well, Bunny was doing it. Maybe I could be an honorary aunt, at least for a few more years. A house in the suburbs? I shuddered, put the car into gear, and drove off.

"HEY, STRANGER!" I used my own key, but knocked as a courtesy before pushing Bill's door all the way open.

"Theda! I was beginning to wonder." Bill was stretched out on the sofa, a baseball game on the TV.

"As long as you were holding off despair." I settled into him and reached for the bowl of popcorn on the table. Popcorn is mostly air, anyway. "Spring training?" I prided myself on my newly acquired knowledge.

"Exhibition game." That seemed to be a clarification, not a correction, so I nodded and snuggled in, holding the bowl where we could both reach in. "So, did you close out the River Bank?"

"Nah." He didn't respond, so I looked up. "Heard a little of what's their names, the Micro Brewsters, but I can catch them again next week. Then I figured, what the hell, I'll go home, change, grab a book." I pointed to the paperback I'd dropped on the table. The book on Cuba remained in the car. "Why, what did you think? That I had another man to see first?"

I was teasing, but the look he gave me made me wonder. "Bill!" I pulled back to look at him, but he'd turned away. Someone was pitching, which I guess made the TV more attractive. "Hey, look at me."

He turned, and I saw sadness in his face. "What is it?" I couldn't help reaching up to stroke his cheek. He took my hand in his and lowered them both to the couch.

"I don't know, Theda. I mean, I trust you, I do." I couldn't help raising my eyebrows at that, but he went on. "It's just that, well, I'm not a kid anymore. I'd like to start thinking about my future, about what I want for the next forty years or so."

"I thought that's what the Last Stand was about?"

"It is, but now that the club's launched, I want to get my other ducks in a row." That phrase bothered me, but I bit my tongue and nodded, waiting. "I want to know I'm in something that's going somewhere. I mean, I've been burned."

So that was it. Before meeting me, Bill had spent close to four years with a woman who ultimately decided that she didn't want to be a cop's girlfriend. I didn't know all the details, but I think he'd even offered to quit back then, only to find out that it wasn't his job that was the sticking point. She'd hared off to the West Coast, looking for the excitement of new relationships, and he'd found out that he missed her cats more than anything about her. But maybe the damage was greater than I'd thought.

"I'm not Laura." I turned to look into his eyes. "You know that."

"I do." A ghost of a smile appeared. "But you do have some of her issues." Before I could protest, he raised a hand and went on. "I mean, Theda, I understand the music thing. I really do. But others of your friends are settling down. Getting married. Having children."

"We've got time." That baby comment hit a sore spot.

"Don't you have a birthday coming up soon?" The smile was broader now. "Now, maybe I made a mistake, but I'd been making some plans…"

"The Boat House?" He knew my favorite restaurant, outside of the Casbah or Petruccio's Pizza, that is.

"I was thinking more of a mushroom, onion, green pepper pizza, with a couple of candles stuck in it. We could clear off some of the bar—"

I hit him with a sofa cushion and he grabbed me, laughing. The rest of the conversation dealt more with the present than the future, but even later, as I sank into sleep, I knew that the topic remained open for discussion.

"Coffee?" I woke to the glorious smell of a fresh pot and the glorious sight of Bill, in his comfy blue bathrobe, holding out a mug.

"My hero!" I tried fluttering my eyelashes, but he'd already snorted and left the room. When I smelled bacon and heard the hissing of the pan, I forgave him.

"Hey babe. Good column." By the time I'd showered and dressed, he had a plate ready for me, sitting right next to the Mail. "What are you up to today?"

"I get to spring Musetta." I leafed through the section. After yesterday's edit, I was a little afraid to read the result. "I hate not having her around."

"Ah," he turned back to the oven. "So that's why you were so eager to come over to my place last night."

"Not the only reason." I opened Living/Arts and sat down to read, pulling the plate close.

"Sports, please?" My mouth full, I pulled out the offending section and handed it across. For a few minutes, we were peaceful, the crunching of bacon—extra crispy—and the slurping of coffee the only sounds.

"Damn." I put down the slice and licked my fingers before drawing the page closer. "Bother and damnation."

"Bad edit?" Bill knew me very well.

"Just an ignorant one." Someone, and I bet I knew who, had decided to spell out some of the phrases in my piece, substituting "hardcore" for "core," and essentially inserting an error. The second, "correcting" Stax Records to "stacks" of records, was just stupid. Jesse, the copy editor, wouldn't have made that mistake. I finished reading and closed the paper, trying to think what to do.

"Bad enough for you to ask for a correction?" Bill knew the routine. He also knew that corrections usually resulted in someone getting disciplined, or at least a talking to. I didn't want Jesse to get blamed, and if someone higher up—someone named "Cash"—had put those errors in my piece, she might be the one to catch flack.

"I don't know." I reached for another slice of bacon. "There's weird stuff going on down there."

"I've got time." To prove it, he stood to refill our mugs. But in that moment, I'd seen the clock. Ten thirty. Soon Musetta would be awake and ready to go.

"Sorry, sweetie." I drained my cup and stood up. "I hadn't realized it was this late. I want to free the kitty, get her home, and give her something to eat."

"Fill me in later?" He put down his own mug and reached over to kiss me.

"You bet!" Even though I could have used more coffee, I felt springier than I'd had in ages. The sun was out. Bill and I were back together, and I was on my way to bring home Musetta. What could go wrong?

ELEVEN

THE SHELTER PARKING LOT was already packed, so I pulled up next to a truck in the loading area and left my blinkers on. A man in a brown uniform was putting crates on a hand cart. By the time he was done, I'd be on my way out, cat in hand. I beeped my Toyota shut as I trotted up the walk, past that back door and around to the front. The waiting area mirrored the lot. Not even eleven, and Amy looked overwhelmed already.

"Hold, please." She nodded as she reached for another button on the blinking phone. In the middle of the room, a little boy started to scream. "Hold!"

"I'm going in." I pointed and mouthed the words, rather than add to the din. Amy looked like she was about to say something, but just then an aide dressed in green scrubs opened the door.

"Martha? Martha Crossington?" An older woman jumped up to follow, and I grabbed the door behind her. "In here, Martha." The aide directed the woman into one of the small offices on the right, but I kept going, stopping briefly in front of the cat quarantine room to squirt some hand purifier from a wall dispenser. Coming in alone was against the rules. But I knew my way around the shelter, and I wanted my cat. Besides, that truck driver was going to need to pull out at some point.

Rubbing the cool gel over my hands and up to my wrists, I passed Rachel's office and made my way up to the cat ward. Inside, cages stacked three deep held a small assortment of animals. Two females with shaved bellies. An old tabby with a bandaged ear, and a black and white kitten that seemed to be shivering with shock.

"Poor baby." Tuxedo cats always reminded me of Musetta. I leaned closer to its cage, but stepped back when I saw it retreat, scared, under a pile of torn newspaper. "Sorry."

What I didn't see was my own pet. "Musetta?" I looked around, but the other cages were empty. "Kitty, you here?" Rachel should have been long finished with her by now. She'd said eleven. Unless—the thought made my stomach sink—there had been a problem. I started to look around, a cold panic creeping up my spine.

Behind me, metal shelving held litter and towels. I pushed them aside. More towels. The other door looked out onto the back hall and right by it, a clothes hamper smelled like somebody had been cleaning up accidents. That was it, except for a row of hooks holding clean coats and scrubs. One had fallen to the floor, and I reached to pick it up.

"Wow?" There was Musetta, in her carrier, tucked back against the wall. "Wow!" She poked one paw out of the carrier's grill and reached for me.

Relief washed over me and I sank down to the floor beside her. Funny, I'd have thought she'd still be groggy. And why wasn't she in a cage? There were several empty ones, clean and considerably bigger than her green plastic traveling case.

"Musetta, did she forget about you?" As my panic ebbed, I began to feel annoyed. "Did someone leave you here all night?" I opened the carrier and lifted my cat up into my lap. She was fully awake. She was also, I noticed with dismay, wet. There was something sticky on her fur. Had she been left here *and* spilled on? I looked over at the hamper and back at my cat.

"Hold on, kitty." I lifted her to examine her more closely. "I need to see what you got into." I ran my fingers through her fur, but there wasn't enough residue to wet them, and her dark fur camouflaged what was left. But at that moment she reached out to paw at me again, I felt the dampness on her cool paw pads,

I also saw, stark against the white of her little sock, the bright red of blood.

"Musetta!" I held her paw up to my face. Blood, or what seemed to be blood, was sunk between her toe pads, but I could see no cuts—and the fact that she put up with me handling her feet made me calm down. A thorough going over revealed no further bloody spots, or any tender parts, although I did get nipped when I insisted on running my hands all along her belly.

"What the hell?" Had Musetta come into contact with an injured animal here in the recovery room or in Rachel's surgery? Yes, the shelter was busy. But this was just too sloppy. Here I was, drying my skin out with Purell while Rachel's patients were swapping blood samples. My fear had turned to anger, and I put Musetta back in her carrier. No way was I leaving her here again. I needed to talk to that vet.

"RACHEL!" I STEPPED out in the hallway, Musetta's carrier in hand. "Where are you? What's going on here? Rachel!" I had to calm down, I knew that, but I was still muttering as a vet tech walked past. She gave me a look. I took the short passage back toward Rachel's office in three broad strides and called through the door.

"Rachel!" I was trying not to yell, but this was ridiculous. "Are you in there?" Musetta peered up at me through the top of her carrier. "Rachel?"

The hall was silent, the bustle of the waiting room a distant murmur. And who knew what was going on in the parking lot? I raised my voice. *Rachel!"*

The woman I knew would have at least poked her head out if she'd heard me, but I was angry and also feeling rushed. I pounded on the door. "Rachel!" Nothing. I tried the handle. It opened.

"Rachel?" Something was wrong. Papers were strewn about, and the little air purifier hummed, but the office was empty. I stepped in. Light came through the open back door, illuminating the kitten poster. But the treatment room looked empty, too.

"Rachel?" I made my way through the darkened office, calling for her. "Rachel?"

Everything was too quiet, and I startled myself by bumping up against something. It was Rachel's desk chair, the one Violet had napped in, lying overturned on the floor. I reached over to right it, grabbing the black nylon back. It was wet. Had something spilled here too? Drying my hands on my jeans, I stepped past the desk, and something caught my eye. There was something odd on the floor. Something lying on the ground, propping that back door open. A pile of white, like a lab coat, only in the light from the treatment room, I could see that the pile was stained and wet and red. It was Rachel.

I knew better than to touch anything. I started to back out, started to yell, to call for help, then I saw a movement. A sign of life. Her eyes were staring straight ahead, but her lips, darkened with her own blood, were forming words.

"What is it? Rachel? What happened?" In a flash, I was on the floor with her. This wasn't a crime scene; this was my friend. "Are you hurt?"

The absurdity of my own words hit me. She was lying there, her body unnaturally still. My hand had landed by the red spot on her coat and the spot was spreading. Hypnotized, I stared at it. Watched it grow.

"Pah." Rachel's voice, barely a whisper, broke the spell and

I kneeled closer. Her eyes were so beautiful, chocolate brown and glistening. Why had I never noticed?

"What is it, Rachel? What are you saying?"

Her lips kept moving, a soft huff of air the only sign of life. "Rachel?" I grabbed her then and held her close, pressing the side of my face up against her mouth. "Rach?"

"Pah. Pah. Pah." Little exhalations, but no words. "Pah!"

I pressed my face closer, trying to understand, and held my own breath, the better to hear. Her lips moved like those of a beached goldfish. "Pah. Pah." And then they stopped.

"No!" I MUST have yelled, because I remember hearing the sound of my own voice. One word. "No!" People came running, so I must have been loud. "No!"

I heard hammering on the door, before someone realized it wasn't locked. Then someone—Amy?—was pulling on me, trying to take Rachel from me. I was shaking her by then, trying to wake her. To make her say more. To bring her back. But the woman in my arms wasn't going to be righted anytime soon. As they pulled me back and took her from me, I could clearly see the slash, like the swipe mark of a giant claw, that had opened her neck. I felt her head flop back against me, her hair loose now and soft. I must have grabbed the knife, too, after seeing it on the floor beside her. I was grabbing at everything then, not wanting to let my friend lose anything more from that horrible wound.

Time slipped by, minutes, maybe more, but it seemed like suddenly more people were in the room. Had always been in the room. That volunteer, a tech in green scrubs. Some of the family from the waiting room, all crowding close, even if they sounded far away. Someone said something about a blade, and I was startled to see it still in my hand, small, but sharp and sticky. I dropped it and watched it clatter onto the floor, right by Musetta's carrier. Time slowed to a crawl. People were yelling. Rachel had been laid back down on the floor. Someone was crouching over her. I looked down at her, too, and the wounds were obvious now. Several long slashes, savage and dark. Suddenly, I couldn't stand it. I staggered back, wiping my hands on my jeans, and heard someone yelp as she scrambled out of the way. My fingers felt tacky. Hot, and as I fell back against Rachel's desk, I grabbed a handful of papers, desperate to cleanse myself of her blood. I looked down at my friend, so still. Everybody was staring, and then Musetta let out a howl.

"KITTY!" THAT CRY woke me out of my stupor and I reached for her carrier. So many people, so much noise. I wouldn't have been surprised if her carrier had been kicked and jostled. But as I reached for the green plastic case, other arms were reaching for me and I found myself pulled out of the room, into the hall, where more arms, stronger arms pushed me up against the wall.

"But my cat—" I didn't get a chance to finish.

"Save it." The voice was deep and tired, and with a flash I realized it was a cop's voice. I'd heard Bill sound like that. "I'm going to read you your rights now."

"But Musetta—" None of this was making sense.

I heard a deep sigh. "The animal will be taken care of." And I realized I wasn't going to get a chance to explain, that I had found her, that I had tried to listen. I looked over and saw the EMTs. One of them was carrying a stretcher. They hurried, hopeful, but I knew what they would find. My friend was beyond saving. She would be carried away, her pretty face covered, and I was under arrest.

TWELVE

"You've got to lock the doors! Whoever did this is getting away!"

Why wasn't anyone listening?

"Miss—"

"Krakow, Theda Krakow." Time was returning to its normal pace and I began to be aware of what was happening. A cop was here. She was holding me, and I was babbling. "I'm Bill Sherman's girlfriend? Bill Sherman, a detective in Cambridge?" That came out of nowhere, and as I heard myself say the words, I realized, for the first time, how grateful I was for Bill's career. Or, his ex-career. He hadn't been gone that long, had he? "But really, I just found her. Whoever did it. Did *her*—" I stammered, unable to say the words "—Don't let them get away."

My grammar had fled, but at least my wits had returned. No wonder Rachel hadn't answered when I'd called. Was this why Musetta was still in her carrier? How long had Rachel been lying there? What had she been trying to say?

"You've got to believe me. I'm a patient. I mean, my cat is. Rachel was going to sneak her in for dental work before the shelter opened, and she didn't do it. So *whoever*, well, whoever must have been in here early."

Something must have sunk in. I couldn't see the cop who held me up against the wall, but I saw her partner, a tall younger man, nod and signal. The place must be swarming with blue.

But, I realized, it was also swarming with suspects. Where had that vet tech been going? How many people had been in the waiting room? That security door hadn't slowed me down any. I stumbled as we walked back through it, and felt the cop's firm grip on my elbow, my hands cuffed behind me. What would Amy think? I'd rushed in like a madwoman. Had she heard me yelling? Had that vet tech, the woman in the green scrubs? But they knew me and would vouch for me. Wouldn't they?

We walked through the waiting room, quiet now, except for the rattle of the printer. Even the screaming boy had shut up, and as I passed, his mother pushed him behind her, shielding him.

"Amy!" She was talking to another cop, a black woman in uniform, but she looked up when I called. "Amy, tell them I couldn't do this." Her mouth opened, but I didn't hear anything, and then I was outside.

There was my car, blinkers still going. No doubt it was headed for the impound lot. And my cat? Who would take care of my cat?

"I get to call someone, right?" I'd have to call Bill anyway, but would he be the right one to come for Musetta? Or should I call Violet? No, Musetta had been through enough. Going from the city shelter to Helmhold House, with all those other cats, would be too much for my sensitive kitty. It was going to have to be Bill. He'd cat sat her before. Ideally, this would all be sorted out quickly.

But "quickly" proved to be relative. By the time I was booked and fingerprinted, my car keys and cell phone confiscated, it was past one and I was past exhausted. I was taken, finally, to a phone, where I had to beg my cell back.

"Just let me look at the numbers, okay? I just don't want to risk not reaching my boyfriend. You might know him, Bill Sherman?"

The officer on duty smiled. He didn't respond to Bill's name, but he heard the other question in my voice. "Don't worry, honey. We'll let you make a few calls if you don't reach someone the first time around."

Still, I tried Bill's cell first. He might still be at the gym. I got his voice mail. "Sweetie? There's been a terrible mistake. Horrible. Rachel is—Rachel is dead." There, I'd said it. "And I'm in jail. Would you, um, come bail me out? And pick up Musetta?" I rushed that in, but the phone went dead. I looked up at the gray-haired officer. He nodded, but I hesitated. Bill's apartment or the club? I really didn't want to explain all of this to Piers or even Reed.

"Bill?" His home machine had answered. "I'm at the Boston police headquarters. South Street station. There's been a huge mistake, but I need you to come bail me out." Short and simple. I was getting this down to a science. "And if there's going to be any delay, would you go to the city shelter and pick up Musetta?"

I hung up and looked over. The smile was gone, but the officer nodded once again. I dialed the Helmhold House and got another recorded message. Wasn't anyone at home?

"Vi, I'm being held by the Boston police and I need to be bailed out. Also, Musetta is at Rach—, I mean, the city shelter. I've called Bill, but only gotten his voice mail. Can you—?"

"*What?* Theda?" Thank God, a real person.

"Hey, Vi. It's, well, it's complicated. But someone hurt Rachel." That was easier to say. "And the police took me in. So, I'm here and Musetta is still at the shelter. I called Bill, but—"

"Hang in there, Theda. I'm going to make some calls and get you out. Pronto!"

"Thanks, Vi." Suddenly, I was very, very tired, and when the officer walked me back to the holding cell, I collapsed on the bench. This was all a huge mistake. Maybe if I took a nap, it would all be over. Rachel would be fine, Musetta would be on her way home, and I'd be facing nothing worse than a Boston tow yard.

IN THE END, it was Bill who bailed me out. Literally, with a bond that put his condo at risk, and figuratively because he was able to arrange for the calendar judge to take my plea that afternoon. For the second time that day, I realized how grateful I was for his ties to law enforcement. Capital cases don't often get bail, he told me, as we waited for some harried public defender to hustle up the paperwork. Hearing the charges was hard. but if it hadn't been for Bill, I'd haven been facing days in that basement cell before an arraignment. I might have been stuck there until my trial.

But Bill had been a cop long enough for some of his colleagues across the river to recognize him, and he called in some favors. Plus, my name wasn't completely unknown in either city. So when the PD pointed out my complete lack of a criminal history, combined with my "strong ties to the community," making a big deal about my help in the previous January's drug case, the judge seemed to buy it, at least to the point of letting me free for now. The numbers floored me. Bill would lose his place if this went bad, but by the end of the day we were out. I couldn't speak, but he drove me to the tow lot and paid to have my car freed from its temporary detention. At least the car's bail was more reasonable than mine.

"You okay to drive home?" His tone made me wonder how bad I looked.

"I think so." The shock had left me drained, and at some level I wanted him to drop everything and take care of me. But, no, he had come through when I needed him. He had a business to run, and I had to stand on my own two feet. "I am." I stood up straighter, shaking off the slump, and reached for my keys.

"Okay." He still looked doubtful. "I should get to the club, but I'm going to check in on you later."

"Maybe I'll come by." I was trying for cocky.

"Maybe you should get a good night's sleep tonight. We're going to have to start talking to lawyers tomorrow. I'll make some calls from the club."

That took the wind out of me, and I nodded, not really aware as he kissed me goodbye.

"Wait, Bill!" He'd begun to head toward his own car. "Did you get Musetta?"

"Violet did," he called back. "We coordinated to free both our girls!" With a smile, he turned and walked off. If he was smiling, my situation couldn't be that bad, could it? I'd already heard what had happened. He'd been at the gym and was picking up his messages when Violet had reached him, frantic and angry. But he'd calmed her down, promising to defend me against the "fascist city-state regime," if she would pick up Musetta and take her to the shelter. I'd been hoping that she'd taken my cat to my apartment, but I guess this way made sense. She couldn't tell if I'd get out today, and I was sure her distrust of law enforcement had made her fear the worst.

Still, it was with a heavy heart that I drove over to the Helmhold House. She would have heard what had happened, when she'd gone to pick up Musetta, and although I knew she'd believe me, I didn't want to talk about it. I didn't want to talk, period. What I did want was to pick up my cat, crawl under the covers, and press my face into the soft, warm fur of her back and hold her there till we both fell asleep.

"YO!" VIOLET MUST HAVE been watching for me. She had the front door open as I beeped my car. "Come on in."

Walking into the little shelter's front door just added to my disorientation, though, and Violet had to beckon me into the small room off the kitchen that Caro used as an office. "Here she is." I started to respond when I realized my petite friend wasn't talking to me. Nestled onto a worn recliner, sat Musetta. She was glaring at me.

"Kitty!" She only flinched a little as I raced over and picked her up for a good squeeze. One small mew and she struggled free to retreat into the corner. "Sorry, Musetta. We'll go home soon." But not just yet. I collapsed into a chair, wondering where I'd get the energy to move again. "Thanks so much, Vi."

"De nada." Violet pulled up Caro's desk chair. "Sorry about the isolation treatment. I didn't want to leave her in her box, but I thought she'd had enough of a shock for one day."

I nodded, looking around. A disposable litterbox had been tucked underneath the desk, a water bowl near my feet. "I owe Caro, too." This wasn't that big an office to begin with.

"You can tell her yourself. " As if on cue, Caro walked in holding a plate with what looked like a cheese sandwich on it. A really good cheese sandwich. One look at my face and she placed the plate in front of me, retreating to the kitchen to fix more. "So, what happened?"

The sandwich was history by the time I finished, and I was halfway through a second, Caro having wisely returned with two plates, both stacked high. "I don't know, I still don't know." I was ravenous, and the combination of eating and talking helped keep the images at bay. "So, well, I guess it looked bad. It all seems unreal to me. I'm just glad you were able to get Musetta."

"I wasn't sure I'd be able to. They were talking about holding her." Violet was finishing up her own second sandwich, cheddar cheese and chutney, and she licked some of the chutney from her fingers. "I guess they weren't sure if she was evidence or not. I don't know, like, maybe she got splattered with blood or something."

"Spattered." I'd learned that much from Bill. The word made me pause. The room spun. Rachel. But another thought was trying to get through. Blood! I didn't want to think about it. Couldn't, but there was something… "Wait a minute, Musetta did have blood on her paws. That's why I went charging into Rachel's office."

"But she was in her carrier, in the cat ward, you said." Violet looked at me, puzzled, a smear of chutney on her cheek. Caro reached over with a napkin to wipe it off. They both waited for me to explain.

"I know. At first, I thought she'd been cut or injured, but she didn't seem hurt. I couldn't find any tender spots under her fur or anything, so I thought Rachel had just been careless, not cleaned up her surgery or something. But maybe it was *her* blood."

"You mean, Rachel's?" Caro asked. "Like, Musetta was a witness?"

I nodded. "And whoever stabbed Rachel put Musetta back into her carrier before fleeing." It didn't make much sense, even in my current state. I saw Violet about to comment and held up my hand. "But, wait, that meant the murderer and I probably missed each other by seconds. Minutes, anyway. And why would a murderer move a cat?"

"Maybe it wasn't Rachel's blood?" Violet and I turned in unison toward Caro. She shrugged. "Just saying. I mean, the cops didn't check it out, right?"

"Maybe they just missed it. I mean, she was in her carrier by the time—when they came in." The same thought hit us all: that blood would have to be tested. Violet grabbed a scissor off the desk and saw me recoil. "To take a bit of the bloody fur."

I nodded. I wasn't going to be good around sharp objects for a while. But I gathered myself and went to pick up my cat. Her smooth black head was damp, but my hands came away clean. Her paws, too, were spotless white. She'd already groomed.

"She must have licked the blood off." Vi lowered the scissor.

I sighed. This was so disheartening. Musetta looked up at me, quizzically.

"You know what they say." I'd almost forgotten Caro, sitting in the corner. "Once they get a taste for human blood—"

"Caroline Williams!" Violet was on her feet.

"Sorry! I just meant, well…"

"I know what you meant." Vi slipped the scissor into a desk drawer and sat back down. "And I know you were just trying to lift the mood. But this is no joking matter. There was evidence on that cat. Evidence that could have shown that the murder had already happened before Theda got there."

I sat back. Evidence. Murder. My cat. Rachel was dead, my cat had destroyed the only proof I had that she had been attacked before I found her. No wonder none of this felt real. I had problems, big problems. But what I needed to do before anything else was sleep.

I MUST HAVE looked like a wreck, because Violet wouldn't let me—us—go until I promised to touch base. But once I got home and freed Musetta from her carrier, I didn't feel capable of speech. Still, I didn't need her, or more likely Caro, breaking down my door. Ignoring the blinking light on my own machine, I was grateful to hear her voice mail pick up.

"Hey, Vi. It's me. I made it home. I'm going to unplug the phone now."

"Theda, wait!" I sighed and took the phone over to the sofa. Musetta jumped up beside me and began kneading my side. "You there?"

"Yeah, I'm here." I moved Musetta's paws down to my leg. Denim was a little less easy for her claws to pierce.

"You'll never guess who just came by." In the background, I could hear Caro.

"Vi, I'm not really up to surprises right now." Musetta, annoyed, turned away and began washing her tail.

"Patti!" I tried to picture the coifed and manicured Realtor in Vi's house. They were neighbors, but I couldn't conjure the image, much less imagine why such a visit was relevant. "She wants an estimate from Caro. Something with her kitchen."

Patti cooked? I thought she barely ate. "Let me guess, she's selling." We'd had enough properties flipped in our neighborhood, and despite her prim demeanor, I'd counted Patti as one of the good guys. No bad news would surprise me today.

"No. I asked her straight out. Turns out, our preppy Patti is getting all domestic. Some new man has entered the picture." That's right; I'd never let her tell me. "He was a client and after the closing he asked her out. He's the one who likes to cook, I bet, but she's trying to play wifey."

"Well, bully for her." My eyes were closing. Musetta collapsed onto her side with a grunt.

"No, no, I'm missing the point. I've got to tell you who her new guy is." I waited with what I hoped sounded like bated breath. "It's Andy Pilchard!"

"Uh huh." Could I hang up soon?

"Andy Pilchard, Theda. Andrew M. Pilchard, of Pilchard and Cohen?" For some reason, that name made me think of the entrance to the Pike.

"Are they over in Allston?" I really needed to get off the phone.

"That's their billboard, Theda! They've got that big sign right by the tolls. You know, 'Heading to Court? On the Run? Call Pilchard and Cohen.' He's the biggest defense lawyer in town. I've told Patti everything that's going on and she wants you to meet him. She was talking about a dinner party, but now I think she's going to ask him to defend you."

I know I groaned, because Vi asked me what was wrong. But she accepted my explanation that Musetta had dug her claws into me and we signed off. I looked longingly at my cat, who was curled up for her own nap.

"Why can't I just forget everything and go to sleep?" She didn't respond, so I reached over and hit the "play" button.

"Theda, you are just the hardest person to reach." Patti. Well, I had her news, and she had mine. I'd call her back in a few.

"Hey babe, just checking in. Did you get Musetta? Are you home now? I've got some ideas about, well, how to proceed with all this." Bill was trying to be delicate, but he didn't have to be. I was grateful for the support and knew that his years as a homicide detective made him an invaluable resource. "I'm making some calls, too." Bless him. "Let me know when you're up and around."

Maybe I could get him to come with me to check out Patti's new beau. The thought made me smile. He tolerated her well enough, but how would a former cop feel about a shyster like Pilchard? I shook my head. Maybe he wasn't a shyster. Maybe he was a good lawyer, who just happened to advertise on billboards. And maybe he was just what I needed. I began to punch in Patti's number, but there was one more message waiting.

"Krakow? Where the hell are you? I can't believe you did this to me." I put the receiver down to listen. "Call me, Krakow. Call me. Now." It was Tim, and I was in the doghouse, and I had absolutely no idea why.

THIRTEEN

I CRAWLED INTO BED, drained by the effort necessary to brush my teeth. Musetta must have known something was off because she jumped up to join me almost immediately and stayed snuggled tight against me until I fell asleep. But I must have started flailing at some point, because I remember her struggling free, the thud as she hit the floor. She'd become Rachel in my dreams, her beautiful eyes glazing over. The spark fading. Maybe I grabbed her, more likely I scared us both with those visions—memories—of death.

"Kitty?" I wanted the comfort of her presence. But unlike her, my night vision sucks, and only the faintest gray showed around the edge of the windowshade. "Musetta?"

Cats, unlike their people, are not sentimental. She'd done her duty by me, and maybe even gotten some necessary comforting of her own. Now she was off about her own business. And I, still bone tired, was wide awake. I shook my head to clear it of those last images. Better not to sleep, perhaps, if it meant to dream.

"Kitty…" I made a singsong out of it as I heaved my aching body out of bed. The last thing I needed was to be freaked out by a movement in the dark. I opened my closet, reaching for my robe. "You there?" A soft head butt reassured me that, in fact, she was, and so I scooped her up and took her with me into my tiny office. Thank God for the Internet, the insomniac's best friend. The Internet and work.

"Let's see what Tim was on about, shall we?" I pulled my seat in and deposited the cat onto my lap. She started kneading immediately, making me grateful for the heavy terrycloth of my robe, as I woke up the sleeping machine. I hadn't had the energy to call my irate editor back, not after what I'd been through. But the idea that I'd gotten something wrong was bothering me. "Clubland" was supposed to be an area where I had control, my safe zone, and when I'd read it, I hadn't seen any mistakes, despite the lousy editing. Still, accidents did happen. As the machine hummed, I stroked Musetta's velvet head. "What did I misspell this time?"

I pulled up the day's paper online. If Tim had entered a correction, it should already be appended to the file. Another plus of online publishing. But no, there was no addendum attached to the story. No "reporter's error." I went through it again, opening my files of notes to doublecheck the spellings, the song titles. They all looked right to me.

"What do you think got Tim so angry, Musetta?" She rested her chin on the edge of my desk, not saying anything. Cats have a knack for comfort, so the position couldn't have felt as awkward as it looked. She was purring, too, which was both a giveaway and an incentive for me to stay where I was. Besides, bed wasn't too tempting an alternative.

"Anything you want me to look up?" She didn't respond to that question either, so I browsed the front page headlines. Nothing there, and I exhaled. I hadn't even noticed I was holding my breath. But I've been in newspapers too long to leave it at that. Metro, that was the ticket, and there it was. Not twenty-four hours had passed, but that was long enough for a news brief, already online and undoubtedly going into the Friday paper. "Vet killed at shelter." I closed my eyes, a flood of dizziness making me grab the edge of the desk. Startled by the sudden movement, Musetta jumped down, and I forced myself to read on. Dr. Rachel Weingarten, 36, had been killed at Boston City Shelter yesterday, the victim of an apparent stabbing. A suspect had been taken into custody, charged, and released on bail, but at least that suspect was not named. I read it again, trying to see through the scant lines to find something I could hold on to.

Rachel was dead on the scene. That wasn't news, though she had been alive, barely, when I'd found her. The "apparent," I knew, was journalese. It meant that no autopsy had been performed yet, although one would be. Maybe they'd find some other cause of death, something beyond those awful wounds.

Like poison? The idea struck me like lightning. Could that have been what Rachel was trying to tell me? Poison? Like what had been put on the cat's food?

No, I shook my head. The contaminant on the kibble had been cocoa, or something very like it. Dangerous to cats, but not to humans. But could there have been a connection? In truth, I couldn't remember if Rachel had even referred to the bad food as "poisoned." She might just as easily have called it "adulterated" or "contaminated."

So what had she been trying to tell me? Had she been pleading? I mouthed the word "please," holding one hand close to my lips. No, that didn't quite work. Had she been calling for Piers? That was closer, but still, not quite right. Maybe she hadn't been trying to tell me anything. Maybe I'd simply been witness to her last breaths, the gasps as life left her.

A wave of nausea hit me. Maybe I was sick. Maybe somehow I'd been poisoned, too. No, that was silliness. I was in shock, probably. Grieving certainly, and, even for me, up way past my bedtime. Still, the quiet was getting to me. Didn't I live in a city anymore?

At times like this, I wished that I had moved in with Bill the first time he'd suggested it. That had been a few months ago, after I'd been through a different rough patch, and I'd rejected the idea without a second thought. It wasn't that I didn't love him. I did. I do. Bill and I were solid, and he was a far cry from the bad boys of my past. But I had to know if it was all for the right reasons. I wanted more time to get used to the idea. Looking back, that had been right around when he was leaving the force. The timing hadn't been good for a variety of reasons.

Besides, I had my friends. That was the great thing about clubland, about the scene. Everyone uses the phrase "family of choice" these days, but we were the real thing. We came together because of shared passions, and we'd seen each other through worse.

Thinking of my friends drove the nausea back. I sat up straighter and Musetta jumped to the floor. Dawn would come, and I'd call Violet and Bunny, and maybe even Tess. Violet had come through for me today, and Bunny was my inside person at the *Mail*. But Violet had Caro now, and Bunny had Cal, and soon would have a little one, too. As for Tess, well, we had been close. But that was before drugs had taken control of her life, and she'd been distant since. Embarrassed, I'd thought. Ashamed of how she'd gotten sucked in and, even more, how she'd hid her problem. Could something like that be going on again? I thought of her at the River Bank, dancing and laughing. What was my life coming to that the sight of my friend having a good time filled me with dread?

I leaned back and closed my eyes. God, I was tired. And then I felt the soft brush of my cat, Musetta had come back and was rubbing her head against my bare shins.

"You're right, kitty. I can't think any more about any of this now." And I followed her back to bed.

FOURTEEN

I WAS SINKING. White arms were dragging me down into a darkness that was warm and thick. I fought back, but my own hands were tied. I kicked. And then woke up.

The phone was ringing and Musetta was on my bureau, staring at me with the glare that only an inconvenienced cat can muster. I'd forgotten to turn the ringer off.

"Sorry." I whispered as I ran past her. My discommoded cat didn't even blink. Of course, blinking is a sign of affection in cats—their way of saying "I love you"—but I think she was also aware of the impact of her full-on green-eyed glare.

"Hello? Hang on!" I hit the machine just as it picked up, and just in time to catch the beginning of a rant.

"Krakow, I can't believe you'd do this to me!" My editor sounded more irate than hurt. I let him spout. "You know what we're up against here. This counts as a betrayal. A personal betrayal. And I've always been on your side."

This was getting strange. "Tim? I'm here." Silence. He must have thought he had my machine. "And I don't have any idea what you're talking about."

Tim snorted. "As if, Krakow." Tim was always picking up his daughters' mannerisms. I guessed they were reaching their teens. "Why didn't you call me back yesterday?"

"Yesterday was crazy." I racked my brain for how to explain. He didn't let me.

"Fine, Krakow. It doesn't matter. It was too late anyway."

My column. "What's wrong, Tim? Has someone complained about 'Clubland'? 'Cause I have my notes."

"And do your notes have the whole story? Everything?"

"Yeah, I think so." I went over that evening in my mind. I hadn't taped the interview because we'd met at the Casbah. Over the last few months, I'd given up on taping interviews in bars. Half the time I'd get them home and not be able to make out more than bar noise and laughter. "Why?"

"Because I'm hearing that there was a story behind the story, if you know what I mean."

I'd settled on the sofa by this point, and reached to pull the afghan over my bare legs. "No, Tim, I don't know what you mean."

"Krakow. I thought I could trust you. Are you going to tell me that you weren't drinking with these guys?"

My head was starting to throb. "No, Tim, I'm not. We were in a bar. They're in a band. I interviewed them over a couple of beers." I pressed my hand to my forehead. "Actually, I think the drummer had a diet Coke."

"Very funny, Krakow. I don't mean the interview. I mean after."

"Yeah." I dragged the word out. What was Tim getting at? "After the show, I hung out with the Mystics for a bit. Why does this matter?"

"Because you hadn't turned your piece in yet, Krakow. That's why. And so when the calls came in that you were more than drinking, that there was some, shall we say, hanky panky going on, that's an issue. Because you were still writing and if you were fooling around with them, well, you could be biased. You could be writing up bands that you, um, wanted to get close to. Don't laugh, Krakow. I have to take it seriously. You're in my department. You're my writer. This reflects badly on me."

"Tim, hold on here." I wasn't laughing. This kind of nonsense had to be dismissed immediately. "This is ridiculous. It was a friendly interview and after their set I hung around to talk with them some more. I wanted to get some more material." I almost stumbled over the last word. Had I liked Liam, the guitarist? Yes, I had. But that was none of Tim's business. "The Infallible Mystics had never played here. Monday was a small gig, just a warm up, and I was previewing the big radio show next week. I needed to see them, and then I needed to talk to them again. I had a score of new questions."

That wasn't entirely true. I'd had more than enough material for my column from our first interview, before their show, and although I had gotten a few extra tidbits, I'd basically hung around because I liked them. Because I could. But I'd never considered such socializing unprofessional. I'd never been questioned about my integrity before. "Where is this coming from, Tim? I mean, people complain about critics all the time. Someone was probably jealous. This isn't like you."

"Well, maybe it should be." He was blustering about. He knew I was right, but there was something else going on. "From now on, we're holding to a higher principle."

"Is this coming from the money guy? Cash?"

"We're under scrutiny now, Krakow. That's all you need to know. And I don't need you embarrassing me." He paused and I tensed, waiting for what would come next. "Now, what's up with the pet poisoning?"

That should have been a relief, but I didn't have the stomach for it. Not before coffee. "I'm working on it, Tim. I'll let you know." With a final harumph, he hung up. I would have to come clean about Rachel, about my own involvement. I had been wrong to not tell him immediately, but I just couldn't face it, not yet. And he was wrong about some things, too. Before I talked to him again, there was more I needed to know, like who had called my editor and slandered me.

"Bunny?" My first mug in hand, I was ready to get to work. "Sorry, did I wake you?"

"No prob." The answer came back half a yawn. Cal had a day job now, doing some kind of graphic design, but I'd forgotten that he worked at home most mornings. "I'll get her."

Another slug and I was feeling halfway human. "Hey, Theda! You guys coming over for brunch Sunday?"

"Bunny, I'd forgotten." The silence at the other end let me know my friend was hurt. "I'm sorry, you wouldn't believe what's been going on." More silence. "Bunny, I'm sort of in trouble."

"What?" I'd caught her in mid-gargle. She wasn't hurt, she'd been getting ready for work. "Theda, what have you—"

"Bunny, I can explain. I was in the wrong place at the wrong time." I really didn't want to get into this. "I'll tell you another time, I promise. But there's, well, there's another thing. Something you can help me with."

She spit and I heard water running. "Bunny, you still there?"

"Yeah?" Was that a hesitation or had she moved into another part of her morning routine?

"Someone has badmouthed me to Tim, and I need to find out who." Silence again, and this time there was no sound of water in the background. "Bunny?"

"I'm here. I'm just, blech, morning's are not my best time."

"Still?" Her lack of answer was my answer. "Hey, I'm sorry. But I'm sort of up a creek here."

A sigh. "That's fine, Theda. I'll be waddling in there soon enough. But can you tell me anymore?"

I stammered a little. "Just that someone told Tim I was inappropriate with a band I wrote about." The rest of it could definitely wait.

"And were you?"

"Bunny! You know I wouldn't. And, besides, Bill and I are back together."

"Well, when you didn't let us know about brunch…" She let the words hang. "I'm sorry, Theda. I woke up sick this morning, and I'm just not myself." Her voice dropped to a whisper. "I'm just dreading this. What if my manifestation of the goddess isn't as the mother? What if this is the biggest mistake I've made in my life?"

"That's the morning sickness talking. You and Cal have wanted this baby for so long, and you're going to be a wonderful mother." I believed it, I truly did, but I was too distracted to sound convincing. "Really! It's just—"

"I know, Theda." She sounded exhausted. "I'll poke around. Hey, you didn't get a chance to ask around for me, did you?" I was drawing a blank. "About a pet psychic?"

"You didn't really—" I caught myself. She did. "I'm sorry, Bunny. I will, I promise. I swear on Musetta's whiskers." That seemed to cheer her up and we parted on better terms.

"Now you try to keep out of trouble, Theda, okay? Blessed be." I took what comfort I could from her final words, and poured myself another cup of coffee for strength.

I should call Patti back. Her offer of an introduction was a huge favor, but the idea of talking to a defense attorney, even a friendly one, just made everything too real.

Maybe I'd get her voice mail. "Hey, Patti, it's Theda. I guess you've heard my news."

"Theda! So glad you got me." I could hear traffic. Patti wouldn't have answered if she were with a client, but she was on her way somewhere. "Do you have a pen? This is Andy's number. Call him right away. I was about to leave a message for you. He had a cancellation this morning." She rattled off a number and I jotted it down reflexively.

"Thanks, Patti. I think I may wait and see what Bill says before I call though."

"Don't be stupid, Theda. Andy's the best, the absolute best! Do you remember the criminal cases with the Big Dig last year? And the MassBay Bank official and that little girl? They were all his."

I vaguely recalled headlines. "I don't think I knew what happened in those cases."

"Exactly!" She sounded excited. "He made them disappear. Here's my showing. Gotta go! Call him, Theda!"

Great, so I was on par with embezzlers and worse. Wouldn't hiring this guy mean I was guilty from the start? I collapsed onto the couch and Musetta jumped up onto my lap, like she'd been waiting. Maybe she had. I stroked her smooth black back and took another sip of my coffee. My cat started purring, leaning into me as if to hold me in my seat.

"You want to keep me here, don't you, kitty?" That resounding purr was my only answer. "Well, maybe you're right." I reached over for the phone and made the call.

An hour later, I was sitting in a downtown office with my head in a spin. "Andy," as I'd been instructed to call him, was a round little man, mostly bald and as innocuous-looking as an accountant. But from the moment I'd walked in, he had grabbed hold of my case like a bulldog. I had thought this would be an introductory meeting. That we'd discuss fees and expectations. But I gather he was either truly smitten by Patti or he had a thirst for justice that hadn't been slaked by his other clients. Before I knew what was happening, he was discussing strategy.

"The key," he said, pacing around an office that looked too bookish for the man himself, "is coming up with a better story." He'd sat me in one of those leatherbound chairs with the brass studs that looks better than it feels, but I didn't know if I was allowed to move. "It's all about which story the jury would rather believe."

"But I'm not telling a story. I'm telling the truth."

He waved me off. "You want some coffee? Jo," he hit the intercom on his oversize desk, "can we get some coffee? Cream?" He'd already sent one assistant scurrying when I'd told him that a public defender had handled my arraignment and bail hearing. The police blotter lay open before him. "Sugar?"

"But shouldn't we figure out first if we're a good fit?" I didn't want to be rude.

"No time to waste. Especially when it's pro bono!" He laughed, but I hoped he was serious. Somehow money hadn't come up. I was trying to figure out a way to ask, but he shushed me, staring at the papers in front of him.

"The weapon was a surgical scalpel, No. 15 blade. That's good." He made a note on his pad and looked up at me. "That argues against premeditation. Something like that would have been around anyway. I mean, it was an animal hospital, right."

"Well, it's a shelter with a clinic attached. But it has treatment rooms and an OR." He was back in the crime report, not listening, so I waited. He grunted and made some more notes, then stood up. "Okay, I have the outline. Now, you walk me through what happened. Tell it simply, just what happened, step by step."

And so I did. Looking up at the bookshelves behind him made it easier, somehow. Andy began pacing, his bald spot wandering in and out of my line of vision. But looking at those books, in their sedate leather bindings, I was able to go through it all. That I'd pushed the door open. That I'd walked back without permission because I was so familiar with the shelter. And that I'd undoubtedly been heard yelling for, or at, Rachel. For a moment, I thought of our confrontation the night before, on Wednesday. I'd snapped at her then, too.

Would anyone remember me banging on the door? How much had Amy, or anyone in that crowded waiting room, heard?

But Andy was questioning me about yesterday.

"No, I didn't see anyone when I went to look for her. Just that one vet tech." He perked up and raced to his desk to scribble on his pad. "But she wasn't coming out of Rachel's office."

"Doesn't matter." He finally sat, the better to take notes. "That office had a door onto a treatment room—and the treatment room led back to another hall, didn't it?"

"Yes." I thought it through. Rachel's office was more like a foyer, opening onto the much-larger treatment room. And I'd seen the vet tech walking down the front hall. She could have come around from the back, if she moved fast enough. "But Musetta was already back in the cat ward."

"What? Walk me through that again." And so I did, telling him about the blood on my cat's fur, the blood that had made me so angry. If someone had killed Rachel while Rachel was looking at my cat, and then replaced Musetta in her carrier, then that person was long gone before I got to Rachel.

"Not long gone. You said Rachel died in your arms?"

This was a bit much. The books started to swim. I needed to be specific. Concrete. "I didn't see Rachel at first. Her office is always a mess, tiny and crowded. Not like—" I waved my hands, taking in the built-in bookcase behind the desk, the wall of windows looking out on Post Office Square. "When I did see her, she was on the ground. And, yeah, she was breathing. I thought she was trying to say something so I knelt down. That must have been when I grabbed the knife, or whatever it was." I remembered the slim, cool blade.

"Did she say anything?"

"She was trying. I can't be sure."

"Dying utterance." He made more notes. "Always good with a jury." He tilted his own pen toward me. Silver, it made me think of that knife. Scalpel, I corrected myself. Rachel had been killed with one of her own scalpels. "Theda?" He was waiting.

"She might just have been trying to breathe." I shook my head. "She was going 'pah, pah, pah,' like, I don't know." I didn't want to say "like a goldfish."

"Pah? Could be Paul or Pat. Definitely not Theda. Did she have a boyfriend?"

"Well, there was Piers. I think they were—"

"Piers!" He didn't let me finish my thought. "Perfect. Maybe this was a lover's quarrel, and you walked in on the sad finale."

"No, that doesn't make sense." I pulled myself to the edge of the huge chair. I needed to make my point. "I'm not even sure they were together. If they were, they'd probably just started seeing each other, and they'd still be in the honeymoon stage. And I know Piers. He's a gentle guy."

"You're sympathetic. That's good." He was writing, not even looking at me.

"No, I'm serious. Piers would not have killed her."

He looked up. For a jolly guy, his eyes were piercing. "But you would have?"

MY HEAD WAS THROBBING by the time I left, and I figured I'd take a walk. Boston's financial district is not my regular stomping ground, and the suits on the sidewalk probably regarded me as oddly as I did them. But after an hour inside, I wasn't ready to head back down into the T. I headed for the new "Greenway," as the city's huge new median was called, to clear my head and gather what remained of my thoughts. One block toward the new park, and I felt better already. Maybe the Big Dig had been a fiasco; the open lawn was still a refreshing sight in the middle of our more generic skyscrapers. And the open air felt great. I spend most of my waking days indoors, in the small back room that I've turned into my office. But there's a world of difference between being inside by choice and being locked up. Out here, with the fresh, damp smell of spring on its way and a midday sun to warm me, I felt human again.

I also realized, perhaps more than before, what I could lose. Pilchard—I found it difficult to think of him as Andy, no matter how often he insisted—had been clear on one thing. The police would not solve this case. They had no incentive when they had me, murder weapon in hand. We would have to get to the bottom of this, find out who had killed Rachel and why, or this would be the last spring I'd enjoy in the fresh air for many years to come.

Well, that wasn't exactly what Pilchard had said. He'd be content with any good alternate theory of the case, I knew that from the way he jumped on the idea of Piers and begun to spin out a story of a jilted lover driven mad by rage. I understood where he was coming from, but I couldn't do that to Piers. He wasn't a murderer, just a guy in a band. He'd lost his girlfriend, he didn't need a friend framing him. What I needed to do was figure out the truth, not a convenient lie.

I found a bench new enough not to be covered with anything suspicious and took a seat, facing the sun. The crime was so far fetched, I wasn't sure how to approach it. Who would kill Rachel? She was a vet, for God's sake. She took care of animals. Did she offend a pet owner at some point? Neuter a pedigreed animal meant for breeding? Overbill? I couldn't see it, but watching the early lunch crew beginning to fill the other benches, I knew I had to go through every possibility. Between our squabble on Wednesday night and my anger on Thursday, I was the obvious suspect. More than the right to picnic was at risk. What could have caused someone to kill Rachel? Had she been unable to save somebody's adored animal?

Or was it the euthanasia issue? Everyone knew the city shelter put animals to sleep. As awful as that was, I also knew it was a mercy. When my beloved James had gotten too sick to stand, so weak that he'd refused to eat, refused to even lick a dab of baby food off my finger, I'd taken him to Rachel. She'd been wonderful, letting me take my time with my darling cat. He was nothing but fur and bones by then, but I held him for what felt like hours, sitting in her office while she steered other patients away. When I'd finally given her the okay, she'd let me continue holding him while she gave him first one shot, to anesthetize him, then another, to stop his heart. And then she'd stood back as I sobbed my heart out, only taking his limp body when I was ready. That had been a miserable day. But Rachel had been the good guy, the one who made the pain finally end.

The letters. We'd all dismissed them as fruitcakes, but it was true that Rachel's hate mail had seemed more serious and a little less flaky than the collection in Violet's blue file. Maybe the answer would be among the crayon threats and crazies. My hands itched to hold that file again. I'd been half asleep when I browsed through them before.

From what Pilchard had said, I might get another chance. The lawyer had run me through what would happen. The police would have taken everything in her office in to examine, he'd said, but Pilchard would get his shot at it, too, with a copy of the inventory to work from. And although Rachel had said the cops couldn't make anything of those letters, not even the typed ones, Pilchard had made vague assertions about his own experts and I wanted my own shot. I knew this city, and I knew the animal scene. Between me and Violet—I stopped, caught breathless for a moment by my own train of thought. Violet had quarreled with Rachel. Violet had been one of the people who'd accused Rachel of faking the new policy, and Violet, in the not-that-recent past, had made connections with some of the more fringe animal rights groups. Could she, maybe, without meaning to, have set someone on Rachel? No, I shook my head. Violet might disagree with Rachel, but they, too, were friends. And even if they had a falling out, Violet had too much respect for what Rachel did—hell, she had too much respect for life—to be involved, even obliquely, in a crime like this.

I was getting nowhere, digging into weird places in my own mind. I'd have to tell Pilchard about the letters, make sure he got them from the police. And I'd ask Vi if I could read hers through again, too. Maybe there was something we'd missed. Some connection. After all, Caro had found them spooky, and they weren't all about my two friends being in love. Beyond that, what did I have?

Musetta. My little cat had blood on her when I went to pick her up, but she'd been unharmed. Could that blood have been from Rachel? Suddenly the sight of those picnicking suits made my stomach flip and I got up to walk, the movement forcing me to breathe and settle down. How could my cat come to have my friend's blood on her? Had someone stabbed Rachel in the cat ward? No, there would have been a trail. The scalpel that killed my friend had been sharp as a razor, and the bleeding would have started immediately. So, had Musetta been in Rachel's office, perhaps on her way to the little treatment room just beyond? Did that mean whoever had stabbed Rachel had then taken the time to bring my cat back to the cat ward? I kicked at the gravel of a newly laid path. None of this made sense. All I knew for sure was that Musetta was the one witness I had. She was the only living creature who could say with certainty that when I had walked in on Rachel, the damage—those horrible wounds—had already been done. And she wasn't talking.

Maybe Bunny's idea of a pet psychic made sense. I smiled despite myself, and found myself imagining Musetta running through her litany of mews to a psychic interpreter as a uniformed detective took notes. "You saw what? Now, are you sure of the time?" But that just made me realize how much I would miss her, if I were locked up. Who would take care of her? My friends, I knew. But Violet had a shelter to run, and only the Siamese Simon seemed as close to her as her old favorite Sibley. Bunny had Pangur Ban and Astarte, as well as a baby on the way. And Bill would never love her quite as much as I would. No, it was unthinkable. I couldn't leave her. I had to fight this. A T stop with a fancy new awning appeared at the end of the block and I picked up my pace heading toward it.

MUCH AS I MAY HAVE missed her, Musetta seemed unfazed by my absence and looked up, yawning, as I came in.

"I'm home!" She blinked and settled back on her perch by the window to continue her nap. "And I'm excited to see you, too." In all fairness, she didn't protest as I stroked her, smoothing out the sun-warmed fur of her back. I even got a bit of a purr before those green eyes finally closed and I left her to slumber on.

The answering machine was blinking when I came in, and I nearly purred when I heard Bill's voice.

"Hey, babe, it's me. I thought about coming over last night, but decided you probably needed your sleep." His voice sounded warm and tender, even on my crappy machine. "How are you doing today? Call me when you wake up and we can start planning. You're not alone in this."

I kicked off my shoes and tucked my feet under me. A nice chat with my honey would go a long way to making me feel human again. As I reached for the phone, Musetta landed on my lap. Either I was warmer than the windowsill or she had missed me after all.

"Hey, you." Maybe I had been too distant recently. "I got your message."

"Just getting up?" I could hear the smile in his voice. Club or no club, he still rose long before I usually did. "Did you sleep okay?"

"I've been out and about for hours." I stroked Musetta, feeling rather proud of myself. "I've got no time to waste, you know. In fact, I've already started on my defense."

"Oh?" Maybe there was something in that single syllable. I didn't hear it.

"Uh-huh. I was talking with Patti's new boyfriend, and he was telling me that the cops wouldn't bother investigating Rachel's murder, so it was up to us to figure out what had happened, for real."

"Patti Wright? The real estate lady?" Bill had met her on numerous occasions, but she'd tried to sell us so many "love nests" that he'd learned to avoid her. "What's she selling this time? A co-op criminal defense?"

"Not Patti, her new guy. He's a lawyer, a big deal, I guess. Andy Pilchard?" I'd meant to build up to the conclusion, but Bill still had a cop's intolerance for the frills of a story. He wanted the facts. "Anyway, I think I've hired him."

"You *what?*" I jerked back, shocked by the volume. Musetta looked up at me.

"I hired him. Or, I think I did. Patti set me up to talk with him, and it seemed like right away he was talking about strategy and how we could come up with alternative theories of the crime." I didn't know why I was explaining myself. I felt like I was apologizing and only moments before I'd been so proud.

"Alternative theories?" He'd gotten quieter, but the warmth was gone.

"Yeah, like who else could have done it." I scrambled to explain. "I told him that she and Piers had started seeing each other, but there was no way Piers was involved." A grunt. "I mean, he's not the type. But I did start thinking about finding out who did do it. That's the best defense, Andy said."

"Andy?" Bill was quiet now. I heard a deep sigh.

"What's wrong, Bill? He's supposedly some kind of top lawyer." I thought about that billboard. It was sleazy, but maybe I needed sleazy now. "I mean, for someone who takes on criminal cases. And he's taking me on pro bono. I think he wants to get in tight with Patti."

"Or maybe he thinks that this is a chance to get in with a cop's girlfriend."

"Ex-cop." Why did I have to remind him? "And what do you mean by that anyway?"

"Andy Pilchard is notorious." Bill was almost spitting. "And even if you don't know who *he* is, you can be sure he found out who you are. Pro bono, my—"

"Bill, hold on! He made sense. Everything he said made sense to me. And I want to get to the truth. I mean, Rachel was my friend."

"This is not a game, Theda!" Bill was shouting now. "You need an honest, professional defense. Not some shyster who's going to tell you to go out and get in more trouble." Either she heard him over the line, or I had tensed up too much for Musetta. She jumped to the floor.

"But, Bill—"

"I'll say it again, Theda. This is not a game. The Boston homicide department is more than competent to investigate what was truly a vicious crime. You're a journalist. You're not a detective. Stay out of police business."

"I can't, Bill." I looked across at Musetta. She was sitting still, but her tail lashed back and forth. "I'm really sorry that you don't understand." I heard a sputter, but I couldn't let him interrupt me now. "It's not just that I want to find out what happened. It's not that I think I've got some special insight. But Bill, if I don't get to the bottom of this, I may end up in prison. This is my life."

FIFTEEN

THAT HADN'T GONE as I'd intended. We'd made peace before
we hung up, but it felt fragile, as if the rest of the fight had
only been postponed. My friend, my lover, my freedom,
they were all slipping away. As if on cue, Musetta started
coughing, not letting up till she'd hacked up a reasonable
size furball.

"Thanks, kitty. That helps a lot." Spurred to action by this
mundane mess, I went for the paper towels. Musetta licked
her chops and sauntered down the hall. By the time I got it
cleaned up, I was feeling a little calmer, the self pity tucked
back with the cleaning solution. Musetta, true to form, was
on her office perch, a paisley pillow right by my computer.

"You trying to tell me I should get to work?" She
yawned, stretching out one white glove toward me. I stroked
her head and took a seat. She was right. What I needed was
normalcy. Usually by Friday, I had at least decided on the
next week's column. Tim knew that, too. His e-mail was
terse, but direct. *"K-Story?"*

I almost laughed. "I wish I knew," I said under my breath
before hitting reply. *"Checking out a few options,"* I typed,
trying to strike a note between vague and optimistic. *"Let you
know Monday or sooner."* I sent it off. Tim couldn't have
been that mad at me if he wanted my story for a line in his
budget. But a ping announced a reply.

"Clubland can wait. What's with poison story?"

I pushed myself back from the desk. Thank God we weren't on the phone. What could I tell him? Yes, there were developments, but the vet I'd gone to question had been murdered? Wouldn't news be covering this anyway?

As if my computer could read my thoughts, it pinged again. Another e-mail from Tim: *"Metro on dead vet. Need poison angle asap. Metro front a possibility."*

Great. I'd wanted normalcy. I'd wanted to keep busy, and here was my editor, asking me to report out a story. Too bad, it was the one story I couldn't write. There was just too much to explain. I stepped away from the computer, letting sleep mode dull its shiny face. I couldn't give in to panic or self pity. I needed to think, and for that to happen, I needed food.

THE CALENDAR HAD only recently left winter, but the thermometer was pushing spring hard. Five minutes after I'd stepped outside, I found myself opening my heavy jacket. The ground was muddy, the trees bare, but between the sun and a breeze so gentle it barely stirred my curls, Cambridge was coming back to life. Daffodil greens poked up between the buildings and a few scattered snowdrops blossomed in a strip of lawn. Did anyone grow crocuses anymore? As I turned the corner, I saw a half dozen buds, some purple, some orange, that answered my question. How bad could things be?

Not entirely rotten, I thought as I pushed open the door to Rutley's Burgers. The weather had been so nice I had made the trek down to the university, hungry for fresh air and also for beef. The aroma that greeted me reassured me I'd come to the right place, and my mouth watered as I envisioned a burger, grilled to perfection, with a thick slice of red onion on top. But I wasn't the only one looking for a late lunch, and so by the time I found a stool at the counter, my order had grown to include sautéed mushrooms, bacon, and a slice of sharp cheddar.

"Hey, Theda!" I'd had my eyes closed as I chewed, the better to appreciate the play of cheese against onion, and nearly choked as I tried to respond.

"Tesh." I nodded, mouth full, and reached for a napkin with my free hand. "Sorry, famished. How are you?" With a twinge of regret I put down my burger and wiped both hands, reaching out to give my friend a quick hug.

"Hungry, but I'm not staying." That was a pity, the slender body I'd just embraced had felt a little too thin, and I could've used the company. "Takeout." Tess nodded toward the ordering station as if she could read my mind. "I had an appointment in the Square, so I'll be eating at my cubicle."

Tess worked at one of the university labs but only crunching numbers. There'd be nothing in her work area that could ruin a good burger or, I guessed, garden burger. "So, how've you been?" I tried to make the question sound casual, but Tess knew me too well.

"Am I still working the steps, you mean?" She smiled as if she'd caught me out. I didn't like that smile, or the bones I'd felt when we'd hugged. "I'm doing okay, Theda. It's hard, but I'm doing okay."

Tess used to be one of my closest friends, but even sisters have to give each other space. I nodded and took another bite, hoping that my silence sounded like support.

"But forget about me. How are you doing?" She leaned on the stool next to mine, and I worked on swallowing. "I heard from Violet. Are you going to be okay?"

"I hope so." That last bit went down dry and I reached for my Diet Coke. "It was pretty terrible. And now, they think—

Well, I've got a lawyer, anyway." An awful thought struck me. "Tess, have you been talking to anybody? I mean, does anyone think…you know?"

She waved away the end of my sentence. "Oh come on, Theda. No matter what else, everyone knows you're not a killer."

That wasn't the reassurance I craved. "No matter what else?" My throat felt tight despite the soda. "Tess, come on. Spill."

"It's nothing." She looked away just when I wanted to meet her gaze. "I mean, everyone knows that you and Bill are on the outs."

I swallowed hard. "They do?"

"Well, you haven't been around that much. I mean, Francesca has pretty much planned the whole benefit without you."

"Already?" My burger was losing its savor.

"Well, not by choice. You've been otherwise engaged." Tess turned toward me, but I couldn't read her face. "Hey, Violet needs something soon or the Helmhold House is going on starvation rations. And Bill had a night free, so, yeah, she went ahead. And besides—" She turned away.

"What?" I heard my voice croak.

"Is that my order?" I hadn't heard the woman at the register yell out anything. Then again I hadn't been listening.

"Tess, what is it?" I reached out. Her arm was definitely too thin.

"I'm sorry, Theda." She looked down at the ground. "I wasn't going to say anything. But, well, you didn't seem to care." I looked at her, unable to form a word. "I mean, when you do come in, it seems that all you do is flirt with Piers."

"Number thirty four? Garden burger with fries?" That time there was no mistaking the yell, and Tess hopped off her stool.

"Gotta run." She leaned forward and kissed me on the cheek. "Don't worry about any of it. Everyone knows you're in transition." And with a jaunty wave she was off.

IN TRANSITION? Was that the same as out on bail, or was it a phrase that Tess had picked up in rehab? I mulled that over as I finished my burger and called for the check, not even finishing my fries.

"These okay?" The heavyset waitress looked at my plate. Either she recognized me or she knew the quality of her chef's hand-cut, skin-on fries. I nodded. "I'll wrap them to go, then." By the time she returned with my change and a brown paper bag, already turning dark from the grease, I had a plan. I'd stop by Violet's. I needed to keep busy, and I wanted to look at her blue file again, anyway. And if I plied her with cold potatoes maybe she'd shed some light on Tess's comments.

I found my buddy at her upstairs desk, the cow-spotted Sibley draped over her shoulders and a ledger opened in front of her.

"That doesn't look like class work." I placed the bag beside the ledger. Violet reached in without looking and grabbed a handful of the fries.

"Not today." She made a pleased noise and glanced up to see what she'd been eating. "Rutley's?" I nodded and she pulled the bag into her lap. Sibley leaned forward to see what his person was eating. "Caro's on me about midterms, but I've got to focus on the real-life stuff first."

I opened my mouth to protest, but she cut me off. "I know, I heard it all morning from Caro. Finishing my degree is real life. But I'm fine. I'm going to pass everything and this June, I'll be out there, cap and gown, with the rest of the Extension crew."

"But, your grades?" I didn't want to push. Clearly Caro had already done that. "Have you totally given up the idea of veterinary school?"

She shrugged, mouth full, and Sibley jumped to the ground.

Caro hadn't finished college, either. But she'd put herself through a rigorous apprenticeship at a small trade school, learning to restore the kind of woodwork that made old houses like this one beautiful. I'd seen how she glowed when Vi made the decision to return to school and finish her undergrad degree. I could only imagine what she thought about Vi dropping all plans to go onto veterinary school. But then, my two friends had managed a serious relationship. Maybe people who could manage to live with their lovers knew something I didn't.

"Right now, I can't see past the next week, Theda. We're hurting."

I pulled a chair up to the desk and looked over at the ledger. Maybe I just didn't understand bookkeeping. "You're going to do a fundraiser, right?"

She nodded again, mouth full, and made a mark with her pencil. I felt a cat twine around my ankles and reached down to pull the chocolate Siamese onto my lap. He stretched out as I stroked his tawny fur.

"Sunday." Something on that page must have been fascinating, the way it held her gaze.

"Sunday? This Sunday?" I stopped in mid pet. "Isn't that awfully quick ? I mean, you won't get any publicity and, well, can it be all planned?"

"Oh, it's all planned." She finally looked up, shooting me a look I couldn't read. "Don't worry about it. I mean, you've had a pretty full plate."

"I know." I went back to stroking the Siamese's smooth coat, as much to calm myself as to please him. Bill had said he'd be meeting with Francesca on Sunday to work on the benefit. But if it was already planned, why hadn't he told me? "I just wish I could forget about everything, about yesterday, and help out with the benefit instead." If Bill would want me to.

"I'm sorry." She put down the pencil and motioned to the last fry. I shook my head. "I still can't believe it. Rachel is gone, and all I'm thinking about is budgeting. I guess this is the one thing I can do anything about." She finished the fry in two bites, a thoughtful look on her face as she chewed. "I've got something for you, though. We're now thinking of a series of fund-raisers, in clubs all over town, and we'll need you to write about the others. Sunday is just kind of our soft launch. Francesca and Tess threw it all together really fast." That was cheering. "We don't even have the bill yet. I mean, the Dividing Lines said they'll play, and Tess is going to do a set, too. But Piers's band was going to headline, too. Though now I don't know. He's pretty much out of commission." We both fell silent, thinking about why.

"So, hey, what's going on with all that?" I knew she meant with my arrest. "Did you talk to Patti's guy?"

I nodded. "This morning. He's taken me on, I guess. He says our best bet is to find out who did it, that the cops won't bother now that they, well, now that they have me." I must have choked on those last words. The Siamese twisted around and nipped me on the hand. "Hey!"

"Don't worry, Theda." Violet reached out to take the cat. "Nobody can really think it was you." The Siamese gave us both an aggrieved look and jumped to the ground.

"I don't know." I slumped in my chair. "Pilchard, Andy—that's his name—really wants me to come up with an alternate theory, even if it doesn't make sense. He was wondering if maybe Piers was involved, 'cause they were seeing each other."

"No!" Violet sat back, her green eyes flashing. "How'd he find out about that?"

"I let something slip." I sunk even lower. "I didn't mean to; it just came out. So you knew about him and Rachel?"

"I'd heard something was up with Piers. But he's a lover, not a killer."

"That's what I told the lawyer. But, well, the cat's out of the bag. So now I've got to find out who really did it, not just let him set up some fall guy who's as innocent as I am.

Besides, I don't want to get away because of reasonable doubt." The words sounded strange to me. Unnatural. "I mean, Vi, Rachel was our friend."

Vi settled back and began playing with her pencil. "Any ideas?"

"No, that's the problem." I felt the tears start to come and fought them back. The key was to keep busy. "I thought maybe I'd look through your blue file, those hate letters again. Pilchard will get copies of Rachel's letters once everything is copied and logged in. But maybe there's some nut out there, something we missed."

"And you want to get started." Violet knew me, knew I was grasping at straws.

"I can't just sit around." I looked around. Not even any of the shelter cats wanted to be near me.

"You can still help with the benefit. I bet Francesca and Tess haven't done everything yet."

I choked. Tess. "I don't know, Vi. I feel like people are talking about me."

She didn't argue, which made my heart sink even more. But she did point her pencil at me. "Hey, weren't you going to get Musetta's teeth cleaned?"

I could have laughed, but at least I no longer thought I'd start crying. "That's kind of lower priority right now, Vi. You see, our favorite vet…"

"I know, I know." She started rummaging through a pile of magazines on an end table. "But I'm serious here. I've just been reading a really scary article on feline dental disease." Aha! So she was still interested in veterinary school. "It's not just cavities and bad breath, you know. There are all sorts of implications about infection, cardiac disease, you name it."

I couldn't hide my smile. "Still reading the journals, huh? I'm glad." I took the proffered magazine. "I believe you. But seriously, Vi, I hadn't thought about rescheduling. I'm not even sure who I would take her to."

"Let me get on it." Violet rooted around on the desk top, this time coming up with a phone book. "How about Dr. Massio? He does have a good rep, even if he does work at WellPet. Let me see if I can get an appointment for you. Meanwhile, if you want to grab that file, it's down in Caro's office."

By the time I came back, flipping through letters, she was giving my name and number to someone. A moment later, she hung up and turned to me. "Well, this is sort of interesting. The city shelter is reopening next week, and Massio is filling in as interim head. Guess that's his idea of community service, huh? He, well, to be honest, nobody there is crazy about having you come in. But I pointed out that this is about your cat, not you. And, well, Theda, I hope this is okay. I said I'd go in with you. We have an appointment for Monday." She snorted, a sort of half laugh. "The up side of all this is that every vet in town has probably had her schedule cleared out."

"Like murder's contagious?" I looked up from the file.

"People are timid, Theda. You know that." I shrugged. "Hey, do you want to come over for dinner tonight? I've got practice at eight, but Caro's making lasagna."

The thought was tempting. Caro could cook and the last forty-eight hours had taken their toll on me, but I shook my head. "I'm hoping to get together with Bill, to be honest." Violet perked up and I felt my smile extending. "Despite everything, we're trying to patch things up." Thinking back on that morning's conversation, I could only hope that was true.

WITH VIOLET'S PERMISSION, I took the blue folder and headed out. I might crave action as a way to avoid thinking, but the truth was that the last two days had wiped me out. As I let myself in, I was cheered to see a "present" awaiting me, Musetta's favorite catnip mouse.

"Kitty, you there?" A peep and a thud answered me, and my cat appeared at the end of the hall. "Musetta." I scooped her up and buried my face in her fur. This close, her purr rumbled like thunder, but when she squirmed around to face me, I jerked my head back. Her breath was getting worse. "We're going to try again, kitty," I told her, recoiling as she reached to touch my nose with hers. "I don't know this vet, but Violet vouches for him."

Would this new vet be gentle with her? I put Musetta down and she immediately began to groom, sticking out one white leg like a drumstick. She looked so vulnerable. Maybe I should cancel. But what Violet had been saying about dental care in cats only reinforced what I already knew. What I really wanted was to see a vet I knew and trusted. I wanted to see Rachel, but I never would again.

On that cheering thought, I collapsed on the sofa, loudly enough to earn a startled look from my cat. But as I read through the letters for what felt like the twentieth time, she jumped up to join me, kneading at my thigh until I lifted the folder and let her onto my lap. Her soft weight made a nice contrast to what I was reading. We all have negative thoughts, angry flashes that fly through our minds. But to take the time and effort to put them down on paper hinted at something else. These people wanted to be heard. They wanted their anger to be felt. Would any of them have gone a step further? Would any of them have attacked a nice woman who happened to take care of the city's unwanted animals?

Maybe I was just too tired. I couldn't see it. Yes, they were nasty. But on the whole the threats were either against Vi and Caro specifically, as a couple, or against the cats. There was that one accusing Vi of witchcraft…I thought of showing that to Bunny. As a peace-loving Wiccan, she'd be outraged. But nothing that seemed to carry over to shelters at large, or unwanted pets. My head was hurting and I put the folder down. We'd get Rachel's letters next week. Maybe something in one of them would reveal some specific threat, something deadly that we'd all missed.

My eyes closed, and just as suddenly jerked open. What we'd missed. That was it. Maybe it didn't mean anything, but at least one of the letters in Rachel's file had been a printout, as if it had been written on a computer. Violet's file were more traditionally kooky, written by hand in ink or, yes, crayon. The neat printing in Rachel's file had seemed better organized. But maybe it wasn't any more sane, simply more serious.

I itched to see those letters again. I had to talk to Pilchard. He might take those threats more seriously than the police would, but he wouldn't know about the difference, wouldn't see that they were in any way unusual for hate mail. I reached for the phone, but the call went straight to voice mail. How far did privilege extend? I left my name and number and hung up.

Or maybe the murder had nothing to do with the shelter or with cats. Maybe it was personal. Had there been another man in Rachel's life? I'd only found out about Piers by accident but she must have met hundreds of men in the course of her days. Other vets or techs. Clients or even the sales reps who came by pushing the latest medications. I tried to imagine her with a fellow professional, someone as clean cut as she was neat. Or was Piers her usual type, a long-haired rocker more sheep than show dog? Rachel had been a private person, always so busy and so caught up in her practice that she and I had never dished about guys or relationships or love. Had she confided in anyone else? Violet knew her well, before they'd fallen out. How long ago since we'd all hung out? Probably before Bill had taken over the Last Stand, I realized, my eyes growing heavy again. Before my own romance had hit its current rocky patch.

The phone woke me with a start and Musetta jumped to the floor.

"Krakow, where've you been?" Tim. I closed my eyes to gather my thoughts. How much did I want to tell him? How much did he need to know?

"Tim, I'm sorry. I've had a couple of appointments. It's been crazy." That was not untrue.

"Well get your priorities straight, Krakow. If you want this job, getting us this poison story would be a good start. At least you could keep me in the loop." A hint of a whine crept into his voice. "I mean, you're my candidate here, Krakow. Help me out."

"Tim," I sighed. "I'd rather focus on next week's 'Clubland'—"

He didn't let me finish. "You need to step up here, Krakow. You pitched this story and some of the editors here smell blood. That's good for you, and good for the paper."

"Tim," I started again. There was no way around it. "I don't think I'll be able to get you the pet poisoning story."

"What? If this is because you're too sentimental or it involves animal testing or something, I don't want to hear it. This is your beat, Krakow. It's your job to get us this story."

Animal stories were my beat? Since when? But this wasn't the time to argue details, like the fact that I didn't exactly have a job, nor was I likely to get one. "No, Tim, that's not what I meant. It's more complicated." I looked around for moral support, but Musetta had left the room. "You know that vet, the one who was killed yesterday?" God, I had trouble even saying it. Had it been only a little more than 24 hours?

"Yeah. Different shelter, right? And she was slashed. Pretty brutal, I hear."

I choked back something bitter. "Different shelter, but

there's a connection. Rachel—the vet—she was doing the lab study on the poison and, well, it looks like the poisoned food might have come from her shelter."

"That's great, Krakow! Pure gold!"

How could I have forgotten the sensibility of the newsroom? Tragedy was our bread and butter. "Yeah, well, Tim, there's a big complication. You see, I don't think I can be the one to report this story anymore. I've been arrested for Rachel's murder, and I'm only talking to you now because I was able to get bail."

I'd never heard my editor speechless before, but I couldn't exactly savor the moment. Instead, I winced every time he sputtered and by the time he signed off, saying he'd get back to me, I think we were both relieved.

The call had focused me. Yes, I needed to talk with Pilchard, but with everything else going on, I'd neglected my one steady gig, "Clubland." And so I grabbed the weekend section and started skimming upcoming club listings. The benefit for Helmhold House hadn't even made it into the ad, and I found myself wishing that Violet had waited a week. Though she had said that this first show would be part of a series. Of course, I hadn't followed up.

"You've reached the Helmhold Home for Wayward Cats." I left a message, but knew I should keep looking. At the very least, I shouldn't focus my entire column on a friend's endeavors. Whom had I seen recently? The Allston Onramps weren't quite up to the level of a "Clubland" profile, though I had thought of writing about them before. I should at least talk to them, talk to Piers. See how he was doing. If something better came up, I'd use his band as a secondary item.

"Bill? It's me." Okay, my message wasn't grammatically correct, but it was my usual.

"Hi, Me." A wave of relief swept over me. Bill had not only picked up, he sounded like himself again. "What's shaking?"

"Not much, I'm just trying to salvage my career." I'd meant it as a joke, but as I said it, I could hear the quaver in my own voice.

"Oh?" Bother, he was on his guard again. "And you'd like my help?"

"Well, I was hoping for dinner." I thought of my empty fridge. I could go shopping. "My place?"

"Want me to stop by Petruccio's first?" I plopped onto the sofa. We were back to normal. "Mushrooms and olives?"

"That sounds like heaven. I'll get some wine." I found myself smiling into the phone. We'd get together and kick back. I'd help him go over blues night bookings. But I had called him for a specific reason. "And Bill?"

"Uh-huh?" I could hear that he had the phone jammed under his chin. He'd be doing paperwork now, figuring out the week's payroll.

"Would you have Piers's number? I ended up catching his band the other night and I may try to fit them into 'Clubland.'" Why was I explaining myself?

"Hang on." He put the phone down and I realized I was holding my breath until he came back and read me the number. "I'm surprised you don't have it."

Was there an edge to his voice? Well, too late now. "Thanks, Bill. So, see you around seven?"

"Yeah, sure, Theda." And he hung up.

When the phone rang again thirty seconds later, I jumped for it. But the voice that answered my breathless greeting wasn't Bill's.

"Krakow." Just one word, that was it.

"Tim? What's up? I've got some good possibilities for next week's column." I didn't, not really, but some instinct was prompting me to cover.

"Krakow." This time, I heard something in his voice. A lack of energy. A deflation.

"I was thinking of the Allston Onramps, but there's also going to be a series of benefit concerts—"

"Krakow!" He was angry. That was more like it. "I'm trying to tell you something."

"Sorry, boss." Could this be about the job?

"Theda, I've got some news." Uh-oh, where was this coming from? "I talked to some of my colleagues here and told them what you told me." He paused. As I waited, I tried to remember if I'd ever heard him use my first name before. "And the consensus is not good. If you were on staff, we'd stand by you. We'd have an obligation to support you." His voice had taken on a peculiar flat tone, as if he were reading or reciting something he'd memorized. "But as a freelancer, you're an independent contractor. However, since you are associated with the *Morning Mail,* in many ways the public identifies you with us. And so, until the current situation is resolved, I'm afraid we cannot continue to use you as a freelancer. You will, of course, be paid for any outstanding pieces." He rushed through that last bit.

"Tim, what are you talking about? What does some legal mistake have to do with my column?"

"Freestanding feature, Krakow." Emotion had crept back into his voice, but it was sadness. "And it's not yours, not anymore."

I GOT THE WINE. I managed that. Not my usual, but a bottle of Chilean that had the double bonus of not only costing half what I'd usually pay while also offering absolutely no temptation. Not that I'd been in the habit of downing a bottle of wine alone on an afternoon. But as Musetta eyed me, sitting once more on the sofa as the light faded and I made no move to turn on either a lamp or music, the idea did cross my mind.

Maybe I should have. By the time Bill showed up, pizza in hand, my mood had disintegrated from shock to something close to despair. "Bill!" I ran into his arms even before he'd put the pizza box down, getting a one-armed hug and some worried laughter in response.

"I'm happy to see you, too, babe. Or is it the Petruccio's?"

"It's not funny." I sniffed and turned away as he put the pie on the table and went to hang up his coat.

"Oh no, what's happened now?" I had his full attention. "Did you hear from that lawyer? Did something happen with your bail?"

"No, it's not that." I heard the peevishness in my tone. I couldn't help it. "I've been fired from the *Mail*. Fired!"

"But you're a freelancer." He slid by me to fetch plates from my cabinet and saw the Chilean red. "Hmm, interesting." I didn't respond and he grabbed two glasses and a corkscrew.

"Well, you know what I mean." He was looking at me, waiting for me to continue. It was hard to say. "They've cut me loose. 'Clubland.' It's gone."

Bill was suitably affronted. "That's ridiculous! You made that column, and they need that column. There must be some mistake."

I shook my head, my eyes filling with tears. "No. I told Tim about my arrest. I had to. He wanted me to write about Rachel. And then he called me back. I'm out. They've dumped me." If he would be angry for me, I could relax. I sniffed. Loudly, and waited for him to notice and take me in his arms.

He did, but he also kept talking. "I guess I can see it. I'm sorry, babe, but it might be a liability issue. I mean, you know you're innocent and I know you're innocent. But if they're employing someone who is under investigation, well, no, someone who has actually been arrested and there's an incident—"

I pulled away, furious. "Whose side are you on, Bill?

They dumped me!" Being angry kept the tears at bay. "I mean, this is what I do. Who I am. Not that you'd know. You've got so much going on I don't even know if you read my column anymore."

"Oh, Theda, that's not fair. You know I'm still struggling to get the club launched, and I do read your column." He released me to lay out the plates. "I thought when I saw how upset you were, it was something serious."

"It is serious. I'm losing everything." Suddenly, I flashed back to our last big fight. I thought of how easy it had been for him to make the switch, from outsider to ready-made player. This was my world, and now he was on the inside. And I was out.

"It's not everything, babe. It's not, as you like to say, 'your life.' What happened with Rachel was about life, and you getting picked up, well, that's a big deal. The column is a gig, and you always find a new gig." He must have seen how those words hit me, how memories of Rachel came rushing back. "Come on, I bet you haven't eaten all day."

He opened the box and separated a slice, holding it up as the strings of cheese stretched down. It smelled magnificent; that burger had been hours ago.

"Theda," he smiled, his voice taking on a singsong tone. "Come here. You know how you get when your blood sugar is low."

He was right, my stomach was growling. He must have heard it and I turned toward him, expecting a hug once he'd deposited the slice on my plate. But he had turned back to the pie, his mind already moving on, as he asked, "Now, isn't that better?"

Maybe if he hadn't been chuckling. Maybe if it hadn't been my column. Maybe we were just not fated to have pizza together, in peace, ever again. But that was the wrong question and suddenly my tears turned to anger. I'm not even sure what I said, but I know that it was pointed, petty and mean.

All I'd wanted was another hug. A "there, there." A promise, no matter how empty, that everything would turn out all right.

What I got was a cold pizza and a bottle of cheap wine all for myself when Bill finally stormed out. He'd tried to comfort me, I knew that, but it was too little, too late. I'd rejected his attempts at reconciliation and he'd grown frustrated, leaving right before it all turned into a full-fledged fight. Hungry as I was, once he was gone, I couldn't stomach more than half a slice. I could barely shove the box into the fridge before collapsing into bed. I needed to retreat.

It couldn't have been ten minutes later that the phone rang. I ignored it, waiting for the answering machine to pick up. I heard my own voice, speaking with a cheeriness that sounded foreign, and I heard the click. I lay there, willing it to be Bill. But it wasn't. Not until the caller identified himself did I place the voice as my colleague—my former colleague—the *Mail*'s staff critic.

"Hey, Theda. I'm sorry to call so late. Is this late? Maybe not for us club rats, heh, heh. This is Ralph. I, uh, well, I'll talk to you when I see you around." Click. Was I so low that I was now considered fair game by the likes of Ralph? I buried my head under my pillow to cry. Musetta jumped onto the bed, and I felt her wet nose sniffing at my hands. But when I reached out to hold her, she drew back, settling finally at the foot of the bed, near my feet and out of reach.

MUSETTA, WITH HER clear conscience, never has problems going right to sleep. But I lay there, going over and over that last scene with Bill. He'd wanted to make up after the morning's squabble, I knew that. But I'd felt so tender and raw that I'd been, yes, I'd been prickly.

I sat up. I should call him. Make a few jokes about how difficult it is to love a porcupine. Invite him to come over. Only this was the second fight of the day. And he wouldn't be at home, he'd be at the Last Stand, with loud patrons and other women competing for his attention.

This called for direct action. I washed my face and put on some nicer underwear for luck before heading out to the club. But the odds of a private conversation looked slim as I pushed open the heavy bar door and found myself in a mob scene. The night, hovering around freezing outside, was hot and sweaty in here, the mood rowdy. Friday night, the first of the weekend amateur marathon. Usually, I'd be at a rock club and I'd be able to sneak into whatever passed for a backstage to get some breathing room. Usually, I'd be working.

I saw Piers behind the bar and waved. He didn't see me, what with all the shouting, and I had to move sideways to get through the crowd.

"Hey, Piers." He looked up, his eyes heavy and ringed under that mop of hair. "I'm so sorry." He looked down and I wondered if he was hiding tears. After Tim's bombshell, I'd forgotten all about calling him and now I was glad. The phone could be impersonal, and he was grieving. I reached to touch him, just to make contact, but he moved away. It must be miserable, feeling this way and having to work.

"Hey, Theda." I looked up and saw Francesca coming toward me, holding two longnecks. "Want one?"

"Thanks." Were these now health food, too? "Crazy tonight, huh?"

She nodded, taking a swig of her own beer. "Weekends. But it's good, right? Keeps the place in business."

"Who's playing?" The line to the back room filled what should have been an aisle between the bar and the booths. A fat guy with red hair was working the door, and I didn't know if he'd know me. Know to let me walk in.

"Reed!" Francesca was beaming. "I figured that's why you came. Isn't this usually a rock night for you?"

I nodded, not wanting to get into it. "Is he on now?"

"Next set. Hey, I've got to run, but I'll catch you later." With a smile, she was off, weaving her way through the crowd. I looked around. No Bill, and I needed a little more reinforcement before I went in search of him.

"So how are you doing?" I'd found a space by the bar, where Piers was squirting soda into highball glasses.

He shrugged. "I get by." Eager hands took the glasses and he leaned past me to take another order.

"I'm just so sorry. I know you were close." He bent over the bar, fishing bottles out of the ice.

"You knew we were close." He looked up, his face unreadable. "Well, that explains some things."

"What?"

"I got a phone call, from some investigator this afternoon."

"Piers, that wasn't me." I rushed to explain. "That's my lawyer, and he's just looking for anything." Even as I said it, I found myself remembering the night I'd dropped Musetta off. Someone had been in Rachel's office. "But, hey, did you see her Wednesday night? I mean, maybe you saw something."

If he realized I was fishing, he didn't respond. "No." He looked down at the bar. "I wish. Rach told me not to come over. Said she was busy. Said she had some old business to clean up."

"Old business?" That sounded awfully convenient. "Nothing else, Piers?"

"Nothing." The eyes that met mine were large with tears. "That was the last—" He dashed his arm over his face. "Well, at least now I know. Thanks. Thanks for everything." His eyes were dry now, all business. "So what are you having?"

"Jameson?" I found myself forcing a smile. "No ice." He was under pressure; this wasn't the time for questions. He poured two fingers in a heavy glass and put it down in front of me, already walking off to see to another customer. "Thanks." I put down a five, and backed into the crowd.

"Tess!" I saw my friend up in the line. She turned at the sound of her name and looked around, then continued walking. "Tess!"

"Theda, it looked like you were busy back there." There was something about her smile I didn't like.

"Piers had been questioned." I mentally smacked Andy Pilchard for getting him into this. "And, well, I felt bad for him."

"So you had to console him?"

I opened my mouth to respond and shut it again. Was I letting Piers off the hook too easily? I looked back at the bar and when I turned back to Tess, she was gone. I took a big swallow of my drink, and reminded myself that I was in a weird mood. It wasn't necessarily my friends. I got in line for the music room.

"Oh, you're okay." The big redhead nodded to me and reached to stamp my hand. I felt an absurd flush of gratitude as I stepped through the doorway. Reed was standing by the sound-board and greeted me with the warmest smile of the night.

"Hello, gorgeous. Come to hear me play?" He slipped an arm around me.

"Wouldn't miss it." I was tearing up. If anyone gave me a full-fledged hug, I'd probably start bawling. I swallowed hard. "You seen Bill?"

"He's in the back." Reed nodded toward the tiny storeroom that served as a backstage dressing room. "Go get him."

I couldn't help but wonder what he had heard, but with that, he gave me a quick squeeze and started to walk toward the corner stage. I straightened my shoulders, took a deep breath and turned toward the back.

"Bill!" There he was, emerging from the backstage room, looking as harried as I've ever seen him. "Everything okay?"

"Theda! Yeah, it's nothing." He started to walk past me, but I put my hands on his arm.

"Bill, I'm so sorry. Everything's just—"

"Theda, I can't talk right now. There's equipment missing." He kept walking, talking first to Reed and then doubling back to the sound board. Reed's smile had disappeared while they were talking, but the big guy on the door had already started lowering the lights so when his drummer started a soft pattern with the brushes, the sax man's smile came back, taking in the crowd before he lifted the instrument to his lips.

"Hey." Bill was deep in conversation with Neil, the sound guy, but I leaned into him, threading my arm around his waist. His arm settled around me and I felt myself relax. This wasn't beyond repair. We were still a couple. I closed my eyes.

And nearly fell over when he stepped away. I must have yelped because he spun around. "Sorry." I felt myself forcing a smile. "It's just been a day." He blinked and I wondered if I was speaking in English. It was up to me, I knew, to try again. "Bill, can we talk? I know you've been trying to help me. I do, and I'm sorry. It's just that I've found out someone's been questioning Piers."

That caught his attention. "But didn't you say he couldn't have been involved? He has an alibi, right?"

"Well, I don't know. I don't think he could have done it. I mean, he says he didn't see her that morning."

Bill snapped. "*He* says. Uh-huh, I get it. You'll take my help if it helps Piers, because *you* don't want to believe Piers could have been involved."

"Bill, it's not that!" I needed to explain how I felt, that I'd dragged Piers into this.

But Bill wasn't listening. "No." He shook his head, backing away. "Not now, Theda. I've got business to take care of."

I couldn't stop the tears this time and ducking my head I

made a run for the back room. If there had been another band in there, readying for the next set, I didn't know what I'd do, but the small room was empty, except for some shelves, an out-of-tune upright piano, and the ratty couch up against the far wall. I headed for the couch, telling myself that since this was a jazz joint the odds were good that the upholstery was vermin free.

But as I walked up, I saw a movement. An oversized black cat darted out from under the sofa and looked up at me.

"Ellis, right?" I sank into a squat, the better to communicate on cat level "And how are you?" The sight of the club cat cheered me immensely and I held out my hand for him to sniff.

Hiss! In an instant the big feline had reared back, mouth open, and before I could withdraw my hand he had swiped at me. I fell back onto my butt as the line of blood appeared on my hand, running along the length of my thumb.

"I'm so sorry!" A friendly voice behind me. Francesca must have come in seconds before. I put my hand to my mouth. Ellis glared, ears back. "At the shelter, he's what we'd call a 'nipper.' 'Not immediately pet ready.'" She sat down besides me on the floor and wrapped her arm around my shoulders. In front of us, Ellis opened his mouth and hissed again as I started to sob.

SIXTEEN

BILL WASN'T A BRUTE, but he was working. By the time I emerged, blurry eyed, he'd been looking for me.

"I'm sorry, babe. Things are just crazy tonight." He held my face in his hands and brushed away a stray hair with his thumbs. I knew he could see that I'd been crying. "For both of us, I guess." I nodded and tried to smile. He was trying, too. Behind him, I saw the doorman walking up.

"You'd better get back to work." I sniffed, but my smile was stronger now. "Can we get together later, though? I mean, I'm sorry about today. Sorry about everything."

"Me, too." He held up a hand to stop the burly redhead from interrupting. "Hey, do you want to go back to my place tonight?" I couldn't remember seeing him look this tentative. "I probably won't get off here till late, but then…"

"It's a date." I wiped my face on my sleeve. The tears were gone, and I had to let Bill go, too.

Reed played well, probably. At least the crowd responded. I found a piece of wall by the corner and clapped when everyone else did, not that I heard anything. As soon as the set was over, I waved and caught a nod from Reed, then made my way through to the front room. I still hadn't been able to really talk to Piers, and I knew that I needed to. Not just to apologize for getting him involved but to understand anything about Rachel. But he was busy, pulling two drafts while two other pints—Guinness, it looked like—waited to settle on the mat. Besides, I couldn't deal with any more rejection. I walked home and hugged Musetta for courage, then drove over to Bill's to wait.

It had to have been three by the time I finally gave up and went to sleep, worn down by the emotions of the day. I know he came home, because I was dreaming of him, and half woke as he slid into bed next to me. "Bill?" I asked, for confirmation that he was real.

"You expecting someone else?" he asked, his voice softer than his words. He put an arm over me and we spooned close, but the rest of my dreams were evil, and when I woke up, he was already gone.

IT WAS AFTER TEN by the time I got back to my own place, but I was as tired as if I hadn't slept at all.

"Wow!" Someone missed me. "Mrow-wow!" I could hear her clawing at the door as I fumbled with my key.

"Hang in there, kitty!" I opened the door to find the belt from my terrycloth robe had been dragged into the hall, where it joined the catnip butterfly and an eviscerated felt mouse. "Is all this for me?"

In response, Musetta butted her head into my shins and threw her weight against me. I scooped her up and hugged her, but she struggled until I put her down again. She loved me, but she wanted her freedom. Maybe we weren't that different after all.

I fed her, first things being first, and then checked my messages. The first message was from Andy Pilchard.

"Where are you, Theda? Don't you know that as your attorney I should be kept informed of your whereabouts at all times?" I gasped. "Just kidding! Got your message. I'm actually calling from Patti's place. She wants you to come over and have dinner with us tonight. And bring your lovely friend, she says. Is that right, sweetie?" I heard Patti's high singsong in the background. "About eight?" At least some folks were happy.

The second message wasn't Bill either. "Uh, hey, Theda?" The voice—deep, male—was vaguely familiar, but I couldn't place it. "I got your number from Ralph. This is Lee Wellner, from the *Weekly Wag*." Great. I was being sought out for interviews now. I could see the headline: When Critics Kill. I reached to hit erase. "Anyway, I thought it was worth giving you a call. I hear you're not doing 'Clubland' anymore, and I was wondering if you would talk to me about throwing my own hat in for it."

I WANTED TO RUN and hide, but there were too many things that needed doing. For starters, I really had to talk to Piers. If I was going to meet with my lawyer later, I wanted to have more to give him than theories. Speaking of which, I dialed Bill's cell.

"Hey, it's me." Was he in the middle of one of his punishing workouts or screening his calls? "We've been invited over to Patti's for dinner tonight. I know it's Saturday." I swallowed, this was not the night to ask a clubowner to play hooky. Not with a club this new. "But I figure it's a command performance for me. Andy Pilchard is going to be there. I could use the moral support." I tried to make it sound like a joke.

Next, I put a call into Violet. "Wuh?"

Damn, I'd forgotten that she'd played Providence last night. "Sorry, Vi. I'll call you back later."

"No, what time is it? I should get up." In the background, I heard a sound. Not quite a scream.

"Violet! Are you okay? What's going on?"

"Huh? Oh, nothing. That's just Simon, the Siamese." She put the phone down and I could hear water running. I hung on, knowing she'd be back as soon as she'd splashed her face.

When she picked up again, she sounded more alert. "Pretty awful, isn't it? I worry about placing him, but every now and then he goes off, and what can I do? He's gotta express himself."

I looked over at my own cat, now napping on the windowsill. Musetta was talkative, but not like that. Still, the Siamese's howling had sparked a question. "Violet, you know the cat Francesca brought over to the Last Stand? He went for me last night, and I don't know why. I didn't know he was a 'nipper.'"

"Ellis bit you? Is he up on his shots?" That had woken her up.

"Wouldn't you know? He came from your shelter."

Simon howled again, and Violet started laughing. "This is too much. But, no, that cat was one of Francesca's projects and she can be weird, what with all her natural cures. I say, if a cat stays, it's got to be vaccinated. Rabies, 'cause that's the law. Distemper, too, and feline leukemia if we can. I mean, I've got the whole community here to think about. But this guy was in and out so fast, so I don't know."

"Well, I think I'll live. He scratched me, no biting. But he'd been perfectly friendly before. I don't understand it. It was Francesca who called him a 'nipper,' as in 'not immediately pet ready.'"

She chuckled. "That's good. I've got to remember that. But, hey, maybe she was trying to convert him to veganism." The Siamese howled again, an unearthly sound. "Don't laugh! She's been trying it. Or it could just be the club. Poor beast's got to be under a lot of stress. Noise, and jazz noise to boot."

I wasn't satisfied, but I had too many other concerns at the moment. Violet anticipated one of them. "So, did you find anything useful in my letters?"

"Maybe." I sighed. "I didn't see anything we didn't see before. But that's actually sort of why I called." She grunted and as I ran through my thoughts, I heard a loud purr start up.

Violet probably pulled her old sweatshirt on and Sibley with it. The cow-spotted cat liked to drape himself around her neck. "But I'm kind of stuck until Pilchard can get copies of her letters," I concluded. "So I'm thinking I could use the time to find out more about Rachel. Who was in her life, you know?"

"You're not still thinking of putting it off on Piers, are you?" Musetta jumped up, alerted by something in the street below.

"What is it, girl?" I walked over. Down below, the street looked as it always had. But right outside, I saw the beginnings of buds on the trees.

"Theda?"

"Come on, Vi. I'm not even going to answer that. You know that was the lawyer. Not me. I just want to figure out what did happen." Silence. "Vi, I'm the one who found her." I shivered at the memory. "I'm the one who is going on trial."

"I can't believe this will all get that far." I couldn't respond. But I was saved by another howl. Either Simon was acting up, or someone had stepped on Sibley's tail. "Look, I've got to feed this crew and make some calls about the benefit tomorrow. I'll ask around about hate mail, too. A lot of my volunteers work with AIDS Action, and the neighborhood groups. Maybe someone knows something about our local creeps. Want to meet at the Mug Shot, say forty minutes?"

"Thanks, Vi. I'm buying." It was automatic. She was helping me, after all. Only after we hung up did I remember that I no longer had a source of income, and that nobody was planning a benefit for me.

SINCE MUSETTA WAS AWAKE, I spent a good ten minutes lunging her. Her latest toy, a bunch of ribbons attached to a wand, served to drive her mad and I had her jumping and circling to reach for the colorful streamers. I let her catch them a few times, too, just to keep her from getting frustrated and

watched her lap and chew at the ribbons before she got tired.
When she turned her back on me, preferring instead to clean
a spotless white mitten, I tucked the ribbon wand into my
desk. I'd heard too many horror stories about cats eating
strings and streamers. This toy was not one I wanted her
dragging around the apartment.

But the diversion did me as much good as it did my chubby
cat. Pilchard was out of the office. I'd see him later, and there
was no point in calling Piers until I had talked to Violet. My
bills, however, were another matter. As I zipped my jacket,
opting optimistically for a lighter coat than I'd worn the night
before, I realized that I should get on it. I'd freelanced for
other publications before. I could again. This afternoon, I
really needed to work up some queries. If I could stay out of
jail, maybe I could make my rent by writing about bathroom
fixtures. Maybe if Lee got my old gig, I could get his.

"Musetta, do you have any idea what the *Weekly Wag*
pays?" She stopped washing long enough to look at me. But
whatever her thoughts, she kept them to herself.

BY THE TIME I GOT to the Mug Shot Violet had nabbed a corner
table. Saturday, and the place was hopping. It was just my imagination, I told myself, that a silence had fallen as I walked in.

"Hey! How're you doing!" Was Violet talking a little too
loudly? I slid into my seat and dumped my coat. "You still
buying?"

With a nod, I stood back up, knocking into a young woman.
"Watch it!"

"Sorry!" This day wasn't starting off well. But I managed
to get two large, double-shot lattes, one with soy milk, and
make my way back without any more mishaps.

"Sugar?" Violet looked up and saw my face. "Never
mind, I'll get."

By the time she sat back down, my paranoia was ebbing. "Sorry, Vi. I just feel like everyone knows, like everyone's looking at me funny."

She snorted. "This crowd? All they care about is getting an outlet for their Powerbooks."

"Maybe, but after last night, I don't know." I sipped my latte. Coffee milk by any other name, it tasted great. "Not just Ellis." I'd seen her about to protest. "But things are still weird with Bill. People are talking about me, linking me with Piers. Who, I think, is avoiding me."

"Well, let me see." Violet wiped a soy milk mustache from her upper lip and began to count on her fingers. "He just lost the woman he'd been seeing. You've brought his name up to your attorney so he's gonna be questioned. And if he *was* interested in you, well, as you say, you're back with your boyfriend."

"And I'm accused of killing his real girlfriend." I finished the list. The caffeine wasn't lifting me like it usually did. "Vi, the only people who aren't avoiding me are Ralph and that creepy guy from the *Wag,* Lee Wellner."

She shuddered. "Oh, now that's scary." Only when I was about to agree did I see that she was laughing. "Come on, Theda. He's just a nerd. What is he, five-six? Maybe a hundred-twenty without those big glasses? Even I could take him. You've had a bad week. A really crappy week, but we'll figure this out. Nobody can really believe that you killed Rachel. The rest of it's just gossip. Piers is a pretty boy. He probably broke a ton of hearts when he settled down with Rachel, and now it looks like you're next in line. Don't sweat it. It'll all blow over."

I hadn't had a chance to tell her. "Even if it does, I'm screwed. Just the fact that I've been arrested is enough for the Mail to have dropped me."

"What?" Heads popped up to stare, and I shushed her. "That's ridiculous. Whatever happened to your rights of due process? Innocent until proven guilty, and all that."

"Violet, please." I was whispering. "I'd rather everyone not know, not just yet."

She glared, her green eyes full of righteous rage.

"It's a newspaper, not a democracy." I kept my voice low, hoping she'd follow suit. "Freedom of the press belongs to those who own the press."

She nodded. Violet had been through enough not to need any more of an explanation. "Speaking of, nobody seems to know anything about any new weirdos. I mean, the Save Cambridgeport group has been getting nasty letters, but that's been true for years."

"Printed as well as handwritten?" She nodded, and my heart sank. "Damn, I really need to see Rachel's letters, or at least to get to work on *something*."

"Don't worry, kiddo. We're going to get you out of the doghouse, and give us both a sense of empowerment in this crazy city." She pulled a legal pad and ballpoint from her old Army Surplus knapsack. "Once that's done, I'll deal with the *Mail*."

AT SOME POINT the caffeine must have finally kicked in. Either that or the camaraderie, but as I walked back home, I felt a spring in my step. The air was still nippy, but now it felt bracing. We had a plan.

For starters, I would call Piers. Trying to talk to him at work was foolish, and it was too easy to misread what was going on in a crowded bar. Then I'd do an Internet search for anything I could find about the city shelter. I could ask Bunny to rummage through the newspaper files as well, looking for problems or scandals. Then, tonight, I'd tell Pilchard about

the letters. It was too early for him to have heard from the
prosecution, or gotten that inventory, but from what Piers had
said, Pilchard's team was already gathering information and
I wanted him to be on the lookout for the file from Rachel's
office. Tomorrow was the benefit, and everyone I knew would
be tied up. But on Monday, when Violet escorted me and
Musetta in to the shelter, she'd ask questions there, too.

Musetta was lying on her back when I came in, her belly
exposed in the feline version of a pin-up pose. But I knew
better than to touch that fluffy white fur.

"You're trying to lure me, aren't you?" I kneeled down to
rub the base of her ears. "You want an excuse to bite me." As
she'd matured, I'd discovered, my cat had become increasingly sensitive to certain types of stimulation. While my last
cat, James, had enjoyed having his belly rubbed, the same
petting drove Musetta into a frenzy. She stretched in response,
pushing her head further into my hand. I reached down to
work on both ears at once and she opened her mouth, purring
with pleasure. From this angle, I could see how some of her
teeth had yellowed, the gums edged with an angry red.

"You need this cleaning, my dear." As if in response, she
reached up to grab my right hand with her paws. I pulled back,
dragging her along the floor until she sprang up, ready to play.

Fifteen minutes later, she was sound asleep and I was
washing two new scratches on the back of my hand. Bill
always teased me about roughhousing with her, coining a
rhyme that he repeated to all our friends: "Pet on the white,
expect a bite. Pet on the black, less chance of attack!" But both
my pet and I had needed the release.

Now I could get to work, and taking Violet's cue, I looked
for a pad to jot down some notes. What did I want to know?
Well, as politely as I could, I needed to find out how things
had stood between Piers and Rachel. I also wanted to know

the history of their relationship, and if he was aware of any other men in the pretty vet's life.

I tapped my pen on the pad. This was going to be difficult, particularly if he suspected I might be involved. But if I could win him over, then he would want to tell me, wouldn't he? Unless he was the real murderer. "Impossible." The cat opened one eye to check on me. "Okay," I modified myself. "Unlikely. Now, go back to sleep, Musetta." She rearranged herself into a coil and did just that, as I reached for the phone.

"Piers, it's Theda. Theda Krakow." We'd become club buddies, but I'd never called him at home.

"Theda." His voice was flat, either with grief or fatigue. It was after noon, could I have woken him? "What's up?"

At least he didn't hang up. "I need your help, Piers." The more I'd thought about it, the more it seemed the direct approach would be best. "I know this is a sad time for you, a horrible time. But I'm in trouble." Silence. "You do know that I didn't do it, don't you, Piers? I'd never hurt Rachel. She was my friend, too."

The pause lasted so long I began to grow afraid. But finally it was broken, by a sigh and a yawn. "Yeah, I believe you. I couldn't see you hurting her."

The wave of relief made me so weak, I was glad to be sitting. "Thanks, Piers. That means a lot. But, you know, my lawyer says that the police aren't going to investigate, now that they have me." It felt so odd to say "my lawyer." "I mean, now that I've been arrested." That felt odd, too.

"You gotta be kidding." He was more awake now. "They can't give up."

Good, I needed him to be angry. "I don't know. I mean, I hope not. But that's why he's asking questions. That's why his investigator called you." Silence. "I'm sorry about that Piers. I really am." More silence. Was I being a fool?

"Look, Piers." I was taking a gamble, but it was the only way I knew to function. "I need your help on this. I want to look into her life, maybe find out who could have done this."

"You think it was someone she knew?" I heard a window open and traffic. Vi had said he had one of those apartments on Commonwealth Avenue, and I could picture him at the window. I wondered if he was wearing a shirt. "Theda?"

"Sorry, again, I just don't know. But if it was just random, why would her killer come into her office at her practice, you know? And it was, well, it was bloody." I swallowed, the image of Piers replaced by something much more horrible. "Anyway, that's why I'm calling. I need to know more about her life."

"Sure." The traffic faded, and I pictured him walking back into a room, maybe sitting down on a couch as ratty as mine. "But we hadn't been together that long."

"When did you start seeing each other?

"Couple of months ago. Let me see, I brought Miss Tish in in December. She had an earmite problem, bad, and I really liked Rachel. I mean, to be honest, rats turn a lot of women off. Then I saw her at a show, something at the River Bank, and found out that she knew Violet. It's funny, maybe because of Vi, I thought maybe she was gay, too. She was just different from a lot of the women I meet."

I knew what he meant. Good-looking boys in bands had their pick of women, but the ones who clustered closest tended to be both younger and more frivolous.

"I mean, she was really pretty. I noticed her eyes right away, and her hair. But she was really strong, too. Tough, almost, and really straightforward."

This was my cue. "Was she seeing anyone else? Or had she been?"

"Had she broken some hearts?" He sounded lighter. The

memories were doing him good. "You'd think. But no, nobody recent. I guess she'd been serious with someone in college, but when they were both in grad school, the pressure split them up. Since then, there hadn't really been anyone. I think he might've cheated on her, she was a real stickler about that."

"Must have been a change for you." I was fishing, but he just laughed.

"No kidding. I mean, I was seeing a couple of girls when she and I first hooked up, and that didn't work for her at all." I waited, my next question on the tip of my tongue. "But they were all casual, and she was special."

"So, that was okay by you? Settling down like that? I mean, you come from different worlds, there weren't any tensions?"

Piers laughed again, sounding totally relaxed. "Are you asking if we fought? Yeah, of course we did. That's why I stopped seeing anyone else. And I started working at the Last Stand as a steady gig to fill in between contracting jobs. She loved my music, really, but she wasn't comfortable with me living from hand to mouth. Get a job, be faithful. She was very clear. But, you know? She was worth it."

"Yeah, I bet she was." I was getting off track. "And you were doing some work for her, too, weren't you?"

"All volunteer. There isn't much contracting work right now. The season hasn't really picked up yet, so I was helping her at the shelter."

"Well, if you were around her at the shelter, you must have seen how things worked there. Were there any problems there? Any rivalries?"

"You're reaching, you know." He chuckled, but more softly. "I guess I don't blame you. I don't know if I can help you, though. I think the staff worshipped her. The volunteers, too. I mean, they had a lot of people in and out. The pay was lousy. Really, even the receptionists and vet techs aren't much more than volunteers. But everyone wanted to be there. All the volunteers down there would kill for a staff job."

We both stopped at that. "Piers?"

"I didn't mean that," he said quickly. "I mean, they're crappy jobs. It's just that everyone who works there is committed to the animals, one hundred percent. And so was Rachel. I think that's why those stories made her so mad."

"What stories?" I didn't dare breathe.

"Oh, you know, about how the shelter was killing animals. That the big campaign was just to raise money. I wasn't really up on that when it was happening last year, but I guess it's a big deal? And Rach spent so much time setting up the fostering program and everything, so to have someone write about the shelter like it was a death camp was pretty low."

"Who wrote the stories?" I couldn't help remembering what Violet had said. She'd been worked up, too. And where there was money, or the hint of fraud, there might be some crazy with a motive. "And where did they get their info?"

"Can't help you. To be honest, I didn't read them. I mean, I've got them here, 'cause they were important to Rachel. It was a couple of weeks ago, something in the *Wag*. That guy who usually writes about music. You know who I mean. He's around."

"Lee Wellner?" I didn't know he did reporting.

"That sounds right. Do you want to see them?"

"Yeah, I'd love to. Would you send me the links?"

He laughed. "You think I'm that wired? I'll just give you the file. I told Bill I'd help out with the sound board problems today. Wanna meet at the club?"

I hesitated, just long enough. "Or we can meet at the Mug Shot. I could always use more coffee."

"It's a deal." We agreed to meet in an hour, and I sat back wondering about this new writer who seemed to be dogging my steps. Writing about animals, poaching my column. Had he also been out to defame my friend? Could he also have written the angry letters? Reporters had done stranger things to make a story bigger. I looked over at my answering machine. I needed to talk to my fellow freelancer. But first, I needed more information.

Bunny wasn't answering her phone, so I left a message telling her to look for an e-mail. The modern age didn't necessarily speed up communication, but at least it could be more thorough. Typing, I was able to explain what I wanted to find out, and why. If there had been anything in the mainstream press about Rachel's shelter, no-kill campaigns, staffing problems or whatever, Bunny would find it.

What was it about Bunny? There was something on the edge of my memory, something we'd been talking about. Not her pregnancy, all was well there. Not the pet psychic idea. Not, I realized with a sick feeling, that job at the *Mail*. The pet food contamination! That was the last thing she'd looked into for me. She hadn't found anything, but I had. That letter, from Violet's files, that made it seem like the bad kibble had come from the city shelter. Rachel's murder had all but driven thoughts of the earlier crime out of my mind, if that was even a crime and not just an accident. But if the bad cat food had come from the city shelter, maybe it and her death were somehow connected. When Piers showed up with the clippings, I'd have to see if he knew anything about the donation, and I'd definitely have to make sure Pilchard knew about it.

In the meantime, I really should write up some pitches. Editors always had a lag time, and if I wanted any income within the month, I needed to stir up some work. I poke around through my ideas file, but all I could think about was Rachel. Giving up, I pushed back from my desk and stared out the window. From the look of the passersby, the day had warmed up nicely. A walk would do me good.

"RALPH!" I COULDN'T EVER remember seeing my rotund colleague drinking anything besides beer. But there he was, at the counter of the Mug Shot, looking somewhat the worse for wear. I'd never called him back. He wasn't stalking me, was he?

"Oh, hey, Theda, how're ya doing?" Before I could answer, he went on. "I mean, I heard. About the column."

Of course, he was the one who had told Lee. He must have known as soon as I did, if not earlier. "Thanks." I couldn't manage more. I stared at the door. Piers had to show soon. But I was being silly. All Ralph had done was pass along the news. "Hey, nothing's settled yet. Maybe I'll get it back when everything is cleared up."

"I hope so. I always thought you did a good job with it." I turned back toward him in surprise, but he was looking down at the floor. "I never meant otherwise."

"Ralph, what are you talking about?"

He didn't even pause. "It's just that I've gotten some reports. You don't know, you're not on staff. But we get evaluated and my last few haven't been great. So when I saw that posting and you were meeting with the editors and everything, I got scared."

He wasn't talking about my arrest. "The Infallible Mystics column! You were the one. You told Tim that I'd been fooling around with the band."

Ralph continued to stare at the floor. I was very tempted to grab his ratty little ponytail and swing him around the room. If only he weren't so fat. Besides, it might upset the other customers. "Ralph, you little…I can't believe you said I was inappropriate. What was it, that I'd slept with one of them or gotten drunk? I mean, when I think of all the times I've seen you drinking with a band." Or flirting, or hitting on anything female. "I can't believe it." But I could. It was only too likely that he'd been getting negative evaluations.

Everyone at the paper was afraid of cutbacks, of drops in readership, of losing some ineffable edge, and Ralph had been plodding on as always for as long as I'd been reading the *Mail*. In the scene, his reviews were so predictable he was almost a joke. He was an institution among my crowd, and friendly enough. But to the bean counters, a jovial drinking buddy wouldn't be considered an asset. I felt my anger melting away. It didn't hurt that he looked crushed, his round face red with shame.

"That's not why I lost the column, Ralph."

"It isn't?" He perked right up. But I wasn't letting him off the hook, not yet.

"It's a long story." His color was fading to normal. "And what you did was underhanded and just plain nasty." He nodded. "But you can do something for me. Something to make amends." I was thinking fast. What Piers had said about Lee stuck in my mind. The Wag writer was showing up in too many places. "You know Lee Wellner?"

He opened his mouth to deny it, the old instincts coming back. "He told me that you told him about my column, Ralph." I was stretching the truth, but my anger made me ruthless.

Ralph grunted, which I took for assent.

"Okay, then. I need you to do some things for me. Concerning Lee and what he's been writing."

"Theda, come on!" His voice took on a particularly unpleasant whining tone. "It's bad enough I made up stories about you."

"Yes, and now you're going to help me get out of the jam you put me in." I should've crossed my fingers behind my back. Hadn't I just told him that he was off the hook? But I scared him. Women did. And so he shut his mouth and nodded. "I'm not asking you to lie again. I'm looking into what Lee was writing about the city animal shelter, particu-

larly about the vet who was killed, Rachel Weingarten. I need
to know what he didn't print, and who his sources were."

He looked taken aback. He'd expected me to ask him to
slam my rival.

"Can you do that, Ralph?"

"Yeah, sure." He sounded anything but. "I guess so,
anyway. I'll probably see him tonight at the Casbah." I sighed.
I'd forgotten that the Moral Imperatives had their CD release
party tonight. If I wasn't careful, it wouldn't be long before I
fell off the musical map entirely. Maybe, if Patti's dinner
didn't go too late, I could make it.

"Good. I may be there, maybe not. But I'll be calling you."
He nodded, his broad face twisted up. I could see that he was
trying to figure out my angle. "Remember, Ralph. You owe me."

Just then, the bells over the front door jingled. "Remember!" I left Ralph looking more confused than ever and walked
over to meet Piers.

"Hey, Theda." He handed me a folder and ordered a large
regular to go. I leafed through a series of articles, neatly
trimmed from a tabloid. Rachel's work.

"Thanks, Piers. I don't know if I'll find anything here, but it
can't hurt." When I looked up, Ralph was still staring. More grist
for the rumor mill, but it couldn't be helped. "Hey, I wanted to
ask you about the work you were doing on Rachel's storeroom."

"Uh-huh?" He paid for the coffee and slipped the plastic
lid off to sip it, wincing at the heat.

"What had been in that storeroom, you know, the one you
renovated? And what did you do with it?"

He shrugged as he pocketed his change. "I helped Rachel
move a bunch of stuff. Cases of litter and pet food. Some bags.
I think she managed to fit most of it in the other storage areas."

"Would she have gotten rid of some of the food, specifically dry cat food?"

"You're thinking of the poisoned food, aren't you?" I must have looked surprised. "Everyone knows what happened at Violet's, that's why we're doing the benefit. You're thinking that food could have come from Rachel's?"

"Maybe." Between his surfer boy looks and his casual manner, it was easy to underestimate Piers's mind. I could see why Rachel had liked him. "Did you ever see any bags of the KittyLuv brand?"

He sipped his coffee again, more carefully. "I could have. I'm sorry, Theda, I just don't remember. But I'll tell you one thing. Rachel was really worried about money."

"So why would she give away a full sack of cat food?" I finished the thought.

He shrugged. "Rachel said that one of the volunteers had been trying to get her to go all natural, but I don't think Rach was into that. I do know one thing for sure." He was looking out the door again. "Rach would never have passed along anything she'd thought would have hurt animals." We both sat in silence for a moment. Finally, he shook himself and turned toward me. "Hey, wanna walk over to the Last Stand with me?"

I was tempted. I did need to pin Bill down about dinner. But was walking in with Piers the best way to approach him? "Why not?" I tucked the folder into my bag and motioned for Piers to lead the way. Behind us, I could feel Ralph staring.

IT WAS EASY TO TALK to Piers, and I found myself relaxing as we made our way down Mass Ave toward the club. The weather helped; if it wasn't sixty, it was getting close and I didn't even bother to zip my jacket as we kept to the sunny side of the street. By some kind of silent consent, we'd left discussion of heavier topics back at the Mug Shot and moved onto music. He had a load of funny stories about gigs gone bad. We were right in the middle of a true tale of woe—a road trip to Pittsburgh, complete with engine trouble and a carsick dog—when we got to the Last Stand.

"I told Johnny, no more petsitting. Nothing on four legs unless it can drum or pull the van!"

Which is why I was laughing as we walked into the club, and for a moment, in the dim interior, I didn't see Bill. He was sitting at the bar, a ledger in front of him. When I did register his blank look, I walked over and gave him a resounding kiss.

"Hey, I didn't know if you'd gotten my message." He looked over at Piers, who motioned to the back room.

"I'll get started, boss."

"What's wrong, Bill?" I took the stool next to him, in front of his ledger.

He was silent for a moment. "Sorry. There's just some oddities. Little things aren't adding up."

"I meant between us, Bill. And as far as accounting, I can't believe you're doing this longhand."

He put his pencil down. "Hey, these are the books I inherited."

"Yeah, and Tess or Bunny or any of a half dozen people we know could have this all on your computer in under an hour. But what about us, Bill?"

Suddenly, the shelved bottles behind the bar seemed to be of intense interest to him. "Bill." I reached out take his hand. "You know I love you and that I'm the faithful type, don't you."

"Yeah." That Grand Marnier must have been fascinating. "It's just that you looked so happy just now. Maybe that would be better."

"Crap." That got his attention. "Piers tells funny stories. He's a nice guy. Now would you cut this out? I've got some serious news for you."

"Oh?" He didn't look totally convinced, but I filled him in, explaining about how the bad cat food might have come from

Rachel's store and how there had been some controversy about her shelter, too.

"So you're saying that someone tried to kill her cats and then gave up and killed her instead?" One eyebrow raised, he was almost grinning. "Theda, I love you and I believe you're innocent. But I think maybe you better leave the investigation to Homicide. I know what you think, but I'm sure they're on the case. Meanwhile, try to get on with your life."

"While I still have one, huh?" I wasn't as confident as Bill that the police were still looking into Rachel's murder, but I wasn't going to convince him. It was time for a truce. "I love you, too, Bill, and we need a life. Would you to come to dinner with me tonight? Pilchard—I mean, Andy—and Patti have invited us over." He opened his mouth to object. "Seriously, Bill, this isn't just social. I don't know if Pilchard is trying to make a big show about how much he trusts me or what, but he is my lawyer. Besides, he might be able to make something out of what I've found."

"And you want to hear what he's gotten in discovery, don't you?"

He'd caught me out. "That had crossed my mind."

"You know he probably doesn't have anything yet." He'd slipped into cop mode, vaguely paternalistic. For now, that was okay. "I mean, he's probably still just beginning to file the paperwork." I nodded. "Most defendants would still be waiting for their bail hearings. If you'd been anyone else, you might not even have gotten out, or not gotten out so fast."

"I know, Bill. You keep telling me. But I have been a friend of the court. And you are my boyfriend. And that's why I'd love you to come with me tonight. Please?"

"I'll be there." I was silent. "Okay, I'll pick you up. But now, please, can I get back to work?" I leaned forward for another kiss, bigger this time, and left him in peace.

I'd just stepped outside, squinting in the unaccustomed sunlight, when I heard a familiar voice.

"Oh, hey!" Tess, still wearing her winter parka, looked as surprised as I was.

"Looking for Bill?" I was feeling generous, and confident. But she was staring past me, down the street.

"No, just doing errands. You know, the Saturday afternoon of a working girl."

"That's right." I'd forgotten what it was like to have a nine-to-five. "But, hey, if you have a moment, Bill's having trouble with his books and I bet most of it would clear up if they were put onto the computer. I was just telling him he should get Excel or something, and he got that deer in the headlights look."

Tess didn't react. Maybe I'd misspoken, assumed too much. "I mean, he might be able to pay you, and it would probably just be an hour's work or so."

"Okay, maybe. I'll ask him." I doubted she'd heard a thing I'd said, but I didn't want to push. I smiled, feeling my face grow a little tight, and waited for her to continue the conversation. "I should run."

I nodded, silenced by her distraction. Well, we were all busy. I had a file of stories I wanted to read, and Bunny would probably be sending over more. I gave her a quick hug, noting once again how thin she had gotten, and watched her walk quickly away, hunched in her jacket like it was still February.

SEVENTEEN

"I STILL THINK THIS is a bad idea." Bill was grumbling as we parked.

"The dinner or Patti's boyfriend taking on my case?" I pointed to an opening just far enough from the corner to be legal.

"All of it." He slid into the space without a question, a sure sign he was distracted. "I don't like that he's taken on your case pro bono. I don't trust him, and I think you'd be better represented by somebody less flashy who was doing honest work for the money."

"And I'd pay him with what?" He started to answer, but I knew what he was going to say. "Bill, you've already signed away your condo for my bail. You're not putting the club up, too." Too much of his retirement money had gone into the Last Stand. "Especially not if you're having money problems there."

"We'd be doing fine. Only, I'm thinking someone may be a little light fingered." I looked over at him. "But I have some ideas." Who would steal from an ex-cop? "And quit trying to change the subject."

"Too late now." We rang the doorbell and adjusted our smiles.

"Theda, Bill." Patti looked good, I had to admit. She was wearing her usual color coordinated outfit, knit slacks topped by a twin set. But her cheeks glowed with something other than makeup and she positively bounced as she led us in. "I'd like you to meet my *friend,* Andy Pilchard."

"Charmed," I said. Bill just stood there, so I took the lead. "And I hear you're an attorney?"

Pilchard, to his credit, laughed as he leaned forward to kiss my cheek. "Good to see you again! Usually I tell my clients to go out, live your life. Be seen. But this is cheery, too, isn't it."

"Most definitely. And have you met Bill?" I had my palm flat on his back, ready to shove him, but it wasn't necessary. He extended his hand and muttered something that sounded like a greeting. Patti took over from there; her years of ferrying clients about had made her a mistress of small talk. For once, I was grateful. I nodded and accepted a glass of overchilled white wine and something orange in a celery stalk. Before long, the conversation seemed almost unforced. Bill and Andy were debating new Red Sox prospects, and Patti was fluttering about, bringing out more appetizers. "It's cheese, but reduced fat, dear. With pimento!"

I crunched down on another of the celery things and let my mind wander back a few hours. Bunny hadn't found much on the city shelter, but she had sent me some interesting articles about the no-kill movement. Most shelters, like Rachel's, were using a combination of programs, from aggressive spay-neuter campaigns to comprehensive counseling, the better to match people and potential pets. Some critics thought the goal was not practical, and some shelters were accused of dumping animals in other jurisdictions rather than take responsibility for unadoptable animals. But nobody called it a scam.

"Theda?" I looked up and realized everyone was standing.

"Sorry." I smiled and reached for Bill's hand. "I was thinking about some articles I was reading earlier. How shelters are reducing euthanasia rates."

"Always working." Patti's voice was chipper as always, but I'd seen the look pass between her and Pilchard. Shelters must be a forbidden topic. I wonder if they'd seen Lee's articles.

Patti was waiting. "Be a dear, Theda, and help me carry these in."

I obliged, picking up the half-empty tray and following our hostess into the kitchen. She must have seen that I was about to raise a serious subject because she cut me off. "Now, I don't want to tell you how to act, dear." She leaned over, lowering her voice to a stage whisper. "But maybe we shouldn't talk about work over dinner?" She handed me a bowl of brussel sprouts. "Bad for the digestion."

I tried, really. And the food helped. Although I'd been anticipating a cuisine as bland as Patti's fashion sense, she did Middle American well. The hunk of beef she'd roasted was rare in the middle, the potatoes crispy, and the brussel sprouts glazed with enough butter to stop an Olympic runner's heart. All in all, the dinner was both tasty and pleasant, with the conversation ranging from the Sox, where Patti showed herself remarkably well versed, to the latest plans for the Boston waterfront. I even bit my tongue when our hostess referred to the "revitalization" of East Cambridge. The Portuguese families that had lived there were mostly long gone, and my complaining wouldn't bring them back.

It wasn't until we'd begun cleaning up that things got hairy. I'd followed Patti into the kitchen, carrying the remaining dinner plates, and caught her separating some of the leftover roast from its string.

"For the kitties?" Patti's two cats had gone from Violet's shelter to lives of utter luxury.

"Shh, don't tell." Patti looked back over her shoulder. "Andy thinks I spoil them!"

"How could he?" I smiled. Patti did spoil her cats, but I approved. "I'll go run interference."

"Hand it over, mister." I stepped into the dining room in

time to take the platter of potatoes from my lawyer. "We're enforcing outdated gender roles tonight!"

Pilchard opened his mouth and closed it, speechless for the first time that night. Behind him, I saw Bill hide a laugh. I quickly deposited the tray inside the kitchen and came back out to the men. "So, what's up with my case, counselor?"

I wasn't serious, not really. But I was wondering how to engage Pilchard, and as soon as the words were out of my mouth, I saw they'd worked. "Theda, I'm not sure this is the time." Bill tried to butt in, but Pilchard wasn't hearing him. Instead, the portly counselor sat back down and poured us both more wine. "Which do you want first, the good news or the bad?"

Bill was staring at me, but the feline was out of the bag. I peeked over my shoulder. Patti was still engaged with cleanup. Maybe I could get this over with before she returned.

"The good?" I smiled, hoping we could keep it light.

"You're in luck." Pilchard sipped his wine, clearly savoring what he had to tell me. "It's early days yet, but I've had a look at the police records and there are two points in our favor." I nodded, trying to hurry him along. "The first is that the murder weapon was most certainly that scalpel. That does away with premeditation." I nodded again, this was old news—and definitely not a good subject for a dinner party. My lawyer, however, was on a roll. "The other plus is that there was a back exit to that office."

That wasn't news, either. I tried to break in, but he wasn't stopping.

"Hey, nobody told me, but don't you see the implications? The killer could have escaped. Could have gone through to the treatment room and out a different door further down the hall. And you didn't!" He was glowing now. "So the worst they can say is crime of passion!"

I felt sick. There had been too much butter on those sprouts.

"And the bad news?" Bill was staring at me in a way I couldn't decipher. It didn't look like sympathy.

"Well, it's not great, but it's not fatal either." I winced at his word choice. He kept on talking. "The staff looks like they're in the clear. Everybody is pretty much accounted for."

"But what about the vet tech I saw?"

He shook his head. "She was taking a delivery. A Fed Ex van had pulled up and was unloading a pallet's worth of cartons. Some kind of bulk supplies. Anyway, she wasn't there the whole time, you must have seen her when she went to check something. But he was there, by the door for a good twenty minutes and she signed off on everything on his electronic clipbboard. That records date and time, too."

"Great." I couldn't finish my wine and pushed the glass away.

Pilchard noticed. "No giving up now. There were a lot of people in that office. We'll break some of these alibis."

"And you're looking into ex-employees, too, right?" I remembered what Piers had said. "I mean, the jobs didn't pay well, but people wanted them."

Another nod. "We're on it. So far, we don't have any former staff who were angry about being fired, but we'll start looking at the other end, at unsuccessful candidates, too."

"Maybe you should let the Boston police do their jobs." There was a growling note in Bill's voice that I recognized, but I had my own objections.

"What about the threatening letters? Have you started to trace them? I'm really interested in the printed ones. They're just different from the usual crazies." I'd meant to hold all of this till after dinner, but we were on the topic now. "And did any of you see the stories in the *Weekly Wag?* They were this close to accusing the shelter of fraud."

Too late, I saw that Patti had returned. Her stare said she'd never forgive me. Ignoring both Patti and Bill, I filled Pilchard in on what I knew. "And so, if Rachel was using it to raise money and some people thought the campaign was a fraud, then maybe that's a motive."

Pilchard shook his head. Patti turned on her heel and walked back into the kitchen. "I don't see it. It's not like someone else would get the money."

"Dessert!" Patti's voice nearly cracked with the force of her announcement as she came in carrying something that looked creamy and bright. "Hope you all saved room!"

"That looks great, Patti." Bill stood to take the tray from her, and leaned in front of me to place it on the table. "Why don't we all get back to this fantastic dinner," he said, his voice a little loud. "Would you like me to slice this, um, cake?"

"Thank you, Bill." Patti returned with plates. "That would be very gentlemanly of you." She shot her date a look. "This is my own invention, a cross between a chocolate truffle cake and Baked Alaska. I thought tonight would be special."

I passed a plate to Pilchard. "And don't forget the poison," I whispered softly. He looked up at me, eyes wide. "Someone poisoned the cat food," I added, by way of explanation.

"Wrong shelter, Theda." Bill plunked a plate in front of me. The baked frosting revealed a suspiciously slick brown interior. If this was going to be our last meal together, it was a bad end.

"Delicious, honey." Pilchard was unfazed. He took another bite as I explained what had happened. "KittyLuv?" He gestured with his fork. "I don't remember it."

"Bright blue and red logo. Maybe it's just listed as kibble or cat food?"

My lawyer took another bite. "I'll check the inventory again. But the problem with these theories, Theda, is that they're all idealistic. People don't kill for ideals. They kill for greed or lust. So we gotta find someone who's gonna profit from this lady's death, or someone else who might have had the hots for her. Or maybe," his fork paused in mid-air, "someone else who had the hots for her boyfriend. Get me some gossip."

Poor wording. I choked down a forkful.

"Coffee?" Patti yelled.

"Let me help you." Bill pushed his chair back so fast it fell with a crash.

"This is wonderful, Patti." Maybe it wasn't too late for damage control. "Do you think I could get the recipe?"

"I'M SORRY, PATTI." We were cleaning up by then. I was scraping plates into the disposal while Patti's cat Aslan licked up the last of the coffee cream from the server. "I just meant to distract Pilch—I mean, Andy."

"Theda, how could you?" She slapped Aslan away from the cream and deposited the fat tabby by his sister on the kitchen floor. "I worked so hard."

"It was a wonderful dinner, really." I couldn't blame her for the ache in my belly. "And, hey, at least because of me the men have bonded." I was trying for humor, but there was some truth to what I said. In a last ditch attempt to salvage polite conversation, Patti had raised the question of the designated hitter. We could hear them going at it in the other room.

"You really ought to be more careful, dear. You know that."

I nodded. "I know, I'm sorry."

"Not just with me, Theda." I looked up. Patti had put down the wine decanter. "Did you see Bill's face when the topic of that woman's boyfriend came up?"

"Piers? But nothing's happening between me and him."

She shook her head. "Everyone is looking for a motive. And, well, I'm in the position to say this to you, Theda. You're not getting any younger, you know. You should be careful about gossip. That is, if you want to hang onto Bill."

I looked down at the floor, unable to respond. Aslan used that moment to start hacking, his round striped body jerking forward in the motion that presaged a furball.

"Oh no, Aslan!" Patti grabbed for the paper towels, but I took the roll from her.

"Let it out, kitty," I squatted on the floor as the other cat fled. "You'll feel better." He did. Cream is just too rich for adult cats. "I'll finish up in here." I looked up at Patti. She nodded and stepped away, wiping her hands on one of a matched set of dish towels that I'd been afraid to touch.

"If only the rest of my life were this simple," I said to the cat. He flicked his tail and exited, leaving me to deal with the mess.

BY THE TIME Bill dropped me at the Casbah we were speaking again.

"Did you see Patti's face?" I was hoping for a laugh.

I got a smile in return. "And that was all a bluff while she fed that fuzzy beachball she calls a cat?"

"Mostly," I confessed. The time had come for honesty. "I mean, I did want to tell Pilchard about the differences in those letters. They weren't complaints. They were threats, and they focused on the no-kill campaign."

"You think he's not looking in that direction." It wasn't a question, and as Bill pulled up to the curb he was looking at me.

"I think he's very…" I paused, searching for the right word, "concrete. That whole thing about lust or greed. I mean, you and I know that isn't always the case." Not that long ago, we'd learned of an accidental killing, I found it hard to call it murder, caused by misplaced idealism.

"You think maybe there's a fanatic at work here?" He put

the car in park and turned toward me. I nodded. "But if someone were so strongly against killing, why would he stab a vet? I mean, whatever else she was, Rachel was a doctor, right? She saved animals' lives."

"If I had the answer to that, Bill, I wouldn't be under arrest."

I got a kiss in response. Things were still tense, but I loved him all the more for it.

The Casbah on a Saturday was packed. Although the night had cooled off, I was sweating by the time I made it back to Brian, who stood sentry over the back room.

"Hey, Brian." I smiled and waited.

"Theda." Without checking the list, he inked a stamp and I held out the back of my hand. I hadn't had to say I was there for the Mail. I hadn't had to pay, either. For tonight, I was still in the inner circle.

But any warm glow I had evaporated as I descended down to the music room and saw my peers. Ralph, his sweaty face glowing in the red stage light, was holding forth, his beer bottle swinging in the air. Lee, meanwhile, was nodding, short and intent, a willing disciple to the older writer. Maybe I was better off out of this.

"Hey, there." Ralph raised the bottle in greeting. Nothing for it but to go over. Ralph owed me, and although I doubt he'd listened half as much as he'd talked, he still might have gathered something to tell me.

"Ms. Krakow." Ralph leaned in for a beery kiss. "You look lovely tonight." I turned my face in time and used the moment to order my own poison, a Blue Moon.

"Theda." Lee nodded in my direction, but for someone who wanted my help getting my old job, he seemed rather reserved. "I hear you want to talk with me."

I took a pull on my beer, stalling while I thought through strategy. He wanted something from me, too. "Yeah, I was curious about some things. But I also got your message. I figured rather than call you back, I'd probably see you here tonight."

He nodded again, a sharp fast movement like a tic. "You know," he paused and removed his glasses, pulling a micro-fiber wipe out of a pocket to clean them, before continuing. "I'm not in the habit of giving up my sources."

I forced a laugh. "Wow, I wonder what Ralph's been saying?" I would have kicked him if I thought he could feel pain at that point. "I'm not asking about sources, I just wanted to know how you came onto that story, the one about the city shelter backing off from its no-kill pledge."

"I hear you used to date a cop."

"I'm still seeing him, but he's an ex-cop now, and this has nothing to do with him." For once, I was telling the truth. "You know I'm friends with Violet Hayes, right? She runs the Helmhold Home for Wayward Cats and they're no-kill, too. We were just talking about this."

"Oh yeah, I forgot." He smiled, but it was a nasty smile. "You're friends with a lot of the musicians you write about."

This was getting to be too much. "Look, Lee, I don't know what Ralph told you. He said he was talking to you, so I asked him to ask you. That was obviously a mistake." I gave Ralph a look I hoped he'd remember when he was sober. "I'm not trying to steal your story. I'm just trying to figure out if there's any truth to the rumor."

"You think I don't check my sources?" Great, I'd made him more defensive.

"I think that sometimes one disgruntled employee can do a lot of harm by spreading a rumor, and that we don't always have the resources to follow up on everything." I was going to add something about the size and scope of the *Weekly Wag*, but figured that would just aggravate him more.

"It wasn't just one 'disgruntled employee.'" I held my

breath, hoping he would prove me wrong by telling me who *had* spread the story. But he was a little smarter than that. "Let's just say my main source was someone who had a long association with that shelter and with other humane organizations in the area. I'm not saying that this person didn't have personal motives. I'm not stupid." That look again. "But I called up the vet in charge once I had my story. She got so upset, I took that for confirmation."

"Well, of course she was upset. She loved that shelter."

"Uh-huh." Lee leaned back on the bar. "She's the one you're accused of killing, right?"

That was it. With a parting glare at Ralph, I stalked off across the room. I wouldn't be chased away, not from my territory. But I wasn't going to get anything useful from this conversation, and I had no reason to take abuse from the short freelancer either.

"Theda, Theda, wait up!" I was heading into the ladies' room to regroup, when Ralph caught up to me. "Hey, I'm sorry about that."

I looked at him and waited. He wasn't getting off the hook that easily. "Lee gets, well, he gets touchy. Some of it is about the Wag. He thinks us daily people look down at him." I shrugged. "And, yeah, I guess I made too big a point of who you are and about your guy and everything. I thought that would impress him."

He looked so downcast, I felt a spark of pity. "It's okay, Ralph. I figured that if he wanted my help getting the column, he'd be a little nicer."

"Yeah, well, that's the problem." Ralph was staring at the wall, so I waited. "He's not just going for the column now. He's been talking to our fearless leaders about that staff position. He considers himself a reporter, as well as a critic. I mean, I know I was out of line suspecting you, Theda, but this time I'm right. Lee Wellner wants both our gigs."

I STAYED LONG ENOUGH to see the band's set and to be seen. I might have lost "Clubland," but I was still a citizen of this world. Which, considering how the dinner party had gone, was a good thing, because it didn't seem like I was fit to socialize anywhere else.

Even Musetta seemed peeved with me. No toys waited for me, and my rotund little cat was nowhere to be seen when I got home. She finally came out as I was getting undressed, tackling me as I was pulling my blouse off over my head and biting—hard—at the top of my foot.

"Yow, kitty!" I hopped away and heard her scuttle. "Musetta, no!" Was Bill right? Had I indulged her to the point where she was becoming a bad pet? I dropped the shirt and saw her crouching, lashing her tail, just out of reach. "Or is it me?"

Without waiting for an answer, I retrieved her ribbon toy. Immediately she hunkered down, ears and whiskers pointing forward as her black butt twitched. There! She jumped and I jerked the ribbons back. She leaped again, paws extended to catch the fluttering toy. For five more minutes we kept this up, teasing and leaping until the jumps became lower and her attention seemed to wander.

"I'm sorry, Musetta." I reached down to dig my fingers into the thick fur around her neck. "You've been all alone, and I've been so preoccupied. It won't happen again."

"Meh." She stretched around to face me. We touched noses and I tried not to recoil from her breath. She'd been lonely. Bored. Was that the problem in Ellis's life, too?

"There are no bad kitties, no matter what Bill says. There are only insensitive humans." She mewed, and I had to laugh. Too many people in my life would have agreed with that tonight. Was I becoming unfit for human company? Now that Musetta was otherwise engaged, reaching carefully around her broad bottom to wash a spot near the base of her tail, I had to take my own question seriously. After all, here it was, Saturday night and not even close to last call. I was home, alone, with no plans to see any other humans. Not entirely true. I reached forward to scratch Musetta's ears and got a look. I'd interrupted her. Tomorrow night was the fundraiser for the Helmhold House. Between Violet's people, the musicians, and Bill's staff, I'd bet almost everyone I knew would be there. But there was a good twenty hours before then, and I didn't even have work to fill it.

Damn the Last Stand! Things had been good between us before Bill had bought that old bar and turned both our lives upside down. Musetta stopped washing for real and stared at me.

"You're right, kitty. We had issues even then." The difference had been that the issues had been Bill's. He hadn't liked my immersion in the rock scene. But I'd been happy, at least until he'd hurt his knee and taken early retirement.

And before Bill? Before then, I'd had my friends, and not just in the clubs. Sundays, for example, we'd meet up at Bunny's house to gorge on French toast and the papers, or hit Chinatown to check out some dim sum place Tess had found, all of us marveling at how she never seemed to gain a pound. Even after Bunny had settled in with Cal, we'd kept up the ritual, and when we'd gotten to know Violet, she'd fit right in, leaving Caro at home to talk music and cats over midday feasts. So maybe it wasn't me. Maybe it was Bill. I looked at Musetta and counted off the reasons. Bill was older than most of my friends. They were rockers. He was—had been—a cop.

Musetta got up to leave. "No, you're right." It wasn't Bill, his age, or his various jobs. He'd let me into his life, and I'd slipped into my new habits willingly. Nor was it the club. Bill was happy with the Last Stand, or had been until this latest round of problems. Had he said someone was ripping him off? But my sweetie was resourceful. He'd figure it out. And we would, too. We needed to adjust and that had been hard, harder than I'd anticipated, but it was do-able. And if I missed my friends it was up to me to reach out to them. No, I needed to be honest.

If I was going to get angry, I should be angry at whoever had killed my friend. That's what had messed things up.

I laughed softly, and Musetta turned to give me one last look. "It's nothing, kitty." God, I was being selfish. Rachel's murder had messed up *my* life? But it had, and if I wanted anything to get back to normal, I had to solve it.

EIGHTEEN

"I STILL CANNOT BELIEVE you didn't tell me. And, would you pass the butter?"

Bunny was on her third pancake and I wasn't far behind. I hadn't thought I'd be able to eat, at first, when Bunny called to remind me I was invited to brunch, with or without Bill. What with everything going on, I had told her about my work problems, but not about finding Rachel or about my arrest. I'd meant to, but going over it all again made it more real. Still, she was my friend, and I needed a morning off. And I was lucky; the Ralph story had bought me some sympathy, and she'd heard about Rachel already, thanks to the combined grapevines of the club scene and the *Mail*. After only minimal fireworks, she and her sweet husband had set to work, feeding me both information and those killer banana pancakes.

"I'm sorry, Bunny." I figured periodic apologies were a small price to pay and handed this one up with the butter. "You know I am. Syrup?"

My large friend nodded. "I figured I'd get the whole story today. You've had a full plate. Speaking of which, another pancake?" I took two more without complaint. "So, tell me again, you think this other writer's source, the one he won't give you, was spreading lies about Rachel?"

"Uh-huh." I licked some syrup off my fingers. Bunny's two cats were sleeping on the windowsill, but I think they would have approved. "I can't help but wonder if there's a connection between the whole no-kill controversy and Rachel's death."

"You do hear what you're saying, right?" Cal poured me more coffee. Bunny was on herbal tea for the remainder of her pregnancy.

"Yeah, I know." Out of guilt, I added a spoonful of strawberries to my plate before drenching the new stack with syrup. "It's just that the policy is the only thing anyone seemed angry about." I'd already told them about the letters, the ones calling Rachel a murderer, and about the search for an unhappy former employee. "But the shelter hadn't fired anyone recently and, I mean, everyone wanted to work there."

"So you're thinking this was a no-kill murder?" The way Cal said it, I had to admit that, as a motive, a shelter policy was a lot more farfetched than plain old greed or lust. Still, I nodded.

"Well, let's think about this." Cal helped himself to another pancake. "What is this 'no-kill' pledge and what did those articles really accuse Rachel of?"

"It's more a goal than a pledge." I needed to stop eating. "Though some shelters say they've done it." I poured myself more orange juice, liquids don't count, and ran through the various programs. "Basically, you reduce the unwanted pet population through service, access, and, education. No Jack Russells for couch potatoes, for example. Or bitey cats where there are kids. But these articles say it was all window dressing, that the shelter was going to keep on euthanizing animals, they'd just find some excuse to say they weren't healthy. And I don't buy that. At the very least Rachel was starting up a foster program, I saw her notes. So I don't know where those accusations were coming from. But, you know, a lot of money is involved. She raised as much as she could on the idea. She needed to, so she could get things moving and take care of all the animals that come in anyway."

"So there wasn't going to be much extra money floating around." Cal looked thoughtful, but Bunny interrupted, stabbing the air with her fork.

"What about the lust angle? From the way you described it, your lawyer was looking at Piers, suggesting that he was jealous of someone else in Rachel's life. But what if it was the opposite?"

"Rachel wasn't the jealous type." I thought of what Piers had told me. "If he had someone else, she would've just ended it."

"But that's just it!" Bunny was so excited now I had a flash of concern about her blood pressure. "He's a guitarist. A boy in a band! He probably had a ton of women. What if one of the girls he had been seeing was ticked off that he'd gone all monogamous? Do we know who he dumped for her?"

I shook my head. Bunny was right in principle, but she'd not taken the extent of his good looks—or his laidback nature—into account. "He said there wasn't any one woman. Nobody serious, he said."

"To *him!*" Bunny used that exuberant fork to grab another pancake. "That doesn't mean that some gal out there didn't think they had potential, didn't think that she was going to be the one." She shrugged. "Might be worth looking into."

"Maybe." I hadn't told my friends that I'd been accused of flirting with Piers. I really didn't want to start asking around about his past affairs. "It just seems like there are other leads. I mean, what about the blood I saw?" I'd stopped talking about the blood on Musetta's fur to almost everyone. But Bunny and Cal were family. I saw them exchange a look. "You do believe me, don't you? Guys?"

"I believe you saw blood." Bunny had a tone in her voice I recognized. "Or thought you saw blood."

"Bun, this wasn't a vision or the goddess sending me a warning or anything." I wanted to respect her beliefs, I really did. But this was important. "This was real blood, and Violet saw it, too."

"But you don't know if it was human blood." Cal's objection had some weight, and I sighed. "I mean, you never were able to get it tested. At an animal shelter, isn't it more likely that she came into contact with blood from an injured animal? Or even that maybe she'd drawn that blood? Theda, think about it. Say it was human blood. What's to say that Musetta didn't lash out at a vet tech or something?"

I shook my head. "Not this much blood."

"So you're saying, what? That the killer stabbed Rachel and then brought her back to the cat ward? Or stabbed Rachel and then went back to the cage room to pet Musetta? I mean, who else would do that except you or maybe Vi? The second part, I mean." I sank back on the couch. That was always where my theory fell apart: the timing. "And another thing." He and Bunny looked at each other again.

"Yeah?" I might as well hear it all.

"I hate to bring this up, but the Bun and I have been talking about it." He paused and looked at his wife. She nodded ever so slightly. "It was Violet who first told you about the rumors, right?" I nodded. "Might it be possible, maybe, that Violet is the one who talked to that reporter?"

"Not likely." I responded automatically, but even after a moment's thought I dismissed the idea. "Why would she go to him when she knows both of us? And she didn't work with Rachel. She runs her own shelter, so why would he trust her as a source?"

"So, you're saying that Violet might have viewed Rachel as a competitor?" Cal spoke slowly, as if he were leading up to something. I saw it coming.

"No, no way." I jumped up and looked over at Bunny. As a Wiccan, she believed that everything good and bad could bounce back at us, only three times as strong. This was slander and I waited for her to protest, too. To hear her deny our friend's possible involvement and add her usual "blessed be." I didn't get it.

"Wait a minute, Theda. Cal has a point." Maybe it was her belly that kept her from rising. Could she be that jealous that I'd called Violet to bail me out? That I hadn't told her until now? What she was saying didn't make sense. "I mean, Violet was the one who first told you about the euthanasia thing, and from what you said, she nearly got into it with Rachel when you went down there with the cat food." She looked up at Cal, unwilling to continue.

"We've neither of us wanted to mention it, Theda, but you can see the logic of it yourself. I mean, who stands to gain if the city shelter loses its big donors? We all know how squeezed everyone is these days, and the Helmhold House is running out of money."

WE HAD PLANNED TO WATCH some movies while we digested, but I couldn't wait to get out of there. As soon as the dishes were on the rack I made some excuse and left. After their bombshell, both my friends had been particularly solicitous. I didn't want coddling. I wanted to believe in my friends, *all* my friends. As I drove home, I replayed the conversation in my head. What they had said, what Cal had put into words, just couldn't be true. First, I couldn't see Violet killing anybody. The girl had only recently started eating meat again. And if she did kill, it wouldn't be for money. It would have to be for something she felt passionate about. To protect somebody; to stop an attack on a friend. Or, the thought crept in, on a cat. No, she wasn't a fanatic. She'd have found another way.

"Crime of passion," was that what Pilchard had said? Not premeditated? I shook my head. Especially now, when so much else seemed to be crumbling, I needed to keep my faith. What had seemed more promising was the idea of other romantic entanglements. Jealousy can be pretty painful, and I could easily see Piers as an object of adoration. And maybe Rachel's past wasn't as dead and buried as Piers had said.

Musetta pounced as soon as I'd opened the door, so I scooped her up and carried her over to the couch. My answering machine was flashing like a strobe and I reached to hit the button while cradling her in my arm.

"Hey babe." It was Bill. Sensing my distraction, Musetta grabbed my forearm and started gnawing on my hand. "Are you up yet? Sorry I didn't get over there last night." We hadn't made plans, but I was glad he'd thought about it. "Things were crazy here. On top of everything else, Ellis bit Neil. Hard. I'm beginning to worry about liability issues." He laughed, but it sounded forced. He owned a business now; it was a real concern.

I gently disengaged my hand and began rubbing the thick fur on the back of Musetta's ruff. Maybe I should think about her training, too. Bill rattled on about the club, and I found myself enjoying the rhythm of his words. Maybe we were finally getting back to normal. "You're coming tonight, right?" It wasn't a question. "Love you."

Musetta reached back to grab my hand, but I kept it behind her neck, refusing to be drawn in. The next message was from Violet. "So, don't know if you heard. There's going to be a memorial for Rachel next Sunday. I guess her family had a private funeral back wherever she's from. This is being organized by Massio, the vet who's taking over, at least for now. I guess they were friends." Interesting. I wondered how welcome I would be. No matter, next weekend was an eternity away. "You're coming tonight, right?"

The third message was more of a surprise. "Hey, Theda, it's Tess." I sat up, dislodging the cat. "I realized I was sort of

distracted yesterday. I'm sorry. I'm sorry about everything."
The pause lasted so long, I expected the machine to cut out.
But Tess's voice came back in time. "I guess I'll see you
tonight, huh?" And that was it.

"What do you make of that, kitty?" Musetta lay on her
back, the afternoon sun warming her belly. "What's going on
with Tess?" I couldn't resist and reached over to the soft white
fur. But this time, when she started to bite, I withdrew. "Sorry,
kitty. We're turning over a new leaf."

With that in mind, I walked back to my computer. First up
was a combination thank-you and apology to Patti. I knew she
didn't check her e-mail often, and that I really should call her.
But this was a lot easier than explaining my behavior of the
previous night. I was tempted to email Pilchard, too. He had an
address on his card. But he'd cautioned me about that on Friday,
stressing that my privacy could be, in his words, compromised.
I wanted to make some suggestions, pass along Cal's idea about
other women, but it would hold till Monday office hours. Who
knew? Maybe I'd have more to tell him after the benefit.

Musetta came into the back room, then, and leaped to her
usual perch on top of my file cabinet. The sun hit at an angle,
highlighting her fur. "You're a beautiful cat, do you know
that?" She blinked once and lowered her head for a nap. I
watched her for a while, the slow rise and fall of her side making her guard hairs glisten. What would I do without her?
More important, what arrangements should I be making, just
in case my trial went badly?

I shook my head. The thought wasn't worth thinking, but
once it had crept in I couldn't shake it. Suddenly, I wanted to
be outdoors, enjoying the air, the city. My freedom of movement. The day had turned fine, and I longed to see if any early
rowers were out on the river. This sun would be sparkling off
the water, catching the little waves brought up by the breeze.

But on the off chance that I still had a life in front of me, I needed to finance it. Let me just get a couple of proposals out, then I'd reward myself with a run and maybe give Musetta a good brushing, too.

An hour later, and I'd managed to work up two queries. I realized belatedly that if I was banned from the *Mail,* that meant that I couldn't pitch the paper's Home section editor. I was halfway into a proposal about container gardens when it hit me that I had to find another market. A quick web search gave me the name of the new editor at *City* magazine, but that meant I couldn't send my summer drinks pitch to her. That went, instead, to a new food and wine magazine that I'd picked up a week ago. I hated writing for startups. Half the time they disappeared before paying, and even when they did stick around they were prone to changing their editors frequently in their first year. But if I got in, now, before everything shook down, maybe *Dish It Up!* would become a regular client. Could I switch from writing about music to writing about food? The thought alone made me hungry again, much to my own amazement. I hit send and contemplated lunch.

But first a run. The weather was perfect. Cool but bright, and I knew I'd work up a sweat by the time I got down to the Charles.

The first tune up was an oldie, and it made me think of that show I'd missed at Bill's. Had that only been last week? It served to get me into a good rhythm, though, and when the next came on I was ready for a sprint. The sidewalk was damp and I kept my eyes down. One wet leaf and I'd wipe out. But it was fine to be outside, wonderful to be stretching and breathing hard. I knew I should be thinking about my case, about Rachel, and the shelter. For just a little while, though, I wanted to enjoy the day. I didn't know how long I had, and I intended to savor every minute.

The river was as beautiful as I'd hoped. I saw an eight-man

boat, oars extended while the coxswain yelled something unintelligible. Further down, two single sculls moved like waterbugs, skimming the surface and leaving hardly any wake. The path wasn't crowded; not like it would be in a month. But the few runners who went by nodded and smiled. We were all glad to be out as winter ebbed. Even the trees looked ready for spring, small hard buds reaching up to the sun. Leaves would follow in just a few more weeks. I hoped I'd be here to see it.

As I passed the Weeks Bridge, I realized I hadn't called anyone back. Well, they'd all assumed I'd see them tonight and I would. But things with Bill were still tender. I would call him, I decided as I left the river and started back up Flagg Street toward home.

BILL WASN'T ANSWERING either his cell or his office phone, but that was no surprise. From all the buzz, tonight's benefit was likely to be the biggest event the small club had seen. And if he had to deal with a fractious cat and some petty theft as well, he was probably running around crazed. I thought of Francesca and their plans for a meeting. Maybe I should stop by, I thought as I showered.

Musetta was lolling about on my sweaty T-shirt when I returned to the bedroom. "Are you claiming me? Or marking yourself with my scent?" She looked at me upside down, drunk on the pheromones, one fang exposed. "Or are you simply a perverse little kitty?"

I reached to pet the smooth place between her ears and she grabbed my hand, pulling it toward her open mouth. "Oh no, kitty. We're trying not to do that remember?" She didn't care and bit me anyway, and I had to laugh. She didn't break the skin and the way she was staring at me, upside down, had a knowing look, like she was testing just how far she could go. I distracted her by reaching down with my left hand to rub the velvet of her nose—and extricated my right hand from her grasp. She gave up willingly. It was all in fun.

She followed me into my office as I toweled my hair. Sure enough, one of my pitches had bounced back already so I spent the next fifteen minutes trying to find a better e-mail address for the new food magazine. Could they have gone out of business already? Just to cover my bets, I made a small change in the story pitch and sent it off to an editor at a national magazine whom I'd had a back and forth with. She liked my writing and had almost gone for another idea. The ball had been in my court last fall, and I'd dropped it. Tacking on a quick personal note—*"Hope you remember me! Sorry it's been so long"*—I sent it off. Maybe losing the Mail wouldn't be all bad. Maybe it would spur me on to greater things.

And maybe Lee Wellner would get my column. The thought dampened my post-run high. Would he end up with that staff job, too? Come to think of it, would he end up taking the shelter story to the *Mail?* Tim and that money guy had sure been interested when I'd told them about the poisoning at Violet's. They'd be suckers for a good conspiracy piece. Of course, if Lee was writing it for them, he'd need more than an anonymous source.

I called Violet. Caro answered. "Hey, Theda. She's at the practice space. They're headlining tonight and she wrote a new song. She'll probably be going straight over to the Last Stand."

"Thanks, Caro. I'll try there. By the way, has she been talking to any press that you know about?"

"She's gotten a ton of calls." Caro sounded both happy and surprised. "I thought it was all planned sort of fast, but, there you go. Word got out." That wasn't what I'd meant, but I'd have to wait to get Violet alone.

Tess wasn't home either, and I was beginning to get the idea. Everybody but me was busy working on tonight's event.

I'D HIT THE GROCERY STORE on the way home. Why did pancakes only make me hungrier? Feeling somewhat creative, I used my one good knife to pare off shreds of that hardened parmesan. Layered over bread, with a good grainy mustard and a slice of turkey ham, it had the makings of a kind of sloppy croque monsieur. "Julia Child, forgive me," I said as I popped it into the toaster oven. The smell drew Musetta, and I offered her a stray shred of cheese. She sniffed it and walked away. "I know, you think human food is gross." I flashed back to the previous night and Patti's beachball of a cat. "And I'm so glad." By the time the sandwich had heated, I'd opened a jar of marinated artichoke hearts and a diet root beer, a feast all to myself.

I pulled the paper over as I sat down to eat. I'd been avoiding the *Mail* for the last few days, but some neighbor had brought the big Sunday edition up to my apartment and I'd have tripped over it if I hadn't taken it in. Still, it looked like a flat time bomb. What dared I read? Sports was an option, but there's really only so much pre-season Sox coverage a non-fanatic can take. Business went the same way. If I had no income, I didn't need to know how to invest it, and none of the books in the review section dealt with music or cats.

With a feeling of dread, I reached for Living/Arts. At first, it wasn't bad. As I worked my way through the first half of the sandwich, I read about a new recording technology. While I used the bread crust to soak up the last of the artichoke dressing, I browsed a piece on dance music. And then, as I took a swig of root beer, I saw it. An Allston Onramps story with Ralph's byline. I choked, spewing root beer all over the band photo. Was he taking over my beat? Mopping up the paper, I did some quick math. The Sunday section pre-prints, which means the article had to have been written early in the week and assigned even before that. Piers might have mentioned it, but, then, I'd never gotten around to telling him I might write about his band. Ralph, however, knew better. I'd seen the fat little rat at the Casbah just last night, and he'd not said a word. Not to me, anyway. Though he'd been happy to badmouth me to Tim.

I chewed on my sandwich. Maybe this was all about the new job, as Ralph had said. Maybe he was scared and felt he had to prove himself. But if that was the case, why had he been talking with Lee? There was something going on here that I didn't understand. I finished my sandwich still hungry, and with too many questions unresolved.

I should have left it there, but I'd put half the artichokes back in the fridge. Two minutes later, I was eating them out of the jar and skimming through news. It was a tiny item. I'd probably have missed it if it hadn't been for the root beer. A spot had soaked through to the front section, making a big blotch right next to a the one-column, two-deck head: "Shelter denies changing no-kill rule." The reporter had talked to Dr. Massio, formerly of WellPet and now acting chief veterinarian of the Boston City Shelter. He'd confronted the vet about the "recent and highly touted new policy ending the euthanasia of healthy animals." Massio, to his credit, had responded that he was still trying to get his feet under him. He said he would try to follow in his predecessor's footsteps, and referred to Rachel as "my dear departed colleague and a close friend." But the reporter had sounded skeptical, choosing words like "deny" and "claim" that the copy desk should have caught and changed. Either someone had been sloppy in the editing, or the reporter had been able to make his case for such a slant, perhaps explaining that a bigger story was in the works. I skimmed down the last paragraph to the end. A story this small had a tagline, rather than a byline putting the reporter's name on top. Sure enough, there it was: LEE WELLNER.

NINETEEN

I STORMED DOWN to the Last Stand with a head of steam. Lee I could understand. I didn't like him, but he was making his own mark. Ralph was another story. He had a staff job, and the unspoken rules said that he should leave me my small bit of territory. But here he was not only poaching on my beat, but doing it before I was fired. Maybe even before he had slandered me to Tim. Who knows whom else he'd been talking to about me. Lee? That would certainly explain the short freelancer's attitude. It was time to stop thinking of Ralph as a harmless old house cat.

Speaking of cats, I had to find out what was up with Ellis, too. I'd been resistant to the idea of a club cat, afraid that any resident feline would end up as Bill's pet and become yet another obstacle between us. But biting was a bit much. Could the big cat have a health problem that was making him irritable? Violet had said the cat had been in and out of her shelter too fast for her to check for any history or shots. Maybe that thick fur hid a wound, an old bite from a street fight, that was driving the cat nuts. Maybe he was diabetic. Maybe he simply needed a quieter home.

A block from the club, I was distracted from my thoughts by a familiar figure. "Tess!" I hurried to catch up. But the face that turned toward me wasn't my friend.

"Oh hey, Theda." Francesca looked preoccupied. "People say we look alike."

"Oh, yeah. Sorry." I searched for something to say. Somehow asking if she'd had brunch with Bill didn't appeal. "Hey, is everything okay?"

She had turned away, and I had the distinct impression that she was holding back tears. "The usual." She forced a smile. "But there's no time for regrets."

"I heard about your pet. I'm so sorry." She turned to me and blinked. "Your cat? Bill told me you'd lost a cat."

"Shiva." She sniffed.

"Shiva, sorry." The Hindu god of destruction was also the deity in charge of bad habits. A good name for a cat. "Bill told me it was distemper?" I thought of the foster program that Rachel had outlined, and wondered if whoever took over the shelter would continue it. "Was Shiva a kitten?"

"No, Shiva was eight years old and healthy as a horse. I make all my pets' food myself." Another one like Bunny. I wondered if they'd met. "But it wasn't distemper." Francesca sniffed again, her voice growing hard. "Shiva was killed."

I didn't know how to respond to that, and, besides, we'd reached the Last Stand. Francesca threw the door open and I followed her in. She kept walking without looking back, so I let her go.

"Little blow up?" Piers was stocking the bar and watching Francesca retreat into the back room.

"I guess so. I was only asking about her cat." I shrugged off my jacket, still stunned.

"Bad idea." He reached for my jacket and stowed it behind the bar. "She got a little nutty there for a while."

"Did someone really kill her cat?" I had a hard time picturing it. "Was it poison?"

"No." He shook his head and reached down to lift a rack of glassware. "That cat was sick. It was her whole natural food thing, if you ask me. But I'm happy to be out of it."

"So, why?" I shook my head, not sure how to even phrase the question.

"Ask her." He turned to take an empty into the back. "Or better yet, don't."

"Theda! Glad you're here." Violet waved from a booth holding up a marker and some blank paper. "Wanna copy out sets and times?"

"Sure." I looked around. Ralph would be here later, I was sure. But right now, it was all friends. "Hey," I held up a blank piece of printer paper. "You didn't get any other comments back about threatening letters, did you?" She shook her head and pushed the master list across to me: four full bands, three acoustic acts to play in between.

"No, nothing. But I'll put out some more feelers."

I grabbed a marker and started copying. Tess was going to open the night and then join in the closing jam, after the Violet Haze Experience set. "You seen Tess? She called and left a weird message."

"She's not due for an hour yet. Though I wouldn't mind if she got here early." Violet looked around. "What was the message?"

"She was apologizing for running off yesterday." I leaned in a bit. "To be honest, I'm a little worried about her."

Violet looked serious. "I hear you. But keep in mind that we've all been worried about you, too. She might just have a lot to catch up on. You know she was doing some work for Bill, here?"

"The bookkeeping?" That was fast. I'd only suggested it yesterday.

"No, odds and ends. Cleaning up and helping set up for the bands." Violet broke into a grin. "She might look skinny but that girl can lift a Marshall stack. Not that Bill would have any use for a Marshall stack, mind you."

"I didn't know." Seems I'd been missing more than I thought.

"Yeah, that's why I was hoping she'd show early tonight. I've got a lot of musicians to load in, and she's only got her twelve-string and a capo."

"If you see her, let me know?" I went back to the list. "Is Bill around?"

She looked up and I followed her gaze. My boyfriend was shuffling in backwards, pushing the door open with his shoulder. I jumped up to help.

"Your leg." He had his arms around what looked like a new soundboard. "What's this?"

"I'm fine, Theda." He lowered the large case to the bar as gently as if it were made of glass. "And this is the latest in mixing."

"I thought Neil did most of that with the laptop." A computer hooked up to the club's antique soundboard not only made mixing easier, it was loaded with songs for between sets, too.

"Oh, you digital people. When am I going to convert you to the warm, living sound of analog?"

I opened my mouth to protest and shut it, smiling. If Bill wanted to become an audiophile and lug tube equipment around, it was his club. "Must be a jazz thing."

He raised one eyebrow. "You mocking me, babe?"

"Never." I kissed him, laughing. "Hey, what's up with Ellis?"

His smile faded. "Not good. Francesca said she was going to try something, but I don't know."

"Rescue Remedy?" More holistic medicine, but the floral drops did have a reputation for calming anxious felines.

"You'd have to ask her." He worked his fingers under one end of the long, black box and looked backward, over his shoulder. "But first, want to help me get this into the back room?"

I reached around to grab the other end. "Lead on, boss."

TWO HOURS LATER, Tess still hadn't shown. I'd done enough lifting so that when someone mentioned getting pizza I was happy to volunteer. Besides, I had to swing home and see to Musetta.

"She's going in for her tooth cleaning tomorrow," I told Bill as I collected my jacket from behind the bar. "So I've got to put her food and water away."

"Poor kitty." I could tell he was on the verge of a crack about her weight and shot him a look. "And poor Theda, deprived of a cat for another night."

"Yeah." The memory must have hit us both at the same time. "It's going to be weird."

"You'll be okay?" He wasn't talking about Musetta.

I nodded. "Violet's going with me." I hadn't told Bill that Musetta was going back to the city shelter clinic, that she'd be seeing the vet who had temporarily taken over Rachel's job. He had enough on his mind. "And tonight will be a good distraction."

"Fair enough. Go spend some time with your little muse. But have that pizza back here by seven. Things will start to get crazy before eight, and I don't want a riot of hungry volunteers."

EASIER SAID THAN DONE, considering that Musetta was in a mood to play. But I called in the order—two veggie, two everything, and one sausage and pepperoni—and tried not to feel too guilty as I removed my cat's food and water dishes.

"Sorry, kitty. Extra treats tomorrow." I kissed her on the head and made my escape, those curious green eyes staring after me. Tomorrow would be odd, I warned myself as I headed over to Petruccio's. But I'd be able to pick Musetta up by early afternoon. And maybe with the start of the new week, somebody would have found out something that would get me off the hook. I wanted Rachel's killer found, but having to worry about my own freedom wasn't helping my thought process.

At least one place still welcomed me. Cries of glee and a few "what took so longs?" greeted me as I walked into the Last Stand, five pies held high. By then, a crowd had gathered. Piers's bandmates were hauling in amps. Sasha, who would cover the bar while Piers played, was loading the cooler, and Reed was helping Neil set up the new soundboard.

"Where are those cords?"

"Coming through!"

"Which one's veggie?" The hustle of prep work, laced with pizza, lifted my spirits. My kitty would do all right without me for one evening. Lifting an "everything" slice, I went in search of Violet.

"Vi? Pizza's here!" I called, savoring the hot cheese. Even the anchovy tasted right. "You want me to bring you one?"

"Can you make it two?" She was sitting in a back booth, going over the set lists with Francesca.

"Wait, is that dairy?" Francesca eyed my slice. I nodded and tried to look guilty. "Well, I should have known to cook. Do you have one without meat at least?"

"Sure thing, coming up." I wheeled around and grabbed three more slices. I might as well keep the girls company. "But what's up? I thought we finished the set lists."

"We did." Violet was a lefty but managed to grab a slice with her right while she kept writing. "But we've got to re-shuffle everyone. Tess was going to open, then play again between Piers's band and mine. But she hasn't shown up yet and she's not answering her phone."

"Tess is missing?" I stood up, ready to run out of there. The last time our friend had gone AWOL, I'd found her on the floor of her bedroom, unconscious from an overdose. "Shouldn't we go look for her?"

"No, no, really." Francesca waved me down. "She's fine. She's just got some stuff going on." I sat back down and waited. "In fact, I bet she'll make it. But just in case."

"Francesca's going to do the opening set." Violet handed me a list. "I'm thinking maybe we won't have anyone play between the other sets, though Reed volunteered." She looked doubtful, and I nodded in silent agreement. Would solo jazz sax be appreciated by this audience? "So, wanna write up the rest of these?"

I hesitated. "Maybe I should swing by Tess's, just in case. I'm parked right near by." I could still picture her as I'd found her, lying so still. "It won't take more than twenty minutes."

"Could you just do these three, first?" Violet pushed the marker into my hand. "I've got to get soundchecks started and then you're free."

I nodded again as she took off, and pulled a blank piece of paper over. Francesca, 8–8:30. The StoreAlls, 8:45–9:15. "Tight schedule." I kept copying, knowing from experience that by the third or fourth band, everything would be running at least a half hour late.

"She does know what she's doing, you know." Francesca spoke so softly I barely heard her. She'd hardly touched her slice.

"Violet?"

A small laugh. "Tess, actually. She and I have gotten close and, well, she just has a lot to deal with right now." I nodded, and kept copying. "She's cleansing her system."

I didn't mean to roll my eyes. I really didn't. I mean, I live in this crazy progressive city because I love it. But Francesca must have seen something because she snatched the paper out from under my marker.

"Your negative attitude doesn't help." Her voice was hard. "And we really don't need your lack of faith." I was about to snap back. Pretty girls are too used to being catered to. Then

I remembered. She'd lost her cat. We'd all lost a friend. I swallowed my words, and before either of us could start to explain, a yell from across the room interrupted us.

"Theda, can you take the mike for a minute?" I left the table to Francesca, who'd turned away. Probably hiding tears.

"Hey, grab that box, will you?" From then on, the night was chaos.

"Did anyone see Neil? I need him pronto!"

"Theda! The mike?"

And so I stood on stage saying "one, two, one, two," carried instruments, and shuttled messages, and before I knew it, the small club was crowded. The empty pizza boxes had disappeared, and the few leftover slices were being eyed by Ralph, who'd shown up with Lee.

"Early night for you boys." I made my way over, trying to hide the anger welling up again.

"Early bird gets the worm." Ralph grabbed the last meat slice, the sausage already curled and congealed. "Wanna split it?" He gestured to Lee, who shook his head and walked off.

"He's still not talking to me, is he?" I took a stool next to Ralph. He kept eating. "Don't think I've forgotten," I said. He turned my way, a string of cheese dripping from his mouth. "You still owe me, Ralph. Big time. You were spreading lies about me and trying to steal my beat." He swallowed. "Ralph, I saw the paper today. The Onramps were my story, a natural for 'Clubland.'" He opened his mouth, but I cut him off. "That was *before* I was fired, Ralph. I know when Sunday goes to press."

For the first time ever in my memory, Ralph put down an unfinished slice.

"The sausage gone off?" He shook his head. Of course, that wouldn't have fazed him. "So what is it, Ralph? You told me you'd help me find out what Lee knows. That's the least you can do."

He sat there, forlorn, looking at the slice. "I can't, Theda."

"Can't, Ralph? Or won't?" He looked so sad I could have felt sorry for him. But I'd done that already once. "This is more than my job on the line here."

He nodded. "I do know one thing. From that story that ran today?" He looked up at me. I nodded; I'd seen it. "Lee says that the vet had another man. Someone from her past was back in the picture."

An old boyfriend. What had Rachel told Piers that night? That she had some old business to take care of? Maybe she was trying to get rid of a jealous ex. "Who?" I grabbed his forearm. "You've got to find out who, Ralph." This was the biggest break I'd had. "Ralph!" But he'd started hiccupping.

"'Scuse me, Theda. Gotta run." He swung off the stool and started pushing through the crowd, propelled by either guilt or pepperoni.

I thought about waiting for him. The big guy had left too many questions unanswered, but I had no idea how long he'd be or in what shape he'd return. Besides, people were lining up to enter the music room. He'd be back there soon enough. I'd never checked on Tess. But Violet's words came back to me. She'd be fine. I needed to trust her. Plus, Violet and all my other friends had worked hard to pull this night together. Truth was, I didn't want to miss any of it.

Francesca was on stage by the time I got in. Most folks were still milling around, talking, so I pushed up front. Francesca might look like Tess, but she didn't have her stage presence, not yet. Instead of singing out—or even into the mike—she was looking down, her heavy hair covering her face. The tune she was picking out on her acoustic was pretty, however. Melancholy and somehow familiar. Nothing I could quite place. Probably a cover, expecting a newcomer to conjure up an original song last minute like this was too much.

Then it hit me. This was her song, the one she'd been working on last Tuesday at Violet's. "Shiva's Lament." I found myself humming along as she came up on the bridge again, when suddenly the song changed. From intricate finger picking, she'd broken into violent strumming. The effect was startling and the couple behind me stopped talking. All around us, people stopped talking and leaned in to hear Francesca sing.

Leaving me…tearing me apart…

I couldn't make out anymore.

"Wow, shades of Alanis." A young guy, his goatee still thin, laughed a little nervously, and suddenly the song was over. Francesca started the next one before the applause had died down, and this one was a cover. Something Irish, maybe the Pogues, having to do with death and loss. Several women were crowding the stage now, nodding as she sang, almost keening, about sadness. Did they know it was for her cat? I smiled, a little ashamed of myself. Didn't I know that mourning knows no limits? I'd lost a cat I loved. I knew how much it hurt. Good for Francesca for being able to channel what were obviously very strong feelings.

As the next band set up, I went to get a beer. Ralph's bellow broke through the muffled roar of the crowd and I started for his end of the bar to continue my interrogation. Just in time, I saw him talking to Lee. The younger writer was almost obscured behind Ralph's bulk. Well, maybe that could wait.

"How's it going?" Bill had come up behind me and his arms around me made me jump.

"Fantastic!" I turned for a kiss. "Have you been back here? Did you catch any of Francesca's set?"

He shook his head. "I've been busy back in the office. She did well?"

"Really impressive. She's got something, but she's got

to learn to look at the audience. The world only needs one Cat Power."

He laughed. Three months ago, he wouldn't have gotten the reference. "Yeah, I saw her go by, but she seemed pretty wrought up. Thought I'd let her catch her breath."

"Pity." I could see no sign of her. "She'd be getting some positive feedback if she did."

Just then the next band kicked in. I recognized the guitarist; she'd served as Vi's roadie for a while but she obviously had chops of her own. With a cool, jumpy rhythm—part reggae, part ska—she and the bassist got bodies moving. Up front, I saw heads bobbing and after the drummer threw in a fast fill a second guitar kicked in. I stretched up on my toes, dying to see more.

"Go!" Bill pushed me forward with a hand on my back. "I'll be here."

It didn't take any more. I was up front and dancing.

"Pretty good, huh?" Vi was next to me, shouting to be heard. "Bassist is a friend of Mona's. I introduced them."

I tried to recall who Mona was again and gave up, succumbing to the music. The guitarist and bassist had their heads together now, singing harmonies into the same mike, her clear voice soaring above his gruff growl. Back again to the syncopated rhythm, and then she broke off for a solo. Old school, all high notes wailing like we were in a stadium. It could have been pretentious, too metal for the room. But the crowd went wild, fists pumping, cheering her on.

Violet and I yelled along, and when the guitarist fell backward, nearly upsetting her drummer's hi-hat everyone cheered. The next tune started up just as hard. This was magic. Post-punk metal, an ironic take on the guitar gods of the past.

I caught myself as I reached for a pad. I wasn't writing about this. I might never write about music again. All around me, sweaty bodies moved. The music continued, but for me the spell had broken.

"You okay?" Violet must have seen my face.

I forced a smile and mimed drinking a beer.

"No, thanks."

I didn't really want one either, but I needed to step away before she saw my disappointment, before my mood infected the night. Just my luck, the crowd parted right beside Ralph.

"Hey!" He squeezed sideways, letting me in. "What are you drinking?"

"Blue Moon." If he was buying. "But, Ralph—"

"Great, huh?" He interrupted, nodding toward the stage. The guitar and bass were playing in unison, necks and notes reaching for the stratosphere. I recognized the tune as something vintage, so did the crowd. The unison line brought a cheer and without a pause the drums and bass kicked in to the next tune. "AC/DC."

"Motorhead," I corrected him. Why was he the staff writer again?

"Oh, that's right. I should tell Lee." I turned in surprise. "Well, Theda, I mean, if you're not doing the column anymore."

"Thanks in part to you, Ralph." I was stretching the truth, but I was furious. "So what gives? Is Lee your new best friend or something?"

"Come on, it's not like that." I glared at him. "You're always talking about the community. He's just getting started. He needs a hand."

That wasn't what he needed. "I'm in the community, too, Ralph. You still owe me." I pushed off from the bar, ignoring both the fresh bottle and the plea in his eyes. "And a beer is not going to cover it."

The band sounded great, but I didn't want to hear any more and headed, instead, for the back room. At least I could tell Fran-

cesca how much I'd liked her set. But when I got there, the room
was empty. Either she'd passed me in the crowd or she'd snuck
out for some air. I poked through the storage area and out the
back. The night had turned frigid, and any intrepid smokers
were probably huddled by the front door. But the air did me
good. I was blowing things out of proportion. Writing about
music was a great gig, and once my name was cleared I could
fight to get it back. But I'd loved the music long before I started
critiquing it, and I could learn to simply enjoy it once again.

That was an easy resolution to keep with this band, and
soon I was back in the groove with everyone else. The room
had gotten even more packed, too full for me to work my way
up front, so I crept up along the side, the press of bodies
making me sweat from the effort. Someone, probably Neil,
had rigged a follow spot and in true rock star style it now high-
lighted that guitarist as she leapt in the air, each descent timed
with a crashing chord. Then it was the drummer's turn, beads
of sweat flying off him like sparks as he moved from one
surface to another, all the while keeping the big bass drum
going at a wildfire tempo. Subtle, it wasn't, but the crowd
loved it and the last loud bang brought a cheer like I'd never
heard in this small room.

Would Francesca go on again? That would be a hard band
for any acoustic act to follow, and I worried for a moment
about the younger performer. Maybe Tess had shown up. She
played solo, too, on a vintage Epiphone that she'd found in a
pawn shop. But she knew how to mike it, and, more important, how to work a crowd. I craned my neck, but the room
was too full.

I did hear a crash as that hi-hat finally went over and looked
up to see a laughing Piers on stage. Either he was helping to
break down or the Onramps were up next. I couldn't recall
what the set list had said, but someone handed up a new bass

drum and it became clear that Piers was setting up. The bands must be sharing equipment, which would explain how the turnover was going so well. I checked my watch. Not even twenty minutes off schedule yet. But, no, Piers jumped down. He was simply helping. A drum and guitar duo came on, kicking into a wiry number that sounded like it had blues in its blood. Only there was something wrong with the setup. The drummer was singing, I could see her face straining, but all we heard was the scratch and scramble of guitar racing against the beat. Neil pushed through the crowd and I saw him crouch down behind her. The guitar kept up the rhythm, a furious strum, while Neil worked and then a voice broke in.

Whatcha whatcha gonna do?
Who's gonna gonna gonna pay for you?

Whoops of joy greeted the return of the vocals, and as much from team spirit as anything, I cheered along. It wasn't poetry, but with the beat it worked, and I watched the band feed on the energy, the guitarist bounding around like his hightops were superballs. By the third tune, he was dripping, his brown hair plastered black against his face, and the room was steaming. Up against the wall, I had a good place, safe from most of the jabbing elbows and stomping feet, but I regretted not taking that beer from Ralph. The bar was all the way across the room. Maybe between bands.

Something cool and wet touched my neck and I jumped. Bill was beside me, laughing, cold Blue Moon in hand. "Forgive me, babe. Couldn't resist."

I grimaced, but took the beer. I'd rather he were playful than angry and the cold brew did taste good. "You read my mind!" I yelled back at him. The pair on stage launched into another song and then another. If they got any more energetic, that guitarist was going to take off. Bill was grinning and nodding toward the stage. The guitarist had indeed gotten airborne. But he'd landed on the drum set, sending the cymbals and floor tom flying. Someone in the crowd started clapping and soon we were all yelling along. If this was their finale, it was dramatic. Might be hard on the equipment in the long run, though.

"Hey, have you seen Tess?" I turned back, but Bill was gone. I could see him above the crowd heading toward the sound board, so I turned back to the stage. As long as I didn't have to pee, I could stay here all night.

Except that Piers's band, the Allston Onramps, just weren't that exciting. Maybe it was that after the last two bands, their nuevo garage rock sounded tired. Maybe it was that new keyboardist. Maybe I was simply worn out, but I found my mind wandering. My case crowded out the power chords, and I found myself going over everything Pilchard had said. Would there prove to have been another man in Rachel's life? Or a disgruntled staffer whose alibi wouldn't hold? I took a long swig of beer and tried to clear my head. I liked Piers, I should be listening to his band. What had Ralph written about them? I'd seen something about "roots" and "basics" before I'd turned the page in anger, but that was all generic. I could have done better.

One tune later, I shrugged. I wasn't going to be writing about them. I wouldn't have the chance, so why stress about it? I looked at the crowd and wondered, could anyone here be a killer? Most of these people were here for the music, or to support their friends. But some were here for the cause itself, to help raise funds for Violet's shelter. The latest crisis had been kicked off by that contaminated food and now, with Rachel gone, it seemed unlikely that we'd ever find out where that had come from or how it turned up at Violet's. Was that sack of dry food intentionally poisoned or had some accident, a spill or drip, made her cats so sick that night? I stared at the stage without seeing it, my mind on that sunny afternoon I'd spent going through Violet's papers. Before Rachel's death, and my arrest, I'd been on the trail of something. Pilchard had dismissed the connection, as had Bunny and Cal, but I just kept coming back to it. Violet's cats had been sickened by bad food, and I thought it likely that the food, intentionally poisoned or not, had come from Rachel's shelter. Sickness and stabbing, cats and women. There was no obvious link, but both were crimes, and both hit awfully close to home. Something was tying all this together. Something had to be.

Someone jostled me and I turned from the stage, just enough to see Francesca off to the side. She stared up at Piers, the stage light making her pale face glow. That was nothing special, every straight woman in the place was probably staring like that. But then he stopped singing and smiled, and she turned away, as if self conscious. Had he seen her? Had that smile been for her? I wished I could see her face but the light now shone on her curtain of dark hair. And as I moved forward, I was jostled again and suddenly wet.

"Sorry, sorry." It was Ralph, and he'd started dabbing at me.

"Stop it, Ralph." I was in no mood to put up with him. I grabbed the cocktail napkin out of his hand and turned back to the stage. But from this angle, I could see farther back, behind the stack that had sheltered Francesca. Lee Wellner was waiting there, almost entirely hidden by the amps. And he wasn't watching the band as they started up a big rousing closer. He was staring at Francesca.

I craned to see more of his face. He seemed so intent, so fixated. But as if he sensed my interest, he ducked back into the shadow. Piers's band had everyone jumping as I dived into the crowd. Lee had put me off with accusations before, but if he knew something about Rachel, about an ex-boyfriend or anything else, I had to find out. I pushed between two dancers and was slammed in the ribs for my trouble.

"Heads up!" A sweaty face, a body bare to the waist, whipped by me. Piers's band had incited an old-fashioned mosh pit, turning Bill's jazz club into a rock madhouse. If I wasn't careful, someone would start stage diving soon.

"Watch it!" Big hands grabbed my arm and pulled me forward and I stumbled, just in time to see a Converse hightop fly by my ear. This was a night! But thanks to that stranger's strong grip, I was through. I pushed my hair back from my face and tried to get my bearings. Where was Lee? I needed to know what he knew. Most important, I needed to find out who his source was. He was going to tell me, or I'd throw him into the pit, glasses and all.

Then I saw him, toward the end of the bar. But the Onramps had finally finished, and everyone who had been dancing was now looking for a drink. I was using my hands by then, finding ways through the sweating bodies. Soon there were just two stools between me and Lee, two stools and about a dozen thirsty patrons.

"Lee!" I called. He didn't hear, the room was still loud and Neil had the between-band playlist turned up. I saw the writer's dark head bobbing, like he was deep in conversation with someone. "Lee!" Nothing. "Lee Wellner! Over here!" That caught his ear. He turned around, a look of shock behind those thick lenses. That's when I saw who he'd been talking with. Hunched over the bar behind him was Violet.

"Vi?" I stood, momentarily stunned, and another three people used the occasion to push past me. "Wait!" I was slick enough to slide between two beefy gents, but in a moment she was gone. I was dumbfounded. Was Violet the source? All the coincidences began to run together. She had been the one to tell me that Rachel was a fake, and that was right about the time that Lee was reporting the same rumors in the *Wag*. She had always run a real "no-kill" shelter, while Rachel did euthanasia. And Bunny and Cal had made another argument, pointing out that Violet was the only one who stood to gain if Rachel's campaign were discredited. Or she were killed.

"What's going on?" I clawed my way through the last of the crowd and grabbed Lee by his shoulder. "Where did Violet go?" I shook him, or tried to. The shoulder I'd grabbed was more muscular than I'd thought. "What are you up to?"

He reached up and grabbed my wrist. "Calm down. What are you talking about?" But even as he said it, he was smiling. He knew something, I could tell. If Violet was involved, so was he. I wouldn't put anything past him.

"Violet, is she your source? What did she tell you? Do you know who Rachel's ex was?" I tried to pull my arm back, but he held it firm. "You've got to tell me!"

"I do? Why, so you can find someone else to blame? Because I got the story and you lost your gig?" He was still smiling, the only man in the room who looked cool. I was sweating and still he held me.

"Let go of me!" I pulled back, but I couldn't get free.

"Or what? You'll stab me, too?" He had my right arm, but at that I swung with my left. He didn't expect it and his glasses went flying, my punch more a roundhouse slap than anything else. "Whoa!" He let go and turned away.

"Okay, now, that's enough!" Strong arms wrapped around me and I started to kick back when I recognized that voice. "Come on, Theda. That's enough!" It was Bill, and he was pulling me away from the bar in a bear hug. The crowd parted for him, and before I knew it, we were in the front room and then out the door.

"I'm okay, Bill. I'm okay." I let my legs and arms hang limp, but he continued to stand behind me on the sidewalk, arms wrapped around me.

Bill held me close and spoke in my ear. "Look, I know you're upset."

"Upset?" I was furious, but I fought the urge to start struggling again.

"You've just lost a friend. It's natural."

He must have felt the tension in me. I had to explain. "And I'm being blamed for it, Bill. And now that little—"

"Theda, stop a moment. Just stop." He released me, but kept his hands on my arms as he moved to stand in front of me. I stood waiting. "You're angry, sad, grieving. I get it. I've been trying hard, Theda, trying to give you slack. But starting a fight isn't going to solve anything."

I nodded. "I'm sorry."

"It's not just that this is my bar." I saw the ghost of a smile and relaxed a little. "But, Theda, be reasonable. He could have you up for assault. And you're out on bail."

The last of the fight went out of me like air from a balloon, and I slumped against him. "Oh. Right."

"Come on, babe." He held me close and this time it felt good. We stayed like that for a few moments. I could have fallen asleep leaning against him, but too soon he cleared his throat. My cue to stand up on my own.

"I've got to get back, babe."

I nodded. "May I come back, too?"

That smile again.

"I promise not to beat up anyone in your club." Before he could respond, I added. "I won't even try to talk to him anymore tonight. I'll talk to Violet, instead."

He checked his watch. "You're going to have to wait, babe. She's going on soon." He opened the door and walked me back in, letting everyone see that we were together as we passed through the crowd. I hoped Lee was watching. "Besides, we've got other things to worry about besides keeping you out of jail."

"Oh?" I looked up at him. "Is it something with Tess?" I knew I should've gone to her apartment.

He nodded, his long face set in grim lines. "It is indeed. I've been over what's gone missing, who was working. Everything. And I think she's been stealing. Small items, petty cash, but stealing."

I felt my face go slack with shock. This couldn't be. I looked up. "Have you talked to her?"

"She still hasn't shown up." On stage, Violet's drummer had started the countdown. Bill leaned in to my ear. "And I really hope I'm wrong, but I think Ellis has gone missing, too."

I stood there, taking a moment to consider what he'd said. Ellis? Had the noise gotten too much? Had he seen that back door and used it? And Tess? That strange message ran through my mind, and I shook my head to clear it. No help for it now. On stage, Violet and her bassist joined in, prompting the crowd to dance and sway. I looked over toward the bar but I couldn't make out Lee. Maybe he had left. Maybe he was still looking for his glasses. I saw someone fly by, a modified stage dive from a bar stool, the bouncer from the front door hot on his heels. If there was any justice at all, one of them would have crushed Lee Wellner's glasses.

TWENTY

BILL MUST HAVE GOTTEN in around four. He'd kicked me out as soon as the music ended, muttering something about "banned for life" that I didn't take too seriously. But he had his hands full. The night had been a success, and the Last Stand was the worse for wear, and so I hightailed it home. It was enough to hear him come in and to feel him spoon up against me. Even Musetta, who seemed to have survived the lack of dinner, obliged, walking over my legs to take up the opposite corner of the bed. I figured I'd hear all the dirt in the morning.

The alarm rang way too early, but fear of waking Bill made me grab it and get out of bed. Musetta was on her window sill by then, getting an early morning start on her birdwatching. But after I dressed, she came over, expecting the food that had been denied the night before.

"Sorry, kitty." I lifted her around her soft middle and she gave a soft mew of protest. "Time to go to the dentist." She lashed her tail twice as I lowered her into her carrier, but accepted the inevitable.

"Meh." As complaints go, that was mild.

"I know. A full meal as soon as you come home. Believe me, I'm not any happier about this than you are." As if in response, she settled down, not even looking up as I carried her out to the street. Violet pulled up two minutes later and as I settled Musetta's carrier in the back, she handed me a large coffee.

"Thought you might need this. There are muffins in the bag." I opened the brown paper bag between us and the heavenly scent of lemon and poppyseed rose to greet me. "Made a stop at the Mug Shot."

"Wonderful, thanks." I broke off a chunk of muffin. It was still warm and moist in the center. I'd been ready to jump on Violet when I saw her. I needed to know if she was Lee Wellner's source, or, if not, why she was so deep in conversation with him. But it's hard to argue with your mouth full. Plus, I thought as I chewed, Violet was escorting us both back to the shelter clinic at an ungodly hour. I'd start gently. "Did you get any sleep last night?"

She shrugged. "A bit. Besides, spring break is over. I've got to get used to sleep deprivation again."

I took a sip. She'd gotten me a latte, a double shot it tasted like. "Still thinking about grad school?"

Another shrug and she reached for her own coffee. "Be nice to have the grades to keep it an option."

I didn't want to push. Besides, I had my own agenda. "So, what did you think of Francesca?" I just wasn't sure how to work up to it.

"She's got the songs, for sure. Did you catch her set?" Violet reached for the bag so I held it up for her.

"Most of it." I paused. Maybe I could work around to Lee? "Great songs, but she sure ran off quickly." I thought of Lee watching her from behind the amp. Had he been the lost lover of the song, or had it all been about the cat?

"Don't be too hard on Francesca. I know she's sort of a know-it-all, but she's had a rough couple of months."

"I know, I'm sorry." A wave of guilt washed over me. I knew that grief first hand. "I heard about her cat."

"Yeah, that was pretty awful. Last week she got a notice about picking up the cremains and that just brought it all up again. You know." I did. Much as I loved Musetta, I still had twinges when I looked at the photo of James on my fridge, and that had been from when he was still sleek and young and healthy. But Violet was saying something about other troubles. "There was a job she thought she was sure to get, and that fell through. She was seeing some guy, too, who turned out to be a jerk."

"Could it have been Lee Wellner?" I couldn't get the image of him hidden, staring, out of my mind. "The writer?"

"No, I don't think so. She never said, but I don't think he's her type." I nodded. Creepy geek isn't particularly sexy.

"Speaking of which, Vi, I wanted to ask you about him." She looked up. "I saw you two talking last night, before your set." Violet was first and foremost my friend, but I had to ask. "And, well, you were the first person I heard saying anything about Rachel, about her dropping the no-kill plan, and that was right when his stories started appearing in the *Wag*."

"Huh." She seemed lost in thought. At least I hadn't offended her. "I do remember seeing those stories, but I'm pretty sure I knew already. Someone had been telling me about the shelter, saying that it was all faked and that they'd keep on killing cats, even healthy ones, for the slightest of excuses."

I gave her a look.

"Okay, and I was pissed off. I mean, Helmhold House has been no-kill since Lillian started it, and here was Rachel getting all this attention. I know, I know," she held up her hands to silence my protest. "It's a different thing. They get tons more animals than we do, and they get the really sick ones, too. But still…"

"So, you weren't Wellner's source?" I had to push. "That wasn't what you were talking to him about last night?"

She laughed. "Is that what you thought? No way."

"It looked pretty intense."

"Oh, ye of little faith! He was pitching me, don't you

know? He was telling me that he could write a big piece on the Violet Haze Experience, like you never could because we're friends. All he wanted was some inside info about some of the women on the scene. Who was seeing who."

"Whom." At least I said it quietly. "So he wanted gossip?"

"He was pretending it would be for the column, but he was just macking on the ladies. Pretty obvious, actually."

Violet was off the hook. I wasn't as sure that Lee's intentions were quite so simple. But by then we'd arrived at the shelter. I reached for Musetta's carrier and spent a moment looking at the building, noting the locked back door as well as the path around to the front. Today the loading dock looked quiet and closed.

My lawyer had commented on all these exits as part of my defense. I hadn't run for it, he'd said. But looking at the building now, I couldn't help noticing how easy someone could have. Three exits that I knew of. A busy shelter with an overworked staff, and a warren of hallways and connecting offices. If Lee Wellner or some anonymous-ex had been in here, it wouldn't have taken them much to duck out again. The question was why? And why, after brutally attacking an innocent woman, replace my cat in her cage? I looked down at Musetta. She was looking up at me. Her look was eloquent. "Please, let me out of this enclosed space," her green eyes said. Unfortunately, our communication capabilities were limited to the obvious. If Musetta had witnessed the murder, she hadn't yet figured out how to tell me or I to hear.

"Theda?" Violet was waiting, so I joined her up the walk to the front door. We'd agreed that she would handle the exchange. I just wanted to stay with my pet as long as possible.

"It'll be okay, Musetta. I promise." The crime scene tape was gone, but the reception area was still quiet for a weekday morning. Only two families and Amy at the front desk. One of the moms was holding the leash of a very large German shepherd, and I could feel Musetta tense in her carrier, suddenly on full alert.

"Hey, Amy." Violet walked up to the front desk while I turned toward the corner, using my body to shield Musetta. "We're here for Dr. Massio? Musetta, uh, Krakow."

Even with my back to the desk, I could feel the intensity of Amy's stare. I turned to smile and she looked away. I guess I could understand how she felt, but it still hurt. Amy murmured something and within thirty seconds a short, stout man in a white coat pushed open the inner door.

"Miss Krakow?" I took in his round face, the touch of gray that lightened his dark hair at the temples, and told myself he looked kindly.

"Dr. Massio?" I stepped forward extending my hand, but caught myself when I saw him step back. Violet stepped between us.

"Dr. Massio. This is Musetta, my friend Theda's cat." She took the carrier from my other hand and brought it to the man in the doorway.

"Ah yes." He looked down at the carrier and up at me again before responding to Violet. "The dental appointment. Very good." Another quick glance at me and then back to Violet. "You should be able to pick her up after two today. If there's any delay, I'll have Amy call you." He backed away and the door closed behind him.

Violet pushed me through the lobby and back out the door. "Wait here."

Five long minutes and she was out again. I'd gone around to the parking lot but couldn't sit still. Instead, she found me leaning back up against her van, trying to enjoy the weak morning sun.

"Well, that was interesting."

I sprang at her. "What? Tell?"

"It's not Musetta. She's fine." Violet unlocked the van and we both climbed in. "But for a private practice guy, Dr. Massio's not bad. He says he'd been looking at trying to do some kind of partnership with the shelter. Turns out, he and Rachel knew each other. They met doing dissections."

"But he looks so much older. You think he might have been a boyfriend?"

"Or one of her teachers." She shrugged. "Though he could be prematurely gray. If I let my natural color show through, I'd have a ton of white in here." I looked over at my friend's purple mop as Violet put the old van in gear. I couldn't see it.

"He didn't even ask if I'd fed her since midnight." Violet just sighed and pulled into traffic.

"YOU SURE YOU DON'T want to hang out?" Violet pulled up to my building. "It's going to be lonely in there."

I grinned. "Maybe not. Bill came over last night." Despite all the drama, it wasn't even ten.

"Enjoy! Come over when you want to, we'll go rescue our girl." With a wave, she was off, and I climbed the stairs, wondering what would be cooking for breakfast.

The answer was nothing, though I did find a note and coffee still warm in the pot. "Gotta finish cleaning up," Bill had written. "Call me."

The blinking light on my answering machine was a little more satisfying.

"Good news, Theda." It was Pilchard. I gathered we were still on speaking terms, despite the dinner. At any rate, he still seemed to be handling my case. "The Fed Ex guy might have seen someone else. My investigator got him to admit that he might have spent a few more minutes in the back of his van than he'd told the cops. And just maybe he saw another doctor go out that exit. Well, he said 'doctor,' but that just means someone who looked official, which means just about anyone. So we're going after the staff again. Someone's alibi is going to be as full of holes as a cashmere cardigan at a moth convention."

I knew I should call him back. If nothing else, I had Violet's nugget to pass along. But the idea of setting up someone else as a suspect, particularly when that someone else was a vet who had Musetta in his hands, just didn't appeal. I'd wait until I found out more, or at least had my kitty home. In the meantime, I tried Bill.

He wasn't at his place or the club office, but I reached him finally on his cell.

"What's up?" He sounded breathless.

"Touching base. You at the gym?" I settled onto the sofa for a chat. It wasn't the same without my feline companion.

"Nope. The club. Back room."

"Wow, still cleaning?" I poured myself the last of the coffee. "Was there any permanent damage?"

"Not cleaning. I'm searching." I heard something go thud, but Bill kept talking. "Ellis never showed."

"You think he got out? He's microchipped, right?" When I rubbed Musetta right behind her ruff, I could still feel the pea-sized chip. But Bill was silent. So much had been going on, I hadn't even asked before. "Never mind, we'll take care of that when he turns up. Do you want me to make up some posters?"

Bill sighed and I pictured him sitting down for a rest. "Not yet. This place is full of corners and cubby holes. I'm hoping last night was just too much for him and that he's wedged someplace that he thinks is safe. I'm just a little concerned, you know? I mean, he's a big cat."

"Say no more." I drained my mug and was already walking toward the closet. "I'll be over in ten, and I'm bringing Greenies."

TWO HOURS LATER, the cat treats were still untouched. We'd ruled out the basement, at least for now. The only door down went from the busy bar area, and it seemed unlikely that a spooked cat would have darted into the crowd to find a hiding place. Instead, I'd met Bill backstage, where Ellis usually hung out, and held the flashlight while he'd looked inside the old upright piano. Next, he steadied a ladder for me up to poke through the broken acoustic tiles.

"You know, this is probably all asbestos up here." When Bill had taken over the bar, he'd removed the false drop ceiling in the music room and the front bar. Back here, it made for a dust-filled crawl space about two feet deep.

"Don't breathe." I tried not to, not just because of the decades of dust. Every now and then, I thought I saw a movement.

"You think Ellis could get up here?" I really didn't want to see anything that wasn't a cat. "You don't think he'd fall through?"

"As the human in charge of Musetta's food supply, I don't think you should talk." I thought I heard a small laugh below me. "But, yeah, I think a freaked-out cat could do anything."

I was glad to hear that little chuckle, weak as it might be. Bill cared more than he'd admit about the fat newcomer. I did one more careful sweep, but there was no way for Ellis to hide his bulk up here. No fur, no large mound of feline. No yellow eyes reflecting back.

"Sorry, Bill." I started back down the ladder. "Nothing up here but us chickens."

He smiled, but the smile didn't reach his eyes. He was being brave. "We'll find him, Bill. I promise."

We moved on to the storage room. Once again, Bill had looked in all the obvious places, but I knew how a frightened cat could compress himself, so together we started to move furniture and I prepared to climb through the ceiling tiles again. Neither of us looked at the back door. Ellis had still been around when the bands loaded in. He was already missing by the time everyone left. Even if someone had stepped outside for a smoke, it seemed unlikely that the cat could have slipped by. Ellis was black, sure, but also as large as a raccoon. A rotund raccoon. Better to focus on the obvious.

"What do you have in here?" It took two of us to move Bill's desk, an old metal beast with drawers on both sides.

"A lot of paper. The old ledgers. A few skeletons." That sad little laugh again. "Watch the cords!" I'd started to slide the back corner, the formica floor was a mess anyway. But I caught Bill's lamp and laptop before they went over.

"Check this out." Behind the desk, only a few inches away from the outlet, a hole had been punched in the wall.

"Oh, that's good." Bill leaned over the top of the wall and shone his flashlight in. "Think he could be back there?"

"I don't know, Bill, I wish I could see how far back it goes." I slid as far as I could into the space between the desk and the wall to look. I am not a wimp, but there was no way I was sticking my hand in there. "Remember that case in New York? The cat that got into the wall of the deli?"

Bill grimaced. "Let's move the desk more."

We'd grunted it out another foot when my cell rang. "Hey, wanna go free a cat?" Violet's voice jumped out at me. For a moment, I was disoriented. Wasn't that what Bill and I were trying to do? Then it hit me.

"Is it time already?" I'd taken off my watch when we'd begun moving furniture and fished it out of my pocket. Just a little past noon.

"Amy called. Musetta is awake and even ate a little. She said we could come by anytime."

My heart leaped. "Excellent!" I looked over at Bill. "But,

Vi, Ellis is missing. You know, the club cat?" I filled her in, hoping she'd hear the concerns I didn't want to put in words.

"I'll come over and help you finish up. I'll bring some traps, too, just in case he got out." She had.

"Vi's coming over." I closed the phone. "She'll help and then we'll go pick up Musetta."

"And maybe some lunch?" I felt myself cheering. He couldn't be too worried if he could eat.

"You got it. Now, would you hand me the big flashlight?"

We spent a good twenty minutes poking through the plaster before acknowledging the obvious. Even spooked, the big cat could not have gotten behind that desk and into the wall space.

"At least I know why the old owners put the desk here," said Bill, pushing the heavy desk back with a grunt. "And in that New York case, people heard the cat in the wall. Ellis would be making some noise by now."

If he still could. I kept my thought to myself as the after hours bell rang and Bill went up to the front.

"Hey there." Violet came back carrying two large box-like traps. "You're a mess."

"Thank you kindly. Do you want to go up in the ceiling tile?" She stared up and looked at both of us. I felt I could read her mind. "Never mind, we can get those. But before we set the traps, we may as well finish this room first."

She nodded, and I think she got that I was humoring Bill. We'd seen no sign of the black cat back here. "What haven't you done?"

"Those shelves." I pointed to a tall metal bookshelf that flanked one wall. CDs and some ancient tapes filled the top shelves, cardboard boxes of bar supplies the bottom. "And the closet."

Vi took off her jacket and rolled up her sleeves to reveal matching wristband tattoos. "Well, Ellis is too large to disappear between those boxes. But that closet looks nice and dark." Taking one of our flashlights, she got down on all fours and began calling for the cat. I moved onto the shelves, poking between packages of cocktail stirrers in the hope of hearing a rustle or even a hiss.

"Hey, what's this?" There was an urgency to Violet's voice that made me start, smacking my head on the metal shelf above me.

"Ow, what's what?" Bill had taken the more sensible path of removing his box from the shelf before diving in. We both looked over to the closet. Violet was leaning in up to her waist.

"This." She stepped back, dust bunnies clinging to her purple hair, and held up a small glass vial. "There's another back there, too."

"What is it?" I reached to take it, but Violet was reading the label.

"Just what I thought. How odd. It's ketamine." She handed me the bottle and reached in to retrieve another that looked identical.

"The animal tranquilizer?" I read the warning on the label: "for use by a licensed veterinarian." Bill looked at me and then over to Violet.

"Yeah, Ketasite's the brand." She examined the silver seal on top. "It's pretty common, but we don't have it lying around. It's a controlled substance."

"You don't think someone used it on Ellis?" I had images of the large cat lying unconscious and being carted away. Drugged and catnapped.

"Why would they?" Violet was examining the label. "This looks unopened. I wonder what the street value of this is?"

"Street value?" I was straining to recall something in the back of my mind, when Bill's training kicked in.

"Special K. The party drug." He leaned back on the desk, and rubbed the back of his neck. "Great. Right here in my club."

I walked over and put my arm around him. He was having a hell of a day, and on not much sleep. "You think someone's dealing?"

Vi answered for him. "This could just be a personal stash. You dry it, snort it. Though who knows how much was back here. Anything's possible."

I couldn't help it, I thought of Tess. She'd gotten so skinny and yesterday, in the warm sun, she'd had her parka zipped up tight. I didn't want to think it, but Bill must have seen it on my face.

"Tess has been doing some work for me and, well, things have been going missing." He rubbed both hands over his face, leaving a gray streak of dirt on his cheek. "Good thing I didn't have her start on my books."

"You think Tess was stealing to buy drugs?" Violet wasn't stupid, but something else was on her mind. Bill shrugged, his face blank, but another idea had flashed through my brain, too.

"You don't think she bought these." I held up the pristine bottle. "You're thinking she stole them from a vet." The full force of it hit me. "You think Tess got these from the city shelter?" She nodded slowly.

"It's possible, Theda. I don't want to believe it either. But somebody was in there early. Maybe she thought the place would be empty."

"And maybe Tess killed Rachel."

TWENTY-ONE

BILL WAS THE FIRST to react. "I need to call some people." He reached for the phone.

"No, wait." I put my hand over his. "We don't know anything. We don't even know if those belonged to Tess." They both turned toward me. "Look, I know her history. We all do. But she's our friend. We have to give her the benefit of the doubt."

"No, Theda." Bill looked grim as he shook his head. "This could mean my license. The club."

"But we're just jumping to conclusions. I mean, think this through. We don't know Tess put these vials here." That got me a hard look. "Even if we did, we don't know where they're from. How would she have gotten into the city shelter? Into the treatment rooms? Wouldn't the drugs be locked up?"

Violet shook her head. "These are from a vet's office. I don't have this kind of stuff on hand, Theda. And you know how crazy the city shelter gets. Plus, we all know how to buzz ourselves in."

She was right, I'd done it myself. "And there's no uniform, nothing to keep her from looking like just another volunteer." I couldn't believe I was saying this, but it did seem plausible. "She could even have put on one of her lab coats from the university and nobody would've questioned her."

"Wouldn't need to. She could've worn Francesca's," added Violet. "Though I thought she gave it back when she quit." I

looked at her, a question on my lips. "A month ago, at least."
Violet kept talking. "You know, when her cat died?"

"So, a few weeks before Rachel…" I hadn't realized I'd
voiced the thought. "We should find Tess."

"You should go pick up Musetta." Bill pushed himself off
the desk. "I can't believe you've forgotten about her. Look,
I'll give you a few hours. I've got to get this place ready to
open, anyway, but that's it."

The discovery of the drugs seemed to have driven all worry
about Ellis out of Bill's head, but he lent a hand as we baited
and set the traps, one right by the back door, the other further
back in the alley. Ellis was an unpredictable feline, but he
deserved a good home. I'd come back and help look for him
later, once my own pet was safe.

I CAUGHT SIGHT OF myself in Violet's rear view mirror, all dust
and disarray, so when she suggested that I wait outside, I
gritted my teeth and agreed. She'd promised me she'd be
quick and although I was tempted to ask her to take her time,
and to grill the new vet about his connections to Rachel, I
wanted Musetta back more. In the meantime, I tried Tess's lab.
She was out, a receptionist told me. Called in sick. No one
answered at her apartment, and I left another message. As I
waited, I thought about calling Piers. Could he have been
lying when he described his last conversation with Rachel?
Or was Tess the "old business," an old friend with a longstand-
ing problem. I hadn't checked the date on those vials.

Another thought made me catch my breath. Could Piers
have been covering for Tess? Could they have been an item,
once, in the old days, or were they again? I knew the rules of
the program: Tess was supposed to avoid any serious commit-
ments for a year, at least. But she was human, and pretty, too,
and he was, well, a boy in a band. I stopped myself. That was

the kind of talk people were spreading about me and Piers, too. But, wait, if she were jealous, or just trying to throw people off the track, she might want to divert attention. A word from Tess could start some rumors. A word from any of us could.

"Here she is!" Violet came out holding the carrier high.

"Musetta!" I was so relieved to see my cat I felt myself beaming. "Thanks, Vi." I looked in at my pet. She was curled up, still groggy, but she opened her mouth for a weak "meh." "You doing okay in there?"

"She's fine." Violet led us back to the van. "She had some bad tartar and the vet has given me a toothbrush and some enzymatic toothpaste." I hadn't seen the small bag until she waved it in the air. "Says if you can't use the toothbrush, just put some of the paste on your finger."

I looked in at my cat. "Musetta, how hard will you bite me if I try to brush your teeth?" Her eyes were barely open, but I imagined I saw a spark in them. "It beats coming back here, doesn't it?"

Cats don't take well to bargaining, and she began to complain on the ride home. Out of consideration, Violet turned down the music. "Everyone's a critic."

"I don't think it's that, Vi." I caught her smile. She'd been trying to cheer me up. "We're good. And I really am grateful that you set this up. I didn't want her to start losing teeth just because my life is jammed up."

"We'll tackle that one next." Violet sounded so confident, I let myself believe. As she drove, I filled her in on Tess's absence from work and my latest fears. I'd barely questioned Piers and just let sympathy sway me. "Am I a sucker for a pretty face, Vi?"

"Well, for this little girl." She nodded back toward the carrier. "But seriously? I still don't see Piers having any part in this. The rest, well, it's a possibility. Look, why don't you spend some time with Musetta? I'll go over to Tess's place, see if I can rouse her."

I paused. Tess had originally been my friend. But maybe she and Violet had more in common these days. Maybe she'd talk to Vi. Besides, I did want to take my cat home and make sure she was comfortable. "Okay, but call me?"

"You got it. And call me, too, if you need anything," she said as she dropped us off. "Always glad to take a study break."

I waved and carried my kitty upstairs. Vets always tell you that cats coming out of anesthesia can be disoriented. They say keep them in an enclosed space until they're fully awake. But my experience with Musetta was that she wanted normalcy as soon as possible. So I put her box down by her food and water dishes, and grabbed the afghan off the sofa to make a soft bed right near by. Then I opened the box and waited for my dear pet to emerge.

"Meh." Her voice still seemed soft, but that was no surprise. The first time she tried to stand, she wobbled so much she lay back down again. But her nose was busy, sniffing at the air and, after the first few steps, at the afghan.

"Yes, that's usually on the sofa." I kept my voice soft. "But let's not try jumping for a while, okay?" I saw her head for her food, nearly keeling over on the way. But she only lapped at the water a bit and then lay down, hard.

"I should leave you be, shouldn't I?" I reached to stroke her and she raised her head. "Why don't I do this?" I lifted her and slid the folded afghan beneath her. That had to be more comfortable than the floor. With a few desultory licks of one paw, she accepted the arrangement and curled up neatly for a nap. When the phone rang, I grabbed it immediately.

"She's not home, either." Violet sounded distracted. "I left a note."

"Do you think we should try to get in?" I could still picture her as I'd found her a few months ago lying on the floor. "At least climb—"

"Up the back to look in from the porch?" Violet was ahead of me. "I did, and nothing. The place looks neat, clean, and absolutely empty."

I sighed. Had our friend gone on the lam? "You think she'll turn up? Get in touch?"

"If not, your boyfriend may sic the cops on her."

With a heavy heart, I let Violet get back to her life. Maybe she'd even study. I sat back to watch Musetta, falling into an almost meditative state. It was so easy to sit there, I barely noticed the afternoon slipping away. My cat's sides rose evenly as she breathed, and every now and then she'd mutter and kick or get up to readjust.

"Today really wore you out, didn't it kitty?" As I sat there, she began to twitch, paws and mouth moving in a dream hunt. But when she turned around and settled into a deeper, calmer sleep, leaving me with only a view of her broad black back, I began to feel like I needed a burst of activity of my own. With a little effort, I rose. I really needed to start running again, regularly, and considered my options. It had been so long since I'd had a Monday without a column to write, I felt at loose ends. It wasn't yet five, early enough still to call Pilchard and tell him my suspicions about the new vet. But if I did, I should also let him know about the drugs and about Tess.

No, once my lawyer heard about her past, he'd put her in the spotlight. I needed to wait, at least until Violet or I had heard her side of the story. At the very least, she might be a friend in need. Even Bill had agreed to hold off, and suddenly I knew what I needed to do.

"Musetta, will you be okay if I leave you for a while?"

In response, one ear twitched. "There's another cat who might need our help." Nothing. So I grabbed my jacket and left for Bill's.

THE HEARTY WELCOME I got was due more to the pizzas I carried than to any help I could offer. But I checked the two traps and put down some cat treats as additional bait, before returning inside to grab a slice. Bill, by that point, had finished searching every nook and cranny of the store room.

"I even went through the basement, Theda." He leaned over the bar to tear off another slice. Nothing diminished his appetite, but I could tell he was distraught. At least he no longer mentioned calling his former colleagues. "Nothing. No trace."

I shook my head. "We'll find him, Bill. Tomorrow, I'll go out looking." Tomorrow, I promised myself, I'd also find Tess, or come clean with Bill about her going missing. I'd also go for a run and eat something other than pizza. "He's a big cat. He can take care of himself."

"Who can?" Ralph had shown up and reached for a slice like it was his right. Bill turned to get him a beer.

"Bill's cat has gone missing." I didn't know how much about Ellis was public knowledge, or if cats might be almost as contraband as drugs. Were there health codes limiting feline bar employment? "But, hey, we never finished our conversation."

Ralph looked up, eyes wide. Trapped. "What else can I tell you?" He wiped cheese from his chin. Bill rolled his eyes and walked down the bar. The early crowd had begun to gather. I heard laughter.

"Lee. What's up with him? And why are you trying to give him my column? You said he's out for your job, too, and yet you're helping him move into the *Mail*."

Ralph put his half-eaten slice down, and stared at it. "Ralph?" Nothing. "Hey, aren't we friends? Colleagues?"

"I had to help him," Ralph's normal roar had fallen to a whisper.

"Yes?" This was like pulling teeth. Ralph looked away. I put a fresh slice on his plate. He ignored it. I stared. "Ralph? You all right?"

"He caught me, okay? I missed some of the headliner. Okay, all of the headliner. I mean, who knew they'd go on at eleven? So, I read some blogs about the show. I mean, I had to file something."

"You missed a show you were assigned to review." He nodded ever so slightly. "And you plagiarized someone else's piece." Another small nod. "And Lee Wellner found out." A shrug. "You plagiarized Lee Wellner?" Ralph's round face crinkled up like a small child's, and I feared a deluge of tears. "How could you be so stupid!" I wasn't helping. "Ralph, you're twice the writer he is."

"I was, Theda. But now, I don't know." The rest of the story came out in a torrent. Threats made, and promises exacted. "You know what the worst part is? It wasn't even the gig he was after, not really." As Ralph talked, his color returned to normal. "He thought writing for the *Mail* would make him a big deal, help him impress chicks."

"Oh, that's the stupidest—" But I stopped. What Ralph said fit with what Violet had told me. Was Lee Wellner's biggest crime that he wanted to get laid? Well, not anymore. "This is blackmail, Ralph. You know that."

"It's the truth, that's what it is, Theda. That little pipsqueak has me over a barrel." And with that he finished his first slice and the second one besides. Confession is good for the appetite.

I would've stayed if I'd thought I could do any good. Not for Ralph. He deserved to stew in his own juice, and besides, even though I understood what was going on, I was still pissed. He'd acted badly, Lee had acted worse, and somehow I was the one paying for it all. But Bill was busy with the first of the blues-night crowd, and I wanted to check in on Musetta. She'd be up and about by now, and as much as I wanted to hang at the Last Stand, a quiet evening together would do us both good.

What I did see when I opened my front door was a blinking message light and a little puddle of what looked like spit. Well, it was coming on spring. Shedding season. I'd probably find a furball somewhere else in the house. I hit "play" and went for the paper towels.

Nothing. The phone picked up and someone waited, and then hung up. I didn't have any more elderly relatives left, but I clicked on the outgoing message. "You've reached Chez Musetta…" Yes, that was still working. I hit "play" again, but got the same blank. Well, I thought as I wiped up the small wet spot, maybe it was a wrong number. Maybe Tess was working up the courage to confess. Maybe I had a secret admirer. More likely it was Ralph, still feeling guilty and wanting to unburden himself further.

They all could wait. "Musetta?" Her food looked untouched. "You want something fresh?" I grabbed the bag of cat treats and shook them. "Musetta?"

I found her, finally, in the back of the apartment. Curled on her pillow on top of my filing cabinet, she looked up and blinked. "Kitty?" I shook the bag, rattling the crunchy treats, but she tucked her head back down again, layering her tail over her nose. This wasn't like her, but I remembered what Violet had said. The teeth cleaning had gone without incident, and she'd woken up enough to eat a little before we picked her up. What I was witnessing was probably exhaustion. "Big day, kitty? Okay, then, I'll let you sleep."

As quietly as I could, I booted up my computer and checked

my e-mail. Nothing there from Tess, either. But three bands, at least, hadn't heard that I'd been fired. Two clubs had sent me their upcoming schedules, and a publicist out in California wanted me to write about a jazz combo. I looked over at Musetta, but she was still sleeping. I'd print that one out for Bill tomorrow. For now, I was making myself worry. Cats sleep a lot. That's simply a fact of their life. Maybe I should take the hint.

Something didn't feel right, however. I grabbed the afghan for myself and settled in with an old movie. I'd keep checking on her until she was up and about. Last call—2:00 a.m.—was usually prime romping time for my kitty.

It was still dark when I woke, so I couldn't tell what had jolted me from sleep. I sat up and tossed the blanket onto the sofa's back and stretched. My shoulder cracked. I needed to get back to working out. But as I bent to limber my hamstrings, I heard it. A low hacking, coughing sound.

"Musetta?" That furball must be giving her trouble. I'd have to pick up some of the medicinal goo tomorrow. "Where are you, kitty?"

Stepping gingerly, expecting at any moment to feel something damp beneath my toes, I moved toward the kitchen and the light switch. I heard another cough and envisioned her bent over, head extended, trying to rid herself of the troublesome fur. "Musetta?" Light on, I grabbed a handful of paper towels and turned back toward the living room.

What I saw horrified me. Instead of one furball, and maybe a little spit, the hallway was spotted with puddles of vomit. And down at the end was my cat. Not sitting up, as she usually would be when coughing up an offending object. Instead, Musetta was lying on her side right near one of the puddles. Too near for a fastidious animal. She'd stopped making hacking noises, but in the light from the kitchen I could see her side heaving as if she labored for breath.

"Musetta!" I ran down the hall, oblivious to the mess, and lifted her. She hung limp, her mouth open slightly as she panted. When she turned ever so slightly to face me, I saw the white membrane, a cat's "third eyelid," half closing over her eyes. That effort alone seemed to exhaust her. Her head fell back, as loose as the warm body in my arms. "Oh, kitty!"

I cradled her in my arms, unsure of what to do. Somewhere I had a feline first-aid book. I'd even prepared a kit, back when I first got her. But that had bandages and a muzzle, in case I had to dress a wound. I looked her over. No, there was no blood, no injury that I could see. Had she gotten some horrible illness, perhaps while waiting for the vet? Was this a reaction to the anesthesia? My mind raced over the options. There was a 24-hour animal ER over in Jamaica Plain. Holding Musetta against my body, I ran for my car keys. We could be there in about thirty minutes at this time of night. Did we have thirty minutes?

Still holding my cat in my arms, I raced to the phone. "Violet, pick up. Pick up!" I yelled into their answering machine. The small body in my arms was shaking, her breathing labored. "Please be there! Pick up!"

"Huh?" It was Caro. I was praying.

"Please, Caro, please tell me that Violet is home! I need her. I need help." I heard a snuffle and something suspiciously like a snort. Was Caro going back to sleep? "Caro! Help! I need your help! I need Violet. Musetta is sick!"

For a horrible moment, I thought she'd hung up. I'd wasted precious minutes. But the line didn't go dead, and a few seconds later Violet came on the line. "What's happening? Theda?"

"Vi, please, I need help. Musetta is sick. I don't know what to do, but she's heaving and she's having trouble breathing."

"Hang on." I heard movement. Violet was up and walking around.

"Is there anything I can do, now? Here?" I tried to look at my cat's face again, but her head was hanging down. Her breathing grew slower and I heard what sounded like a sigh. "She's wheezing. Oh, God. I'm going to take her to the ER."

"She may not have time," Violet said. I started to cry. "Hang on, Theda. I'm on my way."

It made no sense, but I was pacing with my cat when Violet showed up. Musetta was nearly motionless, and I'd held her as carefully as I could as I'd run downstairs to prop open the front door. Now I rocked her gently in both arms, my head laid on her black back to listen as her wheezing grew weaker, as her green eyes closed.

"Please, Musetta, just a little longer." I was whispering, hoping my voice would reach her, would keep her here with me. I counted each labored breath. "Hang in there for me, kitty."

"Take this!" Violet burst in like a stormtrooper, thrusting a plastic IV bag at me. I grabbed it with my right hand and moved toward the closet, latching its attached hook over the back of the door. "Good, now hold her tight."

I wrapped both arms around my pet, but she was beyond struggling as Violet pinched the loose skin on the scruff of her neck and plunged the needle in. A few adjustments, and saline was dripping in. I sat on the floor beneath the bag, cradling Musetta and stroking the smooth fur between her ears. When I looked up, I saw my fear reflected in Violet's face. We waited. Seconds passed.

"Come on, Musetta. Come on!" Violet stared at the cat, checked the saline and back at Musetta again. "Come on."

I bent my head down, kissing that sweet place between her ears. "Please, kitty," I whispered. "I need you." This close, I couldn't distinguish my breathing from hers. I didn't want to lift my head, to see her side go still. I closed my eyes. "Please."

"Theda." It was Violet, her voice soft. I kept my eyes closed, ignoring her. "Theda, look." I peeked. Violet was kneeling at my side, looking into my cat's face. "The nicitating membrane has pulled back."

I leaned over to peer into her eyes. And Musetta lifted her head to look back. "Musetta! You're alive!" She blinked and mewed, soft but audible.

"Barely." Violet checked the IV. "Let's give her the rest of this bag."

Within minutes, Musetta was struggling to get down and so Violet lifted the bag off the back of the door and held it as I gently put her on the floor. Seemingly oblivious to the needle in her back, Musetta started to groom.

"Oh, thank God. Thank you, Violet." I reached to take the bag from my friend, who collapsed onto the floor. My own legs were pretty weak, but the adrenaline kept me standing.

"I'm just glad I got here in time. When I first saw you two…" She shook her head. "What happened?"

"I don't know." I leaned back against the wall. Musetta had started on her feet, and watching her spread her toes to reveal the pink pads filled me with joy. "She never quite woke up from the anesthesia. I didn't know if she was having a reaction or what."

Violet nodded thoughtfully. "Could be, but I don't know. This looks just like what happened with my cats last week. Murray was just that limp, wheezing. I'm wondering if it could have been the poison."

"But she only nibbled a little when she got home." With the crisis past, I felt too tired to think. "Wait. There was something else. You said Amy told you that she'd eaten before we picked her up." Some thought was trying to break through. "The shelter food. That receipt. I remember now. Before Rachel, before everything happened, I found evidence. I don't remember if I got to tell you, but I think that bad cat food came from the city shelter. "

"You think Musetta got poisoned at the shelter?"

I shrugged. It was the only logical conclusion.

"But why? I remember you saying that our bad food might have come from there. But why would anyone there want to hurt Rachel's cats? I mean, me. Me and Caro. I'm used to that. But why poison another shelter's cats?"

"Why would anyone want to hurt Rachel?" I could only answer her questions with my own. "Maybe someone wants all the shelters closed. Or maybe she was the real target. Maybe because Rachel was raising funds that other people could use." I felt awful saying that. That was the reasoning Cal and Bunny had used, and it pointed to Violet. "You know, to discredit her and get the money themselves."

"Oh, please." Violet looked up at me. "It's not like there was real cash lying around. Rachel wasn't as hard up as we are, but she was working miracles on a shoe string, always figuring out discounts and tax write offs." Musetta stopped washing and Violet held a hand out for her to sniff. "Look, I know what I said about Rachel, about her fund-raising. But, well, she did what she had to in order to raise her shelter's profile. I was angry and frightened back then. My cats had just been poisoned. But think about last night." She blinked. The sky outside had turned from black to gray. "I mean, Sunday night. That wouldn't have happened for Rachel. She just didn't have the neighborhood support we have. I mean, she was citywide. It's a different game."

I sighed out the last of the tension and slid down to the floor. Just in time I remembered to keep my hand up, but Violet reached over to take the bag. I hadn't meant to test my friend, but she'd passed with flying colors.

"But if she was that hard up, why give away food?" I could

hear the confusion in my voice. Violet looked at me. So did Musetta. Neither had an answer for me. "That's what I keep coming back to. Still, I can't help but think that the poisoned food was from the city shelter and that Musetta got some of it there." I was so worn out, I couldn't remember what I'd told her so I ran through it all once again. The letter, the bag. Something else began nagging at my thoughts. I couldn't quite make it fit. "Did you know Piers was working on one of the storerooms? She wanted to make it another cat ward, to house more animals."

Violet nodded. "I'd heard."

"Could that be connected? I mean, maybe she had to get rid of some stuff? But how much room does a bag of food take?" We both thought about that as Musetta started on her belly fur.

"Maybe she was getting rid of one particular type of food. Rachel was very into nutrition."

I shrugged. "And poisoned food isn't very nutritious. No, she couldn't have known." I was staring at Musetta. I could watch her groom forever. "Was she dumping it to get into health food?"

Violet shook her head. "Sort of the opposite. I think she was really reacting against the whole holistic organic food thing. She went on a rant about it to me pretty recently."

"A rant?" Her movements were so precise. Her tongue so pink and careful. "Against health food?"

Violet shrugged. I was too tired to make sense out of this. I just wanted to look at my cat. My back-to-normal cat. But one thing still bothered me. "The bag she gave you, if she did give it to you, that wasn't organic or health food or anything. It was KittyLuv, top of the line grocery store stuff."

"I don't know what to tell you, Theda. Hey, take this." She handed me the empty saline bag. "And hold Musetta while I get that needle out. I think this is one kitty that's ready to be let off the hook."

TWENTY-TWO

MUSETTA DID SEEM to be back to normal, begging for treats and then using the litterbox in what seemed to be a healthy manner. But I was determined to watch her and so Violet stayed, too, just to make sure. The two of us sat up talking until dawn, and after a while even I relaxed.

"If you keep petting her to wake her up every time she falls asleep, she's going to bite you. Hard." Violet had broken out my old *Rolling Stones* by then and peered at me over a White Stripes cover.

"She's too well behaved." I continued stroking my cat. "She'll just leave the room."

"Right." Violet's face disappeared back behind the magazine. It was true, Musetta had stopped purring a while ago. I let her be.

"Hey, you think any other cats got sick?" I didn't know how many other cats were in those rows of cages, waiting for their owners to pick them up.

"We'll call, soon's they're open." Violet hadn't turned a page in several minutes. I suspected she was falling asleep.

"I think we should go over there, just to make sure. Besides, I want to see if it was the same brand." A horrible thought hit me. "Maybe in all the fuss, they ended up using the same bag we brought over from your place."

"Doubt it." The page turned. She was awake now. "But I wouldn't mind getting that bag back. I still want to see if we can trace it."

"I'm coming with you." Musetta was sleeping now, and I watched the gentle rise and fall of her side. My fear was almost gone, but I was getting angrier by the minute.

"Theda, that's not a great idea." Violet put the magazine down. "We don't even know if that's what made her sick."

"Come on, Vi! It's the only thing that makes sense. You saw her, you told me what happened with your cats. And I am innocent until proven guilty. I have a right to go to my city's animal shelter."

Violet raised her eyebrows once, but didn't respond. Instead, she propped the magazine back up. Soon, I heard soft snores, but I couldn't sleep. Too much had happened when I wasn't paying attention, and I was raring to set things right.

"COFFEE'S READY!" Violet had slept through the grinding of beans and running of water, and I was tempted to let her remain asleep. But she had an interest in what was going on. It only seemed fair to give her the option.

"Coffee?" She sat up straight. Her hair, however, slumped to the side.

"Yeah, I don't have soy milk, though. We could stop at the Mug Shot, but the shelter opens in fifteen minutes."

"I'm good." She rubbed her face and ran her fingers through her purple hair. It almost stood back up. "How's Musetta?"

"See for yourself." As I poured the fresh brew into travel mugs, Musetta jumped on the sofa next to Violet.

"She's getting big." She pulled the cat onto her lap. "Heavy, too."

"Watch it, Vi. Fat is a feminist issue."

"Fat is a diabetes issue, Theda." She released Musetta, who jumped to the floor. Insulted, I imagined. "Especially for house cats."

"Rachel said—" I stopped myself. "I still can't believe she's gone. We've got to get to the bottom of this."

"Oh hell!" Violet's yell almost made me spill my coffee. "I forgot to tell you. We got another letter yesterday. With everything going on—"

"What did it say? Was it another threat?"

"Yeah, and sort of generic. I don't know, it read like a form letter, like, 'You're a nuisance and the neighborhood should get rid of you.' There was something off about it. And another thing. This one was printed out, like you said Rachel's were."

"Generic? Like someone is trying to cover up?" If only I wasn't so tired. "Vi, who did you tell about those letters?"

"Everyone. I even called over to the shelter to talk to Amy."

"I want to see it, Vi." Musetta head butted me. She looked fine, sleek and peppy, but I couldn't help remembering how sick she'd been. "But first, let's go over to the shelter. Maybe we'll get some clues on who our nasty correspondent is."

"And find out what's poisoning our cats, too." Violet took the coffee mug with her to the bathroom. Five minutes later, we were on the road.

"THEDA, MAYBE I should handle this." We'd taken my little Toyota for its ease in parking and, sure enough, I'd been lucky to squeeze into a half space at the edge of the shelter lot.

"No way, Vi." I slammed the door shut. "I'm too involved."

"That's just what I mean." But height has its advantages and Violet had to scramble to keep up with me as I strode toward the front entrance. "Wait up!"

I did pause, for a moment, by the front door. Unsure of what exactly I wanted to say, I held the door open for Violet. She walked in and stopped short.

"Francesca!" We both looked up. The younger woman was standing right outside the door. From the rings around her dark eyes, she hadn't slept any more than we had.

I stepped ahead. "Is everything okay?" I looked back at Violet. "You don't have another cat, do you?"

Francesca shook her head so that her long curls swung around. "It's Ellis. I'm freaked."

Violet and I looked at each other. We'd both forgotten about the club cat. "Nothing in the traps?"

Francesca grimaced. "Something had been in there. But not a cat."

"Maybe he's been picked up." I tried to sound upbeat. "Are you going in to check?"

"Of course, I'm going to check!" Her voice rose tight and high. "Why else do you think I'm here?"

"Just talking." I raised both my hands and stepped back as she huffed by me. Violet and I followed her into the waiting room. The place was a madhouse. Not yet nine, and three sets of parents seemed to be restraining a half dozen children. One quiet girl was sitting alone, stroking a brown and white lop-eared rabbit. Another unwanted Easter bunny had found a permanent home.

The confusion was compounded by a constantly ringing phone. A volunteer in pink sat at the desk, in Amy's place, trying to make sense of the calls. "Hello? Please hold. City shelter? Please hold." We looked around and saw Amy emerging from a storage closet with a package of paper.

"Amy!" Violet waved to the regular receptionist. "Can we get in to see Dr. Massio? It's sort of an emergency."

Amy looked up at us but kept walking, over to the printer on its little stand. "*You* can." I heard her, so did Francesca, but while the receptionist made her way through the hubbub, answering questions as she walked, we both stepped up to join

Violet. Amy shooed her temporary replacement out of her seat, buzzed the door, and we were through.

The door clicked behind us and I found myself looking down an empty hallway. Something I'd just seen was tickling at the edge of my consciousness, but the hall in front of me was blocking it out. The last time I had been back here, there had been crowds. Cops. My friend…No, it didn't bear thinking about.

"Where to?" I heard my voice crack just a bit.

"Well, Dr. Massio has taken over Rachel's office." Violet knocked, and when there was no answer, let herself in. I hung back. There was no seal on the door, and I knew the room had been cleaned and made over. But I dreaded it. Instead, I dawdled and walked on. To my left, a window in a door revealed rows of cages. One of the cats looked familiar. Large and black.

"You can't go in there. Not if you're going anywhere else. That's now the quarantine area." I looked up. The round-faced doctor had emerged from the storage room down the hall.

I looked back into the room. Another round face looked up at me, this one with a dab of white right beneath his chin. "Ellis?" I opened the door.

"Miss!" The vet came toward me. I slipped in and closed the door. "Miss!"

It was Ellis. I started to unlatch the cage when rude hands dragged me back.

"I said, this area is quarantined!"

"Whoa!" I was laughing. This guy was serious. "It's okay. I know this cat. He belongs to my boyfriend, but he must have gotten out."

"I don't care what you think you know. We have procedures here, and until this animal has been checked for infectious diseases we can't release him. If he checks out, then you can present your credentials, though we'll want to know how he 'got out.'" The round-faced vet made air quotes for emphasis. He didn't believe me.

I started to respond and stopped myself. He was right. This was how a shelter should be run, for the safety of individual animals and also for the pet population at large. I was about to try again, to come up with something that sounded more rational, when I heard Violet out in the hall.

"Found it!" Violet burst into the quarantine room, holding the KittyLuv bag. "It was back on the shelf in the cat ward. Hey," she turned toward the vet. "Did you know that the cat we brought in yesterday got sick on something she ate here? Something like this?" She raised the bag and shook it. The few remaining pieces of kibble rattled around inside. "How did this get out of Rachel's office? Someone's poisoning cats, you know."

"What's going on? This is ridiculous. Amy?" He reached for the door. "I'm calling security."

"Bit late for security, isn't it?" I was thinking of the cat food, but that wasn't how he heard it.

"You!" He turned and stared at me. "You're the crazy lady. The murderer!"

Before I could respond, Francesca slammed into the room. "*You're* the murderer," she shouted at the vet, her voice too loud for the crowded space. "Killer!"

I grabbed her shoulders. Her thin frame was shaking. "Ellis is fine, Francesca. Calm down. We just have to deal with paperwork."

"Don't tell me to calm down!" She pulled away. "I know him. Him and all his type. They killed her!"

"What?" I stared at her. For a moment, all was still, and then the thoughts started tumbling together. The printer. The letters. We were looking for someone from Rachel's past. Someone who might have reason to intimidate her, to try to manipulate her into leaving—or coming back. Someone who had access to the shelter and knew his way around. Someone who could walk right by a delivery man without looking out of place.

"What's your name?" I was struggling to stay calm, but my question came out with an edge. "Your *name?*"

"Dr. Massio. You knew that." He looked more confused than alarmed, but the ruckus was attracting attention. An older woman stuck her head in the door.

"Is everything all right in here, Peter?"

I froze. That was it. "It was you, the one she was calling to. The one she named as she lay dying." I turned to face him once again. Lee might be a creep, but he had no reason to lie. "There was an old boyfriend who'd resurfaced. You wanted her back. She was fighting with somebody the night before she died. I heard it. It was you, and you killed her."

"You're crazy. This is crazy." He turned to walk away. "Amy! Call the cops!"

I needed to see his face, to watch his eyes as he made his excuses. So I grabbed his arm. He wasn't a big guy and I was angry enough so that I spun him around. "I'm not done here." I was furious, but I had to know more.

"Oh, yes, you are!" It was Violet, pulling me away. "This isn't what you think." She hissed in my ear. "I'll explain later. Get out of here, Theda. Go." She shoved me out to the hall, toward the loading dock. "Go!"

Was it my imagination or did I hear sirens? "But Ellis…"

Violet pushed the cat food bag into my arms. "You take this, I'll get the cat. You're out on bail, Theda, don't be stupid." She paused for a moment. "Don't go home. Go to Bill's."

I nodded. Those sirens might not be for me, but Amy was opening the door from the reception area, two volunteers behind her. I was outnumbered, and I ran.

TWENTY-THREE

VIOLET WAS RIGHT, of course. If Dr. Massio set the cops on me, they'd come to pick me up at my apartment. I'd be safer at Bill's. But Musetta was at my house, so I turned down Putnam, thinking I'd pack up the kitty and then hide out. Besides, it only seemed fair to warn Bill first if I was going to be bringing his former colleagues from across town down on his head.

"Kitty!" Musetta bounded down the hall as soon as I got in. I picked up the catnip butterfly that had been left for me and she reared up. "Long bomb!" She took off and I used the occasion to push the KittyLuv sack on top of the kitchen cabinets. We did not need any more incidents, but once I was in there, it occurred to me that I hadn't eaten any food, good or bad, in too long. A quick snack, a phone call, and we'd be off.

"It's me." I sliced open a bagel as voicemail answered. "I'm coming over. I think, well, maybe this is solved."

"Hey, Musetta!" I ate standing, watching her scamper down the hall, and shoved the rest of the bagel half in my mouth as I got her carrier from its shelf in the closet. "Field trip!" I loaded my courier bag with cans and a few toys. "Musetta."

A curious black and white face peeked around the corner, just as the phone rang. I grabbed a few more cans and shoved them in. "Hang on, kitty."

"Hey, you!" But if I'd expected Bill, I was in for a surprise.

"Theda. It's Tess. I, well, I owe you an apology. And an explanation."

"Tess, this isn't the best time." I peered down at the street. Violet's van was still parked outside. No cop cars in sight. "I'm sorry, but I do have to be brief. How are you? Where are you?"

"I'm—I'm getting a tune up."

I collapsed on the sofa, dropping my bag at my feet. I had the feeling I wasn't getting away as quickly as I'd hoped. "A tune-up? Tess, I hate to ask."

"Then don't, Theda. Please. Let me just tell you. Yes, I slipped. But I'm putting myself back together again. One day at a time."

"That's good." I knew I sounded doubtful, but I couldn't help it. She'd looked so skinny and frail the last time I'd seen her. "So?"

"It's my own fault. I mean, I've got to own it. Maybe I just can't do the club scene anymore. Maybe it's time for something different. Let go and let God, you know?"

I'd been right, not that I'd say that exactly. "I was wondering. I kept seeing you out with Francesca."

"It's not her fault. Really, Theda. She's a good kid. But, well, she's bitter about things and that got to me, I think. But she tried to help. She even got me some stuff to help me calm down, to quiet the cravings."

"The ketamine?" From the quick intake of breath, I knew she realized that her stash had been found. Would an animal tranquilizer have the same effect on people? I didn't know, but from what I'd heard about "Special K" as a party drug, I doubted it. "Were you taking that stuff, Tess? Where did she get it?"

"It's from ages ago. I didn't use any of it, honest. I knew that if I started with anything, I wouldn't stop. But I didn't think I could hold out much longer. I had to get away."

"Tess, if she was stealing drugs for you—"

"No, Theda. This is on me. All on me. I'm calling just to make a clean breast of everything and, well, I'll be calling Bill next. I'm taking some time off from the lab and when I'm back, I'll be working to make it up to him, and to you. But now, I've got to take care of myself. I wanted to let you know, so you wouldn't worry, okay?"

"What about your cat?"

A gentle laugh came over the line. "I knew you'd ask, Theda. Don't worry. Francesca's got a key. She'll look after her." And then she was gone.

After she hung up, I expected to feel angry or, at least, disappointed. I'd sensed something was wrong. I'd known it.

But for some strange reason, I found myself feeling proud of Tess. She had screwed up, sure, but she had caught herself. She was getting help. She was…resistant. And it hit me, then, that I'd been wrong about her resemblance to Francesca. It wasn't just that her new friend was bitter, though I believed that. There was a fragility to Francesca that I'd been attributing to Tess. A brittle quality. That was why I'd been treating Tess so gingerly, but I knew I didn't need to do that anymore. Tess was going to make it.

THAT THOUGHT warmed me while I set about searching for Musetta. I knew she couldn't have gotten out, but I'd already checked under the bed and the back of the closet. "Kitty? We should get a move on."

No luck, she recognized the carrier and she knew what it meant. In a desperate bid, I went to get her treats. Violet would understand, just this once.

"Greenies!" A head peeked out, but it was too late. Someone was knocking on my door.

"Coming." Musetta ducked back into my bedroom and I took a deep breath. If the cops were going to take me downtown, I could call Bill and Pilchard. They wouldn't revoke my bail for shouting at a vet, would they? I hadn't threatened anybody.

I opened the door. "Francesca!" I collapsed against the door in relief.

"Hey, Violet sent me over." She walked in and saw the carrier on the floor. "She figured you might come by here to get your kitty."

"She's hiding. She thinks the carrier means a vet visit." Francesca moved into my living room and looked around. I had to bring up the ketamine, but was I breaking a confidence? "Hey, I talked to Tess."

"She called you? Good. I was telling her she should. I figured you'd worry." Francesca got down on her knees to peer under the sofa. "I'm taking care of her cat."

"What about Ellis?" My last sight of the black cat stayed in my mind. He had too big a spirit to stay long in a cage. "Did you spring him?"

She shook her head and moved on to the kitchen. "No, not yet. There's going to be all sorts of paperwork. Violet will handle it."

I looked at the young woman curiously. She'd seemed so upset before. Now she was quite blasé. And did she really think my cat would be hiding on my kitchen shelves? "Can I help you?"

"Oh, sorry. I thought I'd get that food sack, bring it back to Violet when you go over to Bill's."

I joined her in the kitchenette and reached up to the top of the cabinet. She grabbed it out of my hands and laughed a little. "Sorry. We don't want this to go astray, do we?"

"Speaking of, I can't figure how Ellis ended up at the shelter, can you?"

She shook her head. "Who knows? But it's so good you

found him. You know, they kill the cats that they don't think are adoptable. The 'nippers.'"

"So you'd said. 'Not immediately pet ready,' right?" I remembered using the term on Violet. She hadn't recognized it, and then I remembered something else Violet had said. "You worked there, didn't you?" The ketamine must have come from Rachel's clinic, but Tess hadn't stolen it.

"I volunteered there ages ago." Francesca gestured in the air and tried to move past me. "I was up for a job there. A good job, but I quit when they killed my cat. My Shiva."

Shiva, the cat named for a god. Well, we all want our pets to be immortal. "Francesca, from all I've heard, distemper is a very serious disease." I didn't mean to block her, but I wanted answers.

She snorted. "Right. Like Shiva could get distemper. My pets are all natural. Nothing but parsley and alfalfa to strengthen the immune system. Shiva was fine. Shiva was going to be fine."

I thought of the ketamine, of the drugs available in a vet's office. "Did Dr. Rachel euthanize your cat, Francesca?"

"She could've cured her." *Her?* My mind flashed to the shelter. Francesca had accused Dr. Massio of killing *her*. I'd assumed she meant Rachel. Francesca was still talking.

"She was pretending to be nice, then. All sympathetic when she heard how sick my Shiva was. She kept after me till I brought her in." Francesca turned away from me. There isn't much room in my little kitchen and she ended up talking to my refrigerator magnets. "It was a trap. She hated me because Piers and I still had something. I was up for a tech job there, and she made sure I didn't get it. I know why, too. He still loved me. Sure, he fooled around. Nobody could resist him. But we talked all the time, I'd come by when he was working there."

"You were in the storeroom where he was working?" An

idea struck me. I looked at the bag in her hand. "Why don't you let me put that back up on the shelf? It will be safe here."

"I don't think so." She turned to face me, the nearly empty sack clasped to her chest. "I think this is bad food and I should get rid of it."

"Francesca?" I didn't completely understand what was going on, but I knew it wasn't good. "What is it about that bag?"

She held it tight. "She didn't love him. She didn't love the animals. She cared more about name brands and corporate sponsorship. Did you know that new vet got this food for her? Got her a flat of it, like that would impress her. I'd told her, I'd cook for the cats. I'd make them healthy food, but no."

"So, you thought you'd show her, right?" I was edging closer. That bag was evidence. "You'd show everybody that KittyLuv wasn't good for cats."

"I was making a *point*. It was only a little cocoa and cat mint, a mix I found on the Internet. But even when she figured it out, she didn't get it."

I knew then that if I got that bag back I'd find what Rachel had: a small tear or injection point. Fingerprints, maybe, or one of Francesca's long, curly hairs. Old business. And my first instincts had been right. In those last moments, my friend was trying to tell me: poison. I moved closer still.

Francesca was on a roll. "She called me, the night before. I thought she'd reconsidered. But she'd seen the notice from the crematorium. She knew I was going to pick up Shiva's ashes and she was warning me. She told me not to try to come into the clinic. Not to try to see Piers again or to spread any more rumors about him. Not to apply for any job, anywhere in the city, where I'd be working with animals. But it's a free world, right? She was in early, and it was easy enough to walk right in. She was in the treatment room, setting up. That's when it came out. She got all up in my face. Told me it was my fault.

Told me I'd not only killed Shiva but I'd endangered every other cat in the shelter by not vaccinating her for distemper. That I could have killed all Violet's cats, too. Like I'd known she'd give it away. And then I saw it: the needle, the IV. She was about to do it, all over again. She's already taken everything from me once." She paused, breathless from her own retelling, and suddenly started. "Wait, that couldn't be—"

I followed her gaze. Musetta was staring, hunched over, bottom beginning to wag. Francesca must have recognized the motion.

"Musetta, no!" I reached down as my cat pounced. Francesca jerked her foot back, Two thin lines of red showed on her ankle. But this wasn't play for my cat, not this time. I didn't know if it was the smell of the contaminated pet food, the volume of Francesca's voice, or some subliminal signal from me, but Musetta reared up, hissing, and swiped again with claws unsheathed.

"Ow!" Francesca jumped back. I lunged for the bag, and as I pulled it toward me, Francesca fell against the counter. We both saw the knife at the same time, but she was too fast for me. I stumbled backward, into the living room. Not fast enough. I felt a burning and a wave of nausea and looked down. Already, the blood was spreading, the deep color soaking up my shirt.

The clatter of the knife hitting the floor startled me out of my stupor. Francesca threw up her hands and dived for Musetta. "Run," I yelled, the effort cutting the pain fresh through me. Musetta dashed out of the room and I almost laughed with relief when Francesca turned toward me instead.

"No, of course not." She seemed to see me for the first time. "Well, the cops already know you're a dangerous criminal. If anyone questions me, I'll say it was self defense."

I staggered backward, the movement sending waves of

sickness through me, and fell into my chair. The hand pressed against my belly felt hot, but I was shivering. The edge of my vision started to dim. With my last bit of strength I flung my messenger bag at her. Cans flew out, scattering everywhere. She smacked one away and laughed.

"You've just made my case stronger." She stared at my midsection and smiled. I had nothing left to try. "Goodbye."

She was gone, but I was too tired to call for help. As my eyes closed, I felt a thud. Musetta was in my lap, leaning against me, her body warm against the chill. She was purring, and that was all I knew.

TWENTY-FOUR

WHEN I WOKE UP, Bill and Violet were staring at me. I was in a bed.

"Francesca—"

"We know." Violet looked at Bill and started talking. "I'd called Bill, too, and, when you didn't show, he headed over. I had to pick up my van anyway, and I got there as Francesca was leaving. She was bloody, said Musetta had bitten her. But she couldn't explain why she had that bag."

"And I've never known Musetta to draw quite that much blood." Bill was smiling. I didn't think that was funny, but I didn't have the energy to protest.

"I'd figured out something was wrong back at the shelter," Violet continued. "After you took off. I stayed to follow up. I couldn't figure out how the poisoned food could have gotten back into the cat ward. Some other cats had eaten it, too, but they hadn't gotten as sick as Musetta. Ellis was one of them. That's why they were being so adamant about the quarantine. Only, when I started asking questions it turned out that one of the volunteers, that new girl in the green top, recognized him. She was sure that he'd been dropped off Sunday night by someone looking just like Francesca. She said the woman complained that he was vicious. That he bit. That he'd—"

"Never be pet quality." I was starting to wake up a bit. "I know, a 'nipper.'"

"Yeah, exactly. Plus, Francesca had seemed a little hinky about wanting him back, you know?"

Poor cat. Francesca must have wanted to make an example of him. Had she planned to rescue him all along, or would she have let him be killed? She must have known how Bill felt about the big, black cat. Maybe that's why she showed up. Maybe she did have some feelings, after all. But Bill was talking.

"Anyway, after the ambulance came, we figured out what must have happened. I called some folks I know from across the river and they picked her up at her place." I closed my eyes. "She had a set of pink scrubs with blood on them. The Boston DA's office think maybe she was going to use it to frame somebody. You, or maybe Tess."

Violet interrupted from very far away. "She's asleep, Bill." I wanted to protest, but it seemed like too much work.

THE NEXT THING I knew, everything hurt. Bill and Violet were still there, but something was different.

"What time is it?" The sun was too bright for me to have been napping long. I looked around at a white hospital room. An IV dripped something clear into my arm.

"About one." Bill looked absurdly pleased. "Wednesday."

"What?" I tried to sit up. Big mistake. But as the wave of pain and nausea passed, I realized Violet was explaining something.

"Best I can figure, she was trying to make Ellis into some kind of feline martyr. That big old guy's a love bug now. She must have been taunting him or something to make him lash out. What a jerk."

I nodded. Slowly. We'd reached the same conclusion. But something Bill had said stuck with me. "So, it's Wednesday?"

"Yeah, babe." He reached forward to brush my hair from my face, a stupid grin still plastered across his face. I had no idea what I looked like. I didn't think I wanted to know. "You more awake now?"

"Yeah." My mouth felt like a litterbox. I reached for the plastic cup of water on my night table and Bill jumped to hold it for me. "You told me about Francesca."

He glanced back at Violet. "She said we ought to let you know right away. I wasn't sure how much you were taking in." He turned away from me to refill my cup. "We had a bad night." There was a catch in his voice.

I drank some more. The room, everything that had happened, started to come in more clearly. "Francesca came over to get the bag." I closed my eyes to think. "Musetta!" I started, sending off waves of pain.

"Don't worry." Violet must have jumped up. She was leaning over me, almost holding my shoulders back against the bed. "She's fine. Bill has your keys, remember? I went by and checked on her this morning, before visiting Tess's cat. She's eating and pooping like a proper cat."

I nodded again, more easily. Whatever was in the IV must be good. "She wanted to ruin Rachel's life, get revenge. Piers, the job, her cat." The pain was moving farther away. "She fed that story to Wellner. Did she write those letters, too?"

"I don't know, babe. I don't know if we'll ever know."

"I bet she did." Violet chimed in. "I knew there was something odd about the last one we got. Something familiar. I want to see the ones she sent Rachel. I've read her lyrics, maybe I can tell from the style."

"Let me know." Something else was nagging at me. "But there's something else. Rachel had Musetta in the treatment room. Why did Francesca bring her back?"

"We've been trying to retrace her steps." Bill had been talking to his colleagues. "Best we can figure, she'd grabbed the bag and was making for the back exit when she ducked into that room full of cages." I looked at him, the question in my eyes. "We found a white coat in her apartment. A long lab coat. She probably used it to cover herself."

"So she went in there for the coat?" I tried to picture the shelter. That back hallway would have led her from Rachel's past the cat ward to the back door and the loading dock.

"It's possible. She would have been a mess." He cleared his throat. I shut my eyes and saw Rachel once again. Yes, there would have been a lot of blood to cover up. "And don't forget, the shelter was taking a delivery. Maybe somebody was coming up the hall."

"And she didn't want to be seen with the poisoned food, just in case anyone remembered the bag had been in Rachel's office, so she stashed it. But why take Musetta? Why move her at all?" I remembered finding my cat behind the lab coats, slunk down in her carrier and covered with blood.

"Camouflage?" Bill shrugged. "Some misguided humane instinct? That might stay a mystery." He spoke so gently. "I'm sorry, babe."

"You guys don't know, do you?" Violet looked at me and then at Bill. "Shiva, Francesca's old cat, was also a tuxedo cat. A big black-and-white girl, with a fluffy white chest and the booties, just like Musetta. If it weren't for that white splotch on her nose, Musetta could have been Shiva's twin."

"She wanted my cat." I couldn't keep my eyes open any more. Those were good drugs. "But she didn't follow through."

"Maybe she heard you coming?" Violet sounded far away.

"Maybe she had some sense left." Bill's voice seemed to be fading. "Musetta at her place would have been evidence."

"Or she'd thought she'd already saved her. Saved Shiva." I didn't know if I was being clear, but nobody questioned me. I could barely form the words. "Everyone knows cats have nine lives."

EPILOGUE

WHATEVER MUSETTA HAD witnessed, my cat didn't have to testify. Pilchard came by the next day to tell me that papers had been filed and the charges would be dismissed. I was in considerable discomfort by then. Not pain exactly, the drugs were too good for that. But the doctors were weaning me off them and along with a clear head came a combination of aching and itching that I wouldn't wish on anyone. Still I was grateful for the news. If Bill lost his condo for me, he and I would never get back together.

Bill was there when Pilchard dropped in, and I was relieved to see that the two were on speaking terms. Maybe Pilchard had taken my case to get in with the cops. Maybe that would help patch things up with Patti. I was too busy trying to stand up without moving my belly to care.

"Okay, I think I'm good to go." I'd managed to slip into sweats earlier. It felt good to be wearing clothes again. Now I gingerly set both feet onto the floor.

"Babe, are you sure?" Bill reached for me. Pilchard blanched and stepped back. I grabbed for the windowsill.

"I'm sure, Bill. When the doctor makes her rounds, she's going to find me up and about." I took a step and then a breath. Both worked. "I've got a cat to get back to."

"She's fine, Theda." Violet walked in with Caro. "Though I'm sure she misses you, too."

"Hi, guys!" I waved. That was too much and I didn't complain as Bill helped me back into bed. "What's shaking?"

Caro didn't speak, just handed me a copy of the *Mail*. I grimaced, I'm sure, but it wasn't reaching forward that got me. Today was Thursday, I knew that much. Last week, I'd had a column in this issue.

"Please, I don't think I've had enough drugs for this." I pushed it back.

"No, really, Theda. You need to see this." Violet was being unusually insistent. Caro just smiled. I picked it up. There was probably a story on Rachel in here.

"No. Arts." Violet took the paper from me and thumbed through it. "Here."

"What?" There was nothing. A gallery review. Something at Symphony Hall. New DVD releases. "What am I supposed to be looking at?"

With an exaggerated sigh, Violet leaned over and pointed to the lower right corner of the page. Right where "Clubland" usually ran. I guess I'd avoided looking there, but now I saw a small box, enclosing one sentence.

Clubland will return from hiatus next week with in-depth coverage of the local rock and pop scene.

"So what?" I felt a bit of a glow, but I had to be realistic. "Maybe they're just getting Lee up to speed. Or Ralph."

"Nobody's seen Wellner. And Ralph's on leave." Violet smiled. "Word is, maybe permanently."

"Poor Ralph." I hadn't realized I pitied him till that moment. Maybe I even liked him. My friends looked astonished. "He's just part of our world, you know?" I knew then I'd be working to get him reinstated.

"But think what this means for you." Caro, ever practical, finally spoke up. "You can have your column back, and now there will be a music job open."

"Assuming I even want it anymore."

I couldn't understand why they were laughing.

THREE NIGHTS LATER, I was on my way to the Last Stand. I'd given in, as my friends knew I would. Tim had left a good dozen messages for me and I'd agreed to get him something for "Clubland" by Tuesday, in order to make his in-print announcement come true. He'd acted precipitously, so I used my bit of leverage for a $25 buck per column raise.

I also made it clear to Tim what I thought about Ralph. I couldn't tell Ralph, though. The staff critic was still incommunicado. Word was, he'd gone off to visit family in Ohio. Tim wasn't talking, so I couldn't tell if Ralph had confessed or been ratted out. Lee Wellner's byline disappeared, too, from every paper in town. I didn't expect it back. Plagiarism is a sin, but blackmail is a crime.

At least I had an obvious "Clubland" for my first week back. Bill had booked that old soul act, Buzz Grammers, again. The septuagenarian lived up in Maine, but insisted on driving down for the interview. I was still hurting. I really hoped I'd be up to hearing his set come next week. But since I was off the Percodans, I'd decided to treat myself to a pre-interview beer.

"Hey there!" Piers was behind the bar. He looked up with a wistful smile when I raised my arm, very slowly, to wave.

"Theda. I was wondering when you'd get back. Blue Moon?"

I nodded and slid onto a stool. I'd almost mastered the trick of not moving my midsection too much. "How're things?"

"They're okay, I guess." Piers pushed my beer over without meeting my eye.

"Piers?" He looked up. "I'm so sorry. Really. I miss her, too."

He grabbed a glass and started wiping it. "Man, I think about her all the time. And I think about Francesca…" The glass was definitely dry. No matter what rumors Francesca had tried to spread, he had loved Rachel.

"You didn't know, Piers. I mean, it could have been anyone."

He gave a sad, little grin. "Yeah, but it wasn't. It was me." He put the glass down. "I mean, for so long, I just let everything roll. Then I go and get serious. Decide to commit, and what happens?"

"You didn't kill her, Piers." I wasn't sure how much was public knowledge, or what Bill or Violet would have passed along. Just then Ellis appeared and nuzzled my shin. He'd become a regular darling since his rescue. I reached—very carefully—to rub his ears. "Francesca blamed Rachel for a lot of things, not getting that job and her cat's death. I mean, she was crazy, she'd poisoned the cat food."

Piers leaned on the bar and looked down at the big black feline. Maybe he'd needed to hear that, or hear it again. "Yeah, and I remember thinking just how smart Rachel was, giving that up."

"Excuse me?" I hadn't had a beer in ages. Maybe it was going to my head.

"It was when I was working on the storeroom, a load of that fancy brand came in." He put the glass back on the rack. "You'd asked me, but I didn't remember then. I think her ex, that other vet? He'd set up a fancy donation for her." He snorted. "Like she cared. But we'd spent a couple hours moving everything when those bags came in. I stacked some of them, but there really was no more room. That's when she said we should give them away. It was the pricier stuff, so she could get a better tax break on it. Like I said, she was so smart."

I put down my beer. Finally, it all made sense. "Thank you, Piers." Someday, I'd explain it to him. In the meantime, I had to trust in his essential optimism. He'd bounce back.

"No probs. You want another?" Maybe talking it out was all he'd needed.

"I'm good, Piers. And I've got to get ready for work."

THREE WEEKS LATER, I turned thirty-four. We'd mourned our friend with a big community service, and maybe I'd buried some of my own ghosts there as well. "So much for the Jesus year," I announced as Bill and I walked into my place. We'd gone out for dinner, and I was in a mellow mood. "I survived it after all."

"Survived and thrived," said Bill. Musetta came bounding down the hall, but he grabbed her before she could attack. "Despite this chubby little killer here."

"Watch who you're calling chubby." Whether it was age or the enforced inaction of healing, I'd begun to develop a certain softness around my waist. I reached for my cat and Bill poured her into my arms.

"Meh." She squirmed, uncomfortable at being passed around.

"I know, Musetta. What a rude man." I kissed the top of her head and set her down.

"So, you going to take the job?" Bill hung up his denim jacket. Spring had finally arrived in New England.

"I don't know yet." I handed him my sweater. "It is tempting." Ralph had returned, only to announce that he was leaving the Mail to freelance back in Cleveland. We'd thrown him a party at the Last Stand and he'd gotten so weepy I was pretty sure the move wasn't entirely voluntary. Since then, Tim had been wooing me to take on the staff critic role. The other job, for an arts writer, had disappeared, victim of a "temporary hiring freeze" nobody expected to end.

"'Cause I was thinking." Bill leaned back on the wall. "If you want to stay freelance, I understand that. And, you know,

I could cover you on my health insurance plan. If we get married."

"Wait a minute! Is that a proposal, Bill Sherman?" I looked up at him and he drew me close. He could do that now without it hurting.